one of the good

Books by Maika Moulite and Maritza Moulite
available from Inkyard Press

Dear Haiti, Love Alaine
One of the Good Ones

MAIKA MOULITE AND MARITZA MOULITE

ONE
OF THE
GOOD
ONES

Recycling programs
for this product may
not exist in your area.

ISBN-13: 978-1-335-14580-2

One of the Good Ones

This edition published by arrangement with Harlequin Books S.A.

For questions and comments about the quality of this book, please contact us at
CustomerService@Harlequin.com.

Inkyard Press
22 Adelaide St. West, 40th Floor
Toronto, Ontario M5H 4E3, Canada
www.InkyardPress.com

Printed in U.S.A.

CONTENTS

To sisters. And sistahs. All of us.

PART I

"There will be a day sometime in the near future when this guide will not have to be published. That is when we as a race will have equal opportunities and privileges in the United States. It will be a great day for us to suspend this publication for then we can go wherever we please, and without embarrassment."

—VICTOR HUGO GREEN

QUOTE FEATURED IN
THE NEGRO MOTORIST GREEN BOOK
1948 EDITION

HAPPI

She was mine before she was anyone else's. All mine. Partly mine. Now she belongs to you and them and shirts and rallies and songs and documentaries. They say she had A Bright Future Ahead of Her and She Was a Star Whose Light Burned Out Too Soon. She Was Going to Make a Difference. That's all true, but it's not the Truth. Kezi was more than her brains and her grades and her voice. She was more than her future. She had a past. She was living her present.

She could have been mine.

Should have been mine.

She was my sister before she became your martyr, after all.

Even as I sit as still as a lion stalking her prey, inside, I'm racing. My mind is buzzing with the thoughts I don't say. My heart is knocking erratically against my sternum and is always one beat away from bursting through my chest. I should be used to it. But you never get used to strangers sliding their arms over your shoulders in solidarity, to apologize for something that isn't their fault. Not when Kezi being gone doesn't feel real to begin with. How can it, when I didn't get a chance to see her face one last time before they incinerated her body and put her essence in an urn?

My parents are already inside the auditorium, seated in their place of honor in the front row. I will join them eventually, but not until the millisecond that I have to. When everything went down, we made an agreement. I will play along and be a cheap carbon copy of the daughter they lost, a constant reminder to the world that she was One of the Good Ones. But before the lights shine on us and cell phones are trained at our brave, heartbroken faces, I will be me. The Prodigal Daughter.

I glance at my own phone. Nothing. *New phone, who dis? I guess.*

I sink into the hard bench outside of the Harold Washington Theater where the National Alliance for the Progression of Black People's Chicago chapter is hosting its annual Salute to Excellence ceremony. I try to breathe. I don't want to salute anything. I don't want to be in there. I just want to pretend that this slab of wood is a cloud, that I'm a regular girl lying outside and soaking up the final drops of sunshine at the end of a mundane day. They call it the golden hour, a photographer told me a few weeks ago, when we were waiting for my mother to be finished with makeup for a photoshoot that *Essence Magazine* was doing about "America's New Civil Rights Leaders." The new normal.

He was fiddling with his camera, removing and reattaching

the giant zoom lens of his Canon, and was apparently one of those people who couldn't stand silence. Others see me and can't help but speak. I can read the panic in their eyes when the realization crawls into their psyches: *Come on, say something nice, don't sound stupid.* But instead of the *I'm so sorry*s and the *You're so brave*s, he prattled on about the magical moments just after the sun rises and right before it sets. It was a breath of fresh air, actually.

"Way less shadow," he said. "Nowhere for your subject to hide."

"I think my sister mentioned it to me once," I volunteered. "She was a YouTuber."

His eyes widened in terror. *Of course.*

"Oh yeah! Oh, man. I'm so—"

"It's fine." I had spoken too soon.

That was then. Now I'm wondering how long you have to sit outside to get a tan when I sense the shifting of light through my closed eyelids. Someone is standing over me and blocking the sun. My heart is no longer knocking at my chest; it is about to crack through my rib cage, my guts, my skin, my top. Like a bullet, only bigger. My eyes spring open, and I hurl my purse across my body reflexively. *Dumb, dumb, dumb. Any deranged rando can recognize you out here and—*

"Ow!"

It's even worse than I thought. It's Genny.

"What are you doing here?" I ask. She's an integrative biologist and basically lives in her laboratory. Mom, Dad, and I had been visiting Chicago for a few days, but Genny stayed behind in Los Angeles. I didn't mind.

"I just got in," Genny says as she rubs her shoulder. Bummer. I was aiming for the face. She hands me my bag. "Why are *you* not inside? They're about to start."

"This is my alone time," I say. I stretch with my arms wide above my head until I notice a blond man parked in a car across the street watching in interest. Our eyes meet. He smiles. I frown and hunch over instinctively. We are never alone.

Beep. Beep. Beep.

"And that's my cue." I stop the alarm and switch my phone to silent. Any messages from Santiago will have to wait. Not that he's gonna answer anyway. "Sorry," I mutter.

She shakes her head. "Naw, I get it. I shouldn't have surprised you like that. I don't know what I was thinking."

We're never on the same page. This is weird.

I shrug as I heave myself up to smooth the black cigarette pants I convinced Mom to let me wear and adjust my tucked-in ruffled beige blouse.

"I thought you said you couldn't make it." I glance at her from the corner of my eye. She's rolling an enormous hardside spinner suitcase back and forth on the sidewalk. It's a sensible black, of course. But surprisingly large for an overnight trip. And *I'm* supposed to be the vain one.

Genny pauses midspin.

"I moved some things around... Kezi was always going on about how important Chicago is to Black history. She told me over lunch that Obama moved here before law school partly because of this guy." She looks at the doors of the theater behind us, at the clunky neon letters that spell Harold Washington, the first Black mayor of Chicago.

"Oh. I thought it was because of Michelle's pheromones." She blinks.

Over lunch.

I hate when she does this. Gushes about all the sisterly things they had without me. Resentment oozes through my pores when I remember that so many of Genny's memories with our middle sister are more recent than mine. I was only a year younger than Kezi and had lunch with her exactly once since starting high school. Genny and Kezi were about seven years apart, and they had a standing weekly date.

I hate myself for wanting to compete for the title of Closest to Kezi. And for what? I lose every time. None of that will bring her back.

We enter the theater, and I don't stop to wait for Genny, who is asking an usher to store her luggage someplace safe. I keep walking, on the brink of jogging, anything to make the gazes that follow me down the aisle of the auditorium a blur, inhuman. I plunk down into my seat with none of the grace and class that years of ballet, tap, and jazz lessons would suggest I have. Or what seventeen years of having Naomi Smith as a mother would demand.

"Let the public consumption of our misery begin," I whisper as I cross my arms.

"*Tut.*" My mother doesn't need to use real words for me to understand her. Clicks and side-eyes suffice to get her point across: *You better get your act together, girl.* She turns in her seat and grabs my father's hand. Their fingers meld into one on her lap. I ignore the flash of a camera that goes off to capture the very casual, completely unstaged exhibition of their courageous love.

The lights dim and funky soul music jingles to life as Genny slips into the empty seat beside me. She looks forward decidedly and remains silent, but I know the *tap, tap, tap*ping of her index finger on her armrest is because she wants to tell me off for abandoning her outside with the overly chatty usher. But she won't. Because acting right in public is first nature to her. It doesn't have to get nose pinched and poured down her throat, like with me. It's another thing she and Kezi have in common.

Had.

"Yes, welcome, welcome!"

The president of the NAPBP's Chicago chapter stops at the acrylic podium and nods at the applause filling the room. He adjusts his baby blue silk tie and smiles so wide that his lips practically reach the back of his head.

"Welcome to our annual Salute to Excellence ceremony! We are so blessed to have the individuals that have rocked this city and our nation—" he bows slightly in my family's direction "—with us here this evening."

Applause.

"Yes, indeed, these people have shaken up our communities and given us a whole lot to think on. You know, I've stayed up nights pondering who we are."

Pause.

"What we deserve."

"Preach!" a woman shouts from the back.

"And what we will no longer stand for."

"Tell 'em!" I turn to witness a man in the middle row jump up from his seat.

The chapter president pulls out a handkerchief from deep within one of the many pockets of his pinstripe suit and mops the sheen of sweat that has somehow already sprung up on his forehead.

"We have a ways to go, it's true. But right now, we celebrate the accomplishments we've made."

This all sounds good. The crowd is inspired. My parents' previously intertwined hands have even dissolved from their unity blob to clap emphatically at the man's words. But I'm still without a sister. I still can't reconcile what happened to her, only three months out. I don't know if I ever will. I bring my hands together robotically as the show begins in earnest, first with a stirring rendition of the Negro National Anthem, where everyone but me seems to know there are second and third verses.

The show drags along. There are spoken word poems and both high school *and* HBCU marching band performances. Certificates of academic achievement for recent graduates are passed out. Genny's hand, the fingers of which have long since stopped pattering in annoyance, has just inched its way closer to where my elbow lies on the armrest between our seats when the students on stage whoop in self-congratulation. I jerk my arm away. She glances at me in simultaneous pity and irritation. There are other various demonstrations of salutation-worthy excellence, and then it's finally time for the keynote speaker.

"Our next guest never planned on being famous. She never thought that she would be called to carry the load that she walks with each day. She never imagined that she would receive the phone call that every parent dreads, but that so many Black moms and dads are forced to answer far too frequently in this country."

The once celebratory crowd now settles into a familiar hush, the quiet that's reserved to show respect. To acknowledge that someone strong is about to speak. My mother smooths her skirt in her lap as she waits for the man to finish his intro. She lets out a shaky breath, and my dad gives her knee a gentle squeeze to bolster her strength.

"Naomi Smith is a resident of Los Angeles, California, and co-pastor of Resurrection Baptist Church along with her husband, Malcolm Walker Smith. She is the mother of three beautiful young women—one of whom is no longer with us today. Keziah Leah Smith, known to her friends as Kezi, died senselessly by the hands of the very people who were supposed to keep her safe. Her death in April following her unjust arrest at a social justice rally has shaken us to the depths of our souls and beyond. And yet, Naomi has stepped forward with a grace and resolve that is truly admirable, speaking for so many families that have been forced to walk down this treacherous road. Today, she will receive the NAPBP Courage Award on behalf of Kezi."

Mom stands and releases another slow exhale through her lips. Dad looks up at her from his seat with an encouraging nod and smile. As she makes her way onto the stage, the crowd begins to clap. It starts slowly at first, as if people are afraid to make too much commotion. But soon everyone is on their feet, hands smacking together thunderously as the chapter president opens his arms wide and then envelops her in a hug, perfectly angled for all the cameras to catch. Mom takes her position behind the podium and smiles as everyone eventually stops their applauding to take their seats. As she begins to address the audience, she isn't Mom anymore. She's the family spokeswoman. The practiced public speaker. The polished preacher addressing her doting congregation. To some, the way that she has stepped into this role with such dignity and speed could be explained only as divinely ordained.

"I'd like to start off by thanking the NAPBP for inviting me and my family here today. It is a great honor to be among some of the most hardworking people of our generation, and I humbly accept this award on behalf of my daughter Kezi. Lord. Sh-she should have been here." Mom pauses to clear her throat.

"The day that Kezi was born, I looked down at her and she beamed right back up at me. She was all gums then, of course, whooping and hollering like a little tornado. But even as she sighed her first breaths on this side of creation, she stopped long enough to grin and gurgle at me and let me know that she saw her mama. That was Kezi. Outspoken and ready to shout from the mountaintops, even when she didn't have the words yet. But she was aware enough to stop and acknowledge me for bringing her into this world.

"Unsurprisingly, Kezi grew up to be a champion for the people who can't speak up and the ones who get ignored when they do. She made it her duty to whoop and holler for the overlooked. When she told me that she had created a YouTube channel to do her part to fight injustice in this country, all I could do was look at her and nod. Now, I'm not one to be speechless, let me tell you—"

I snort loudly from my seat, and Genny nudges me harshly in the ribs.

"—but so often, Kezi would say something that would stop me from forming my next thought. Just like that, any words would be taken right out of my head, and I'd just gaze at her in awe. Don't get me wrong, I thought that was a hefty task to undertake on some website. But if anyone could do it, it would be Kezi. And not only would she do it, she'd be great at it. And she was. She had thousands of followers, got to write amazing think pieces—she even had the chance to speak on TV once. Major organizations like yours recognized her work."

She nods once at the NAPBP president. Then to her captivated audience.

"But online activism wasn't enough for Kezi. It wasn't long before she wanted to do things in the real world, march in the streets and wave signs and scream and shout to be heard. And this scared me. Rattled me to my core. Every day on the news, I was seeing someone get beat up, shot by police, worse. I didn't want that for any of my children. No—"

Mom pauses again to clear her throat, and I see my dad straighten up in his seat.

"No one does," she whispers. Stops. The room freezes too. I glance at Genny—this part of the speech is new.

"My own father lost his dad at a young age, you know. My grandfather never got justice. He was yet another Black man lost to the mysteries of the night in the Jim Crow South. But at least he was around long enough to fall in love. Cultivate a family. Get to know himself a bit. M-my daughter will never have that."

These past few months have been a never-ending performance for Mom. She's been reciting the same lines over and over again on an endless loop of repetition. But that just meant that she was always on point. You could ask her any question, and she'd be ready, because she knew how the show ended. Booming applause. Tear-filled eyes. Deep breath sniffles.

My mother is a natural speaker who can draw in the crowd, pull them right up against the door to our pain and then guide them back out, farther away from what we had experienced and closer to the promise of hope. To a day when things like this didn't happen anymore. She has gotten particularly good at separating herself from these moments. She's playing a part, after all, her true expressions of grief folded into a tiny box only to be unleashed in the privacy of her home. Uncorked with a bottle of wine. They never see that.

Until today. Right now.

The room is as silent as death as my mother mourns. The unbreakable barrier between her heartbreak and the public shatters into a billion shards. I feel the pricks in my own eyes.

"My baby," she gasps. "Kezi."

A wail as deep as the ocean and just as blue escapes her lips. I am suddenly hot, my blood rushing through my veins and arteries, not nearly fast enough to my brain to tell me what I should do. Because I have to do something. Genny looks stricken, equally uncertain how to react. Her fingers find the loose rubber band she's taken to wearing on her right wrist. She snaps it hard against her skin. Again and again and again. The flush spreads up her arm.

I wonder how bruised Kezi was when she died. How long she screamed before her throat burned and she couldn't anymore. If she even screamed at all. But I can't wonder long. Wondering takes me there with her, and she keeps leaving in a blaze of agony, over and over.

The worst thing that could ever happen to my family did happen, exactly one hundred days ago. Each day has brought one more brick on our backs, added one more link in the iron chains that unite us through blood and fire. Politicians make promises about what they plan to accomplish during their first one hundred days in office, that period of time that is still early and hopeful, yet substantial enough to make a difference. But no one talks about the first one hundred days into a death. How you still expect to see your sister unceremoniously dump her textbooks on the kitchen table. How your nose still anticipates smelling the avocado and honey hair mask she does while editing videos on the weekend. Or how her room has become an untouched museum. A shrine. A crypt.

She can't be dead.

Speaking about her in the past tense still feels weird on my tongue.

If I just close my eyes—

We're still here.

My dad is the muscular and mute type. He is content to

stay in the shadows and let my mom be our collective voice. But that won't fly today. Not when she is standing before a crowd of hundreds and about to collapse with exhaustion. With despair. Because even in a perfect world from here on out, even if all her speeches and interviews lead to not one more drop splashing into the rivers and seas of the blood of the innocent, Kezi will still be gone.

So Dad makes noise. He leaps from his chair and calls out to his wife.

"It's all right, Mimi."

It doesn't take him long to reach her, to wrap his broad arms around the shuddering body of the only person in his life who knows what it feels like to have a part of your human legacy extinguished. Genny, who shuns most attention, walks purposefully to the stage as well. To be the brace to the family backbone.

I know what I should do now. I don't need to look to my left or my right or behind me to realize that these people expect me to join my family and share in our communal torment. To help us hold each other up. But only a tissue-thin wall stands between my aching sadness and the withdrawn mask I wear.

So I can't. I can't keep my end of the bargain.

I rise from my seat too. Genny's eyes find mine. Even as I turn my back on my oldest sister and parents onstage, as I drag my feet down the aisle, slowly enough that every shocked face remains in focus and human, I know her gaze still follows.

Something to know about me is that I hide.

I burst through the double doors.

I run away.

2

KEZI

I must have died and gone to hell.

Right?

Because why else would I have heard that *outrageous* bleating from my alarm at 5:30 (in the morning!) and chosen to wake up? It was mid-April of twelfth grade. I should have been suffering from a severe case of senioritis that could be cured only by sleeping in. But there I was, doing my Monday morning countdown to study.

"Eight…seven…six…five…four…four…four…three… why, oh, why…two…ONE!"

I yanked the covers shielding my head down to my waist and leapt out of bed before the just-right firmness of my mattress and perfectly fluffed pillows could lure me back into their warm nest.

Bang bang bang.

Couldn't even blame her. I dragged my feet over to the wall I shared with my baby sister, Happi, and knocked twice. Two syllables. *Sor-ry.* (For counting so loudly that I woke you up while I was trying to wake myself up.)

Silence.

I slipped on cozy padded knee socks and plodded to my desk, where my notes were spread neatly across my laptop, right where I'd left them the night before. Mr. Bamhauer, my AP US History teacher and the miserable Miss Trunchbull to my precocious Matilda, was a stickler for the "old way" of doing things and insisted our notes be handwritten on wide-ruled paper so that the letters were big enough for him to see without his glasses while grading.

I skimmed over the major moments of the Civil Rights Movement that I knew the Advanced Placement test makers were likely to ask about when I sat for the exam in less than a month: *Brown v. Board of Education of Topeka. Emmett Till. The March on Washington. The Civil Rights Act of 1964. The Voting Rights Act of 1965.* Each bullet point was like a twist unscrewing the faucet of my brain, flooding my skull with facts. To me, *Brown v. Board of Education* wasn't just some case. It was the rebuttal to *Plessy v. Ferguson*, the racist court decision that dictated the "separate but equal" ideology. It was one of many nails in the giant coffin of Jim Crow laws and had ushered in the legacy of the Little Rock Nine. But before the Nine, we'd had students like Linda Brown, the Topeka One. Mr. Bamhauer lectured about the past, of course…but he made it stale and removed. To him, the people involved in all this world-changing were just names and dates in a book. Nothing more. They hadn't had souls. Or dreams.

Brown v. Board of Education propelled my thoughts directly to that little girl. I envisioned how Linda Brown must have felt when she'd learned at nine years old that she couldn't go to the school down the road, the one her white friends in the neighborhood attended, just because of her skin color. I felt her heart hammering when she saw how shaken up her daddy was on the walk home after his talk with the school principal. I imagined the hushed conversations Oliver and Leola Brown had over the kitchen table when they decided to move forward with the case, knowing what it would mean. I thought of all the parents hunched over in exasperation, fear, and determination, the folks in Delaware, Washington, DC, South Carolina, and Virginia, who decided they could no longer accept segregation either.

I drank in American history, in all its problematic glory, like water. It was mine after all. My dad's grandmother Evelyn had embarked on the Great Migration to California after her husband was killed overseas in World War II. He died for a country that didn't think he deserved to call it home. My mom's grandfather Joseph had been killed right here in America's Jim Crow South. And their tales were just the family history that had been passed down.

I wasn't much of a morning person, but once I rubbed the crust out of my eyes, I couldn't close them again. Not with all these stories of individuals insisting they be remembered calling out to me at once. I had to listen to them.

After almost an hour of studying, my alarm rang again to drag me out of my bubble. I walked back over to my and Happi's shared wall and knocked out another syllabic message: *Hap-pi! Wake! Up!* Her groan was loud and miserable. I chuckled. The only human being on earth less of a morning person than me? Her.

As I waited to shower, I checked the email account I used

for my YouTube page, marking off the usual spam, replying to short messages, and noting the invitations and requests I had to think on more and get back to.

But then. I paused.

Oh Kezi. I was reading this ridiculous article about parasocial relationships. It was describing those pathetic people who feel like they know media personalities but don't. You know, those freaks who get excited when they catch a glimpse of a celebrity's baby or read every interview to see what brand of shampoo they use. Like that would make them closer. I thought it was fine. But I stayed up all night. All night. All night wondering if you would see me that way too. Like some random weirdo on the internet.

But I told myself over and over, she's much too good, way too smart, to not realize that some of her subscribers are more special than others. And I'm more than a subscriber. I'm a supporter. A lifeline. We get each other. No one understands the struggle and what you're fighting for like I do. But all night I thought of this. Going insane. Running in circles in my mind until I tripped on something that made me stop. It was something you said, actually.

I tried to swallow but couldn't get past the sand in my throat. Nausea washed over me in waves, and I clutched my stomach to steady myself.

You said: We're in this together. You remember that, don't you? It was that youth panel you spoke on two weeks ago at city hall and you made this beautiful, beautiful comment on how to have hope in the face of hopelessness. You promised that "even in the darkest moments, when you feel completely alone, like you're the only one who cares, just remember that I care. Our community cares. And the people who came before us and behind us and the ones who come up beside us care too. So long as we keep caring and trying, there is hope."

I cried when your words came to me. And I'm going to sleep well tonight knowing that I'm not alone. I'm not hopeless. I have you.

There was a video attached to the email, sent from an address named *mr.no.struggle.no.progress*. My eyes widened and my pulse pounded against my ears when I registered whose face was in the thumbnail. Mine. I clicked on the preview button with a shaky hand and watched myself at the event the email sender mentioned. There I was, speaking animatedly and pronouncing the very words this stranger had taken the time to transcribe. The camera panned slowly across the room as my voice continued in the background.

I remembered that day. I almost hadn't made it in time, because Happi's audition for our school's Shakespeare play had gone longer than planned. Instead of taking my sister home after her tryout, I had dragged her with me straight to the panel. There she was in the video, seated between Derek and Ximena, who'd also come to show their support. The customary sounds of an audience wove in and out of the audio, a fussy baby babbling merrily, a chorus of a dozen sheets of paper rustling, a sniffly man's sneezes punctuating every few sentences.

The camera continued its survey of the room, and I noticed a group of people standing along the back wall. The space had been remarkably packed for a city hall meeting, and I recalled that quite a few members of the audience had come because they were subscribers to my YouTube channel, *generationkeZi*.

When the meeting was adjourned, more than half in attendance had made a beeline to where I was seated, to chat. I'd greeted a lot of people, but others had stood on the sidelines and watched from afar, never approaching.

Who sent this message? A fan I hadn't gotten to speak with? The cameraperson? A local citizen who was feeling particularly inspired?

The slow creak of the bedroom door opening diverted my attention. I spun in my chair, not even sure when I'd grabbed the silver plaque I'd received from YouTube for reaching one hundred thousand subscribers, noting the instinct I had to hold it in the air menacingly.

"Bathroom's all yours," Happi said, pausing midyawn to look at me strangely.

"Thanks, I'll be right in," I replied to the back of her head as she stumbled to her room.

Instead, I gripped the plaque in my lap and sat there, frozen.

Him again.

3

KEZI

I closed my eyes. Breathed.

In…three…two…one.

Hold…two…one.

Out…four…three…two…one.

I stayed like that for a couple of minutes, finally putting to use the guided-meditation app Genny had made me download months ago, until the tension in my shoulders slithered out of my muscles and into the atmosphere.

As I slid on my shower cap and let the warm water pitter-patter against my goose-bumped flesh, I gave myself a talking-to.

Chill.

You are here. No one is going to get you.

Lots of people online receive weird messages from randos. What are you going to say?

Someone sent a couple of emails gushing over you and wished they knew you better?

Oh, they quoted something you said at a public event?

Who would you even tell?

Not Mom and Dad, for sure. They would cut all access to the internet before you finished your sentence.

All for nothing.

Chill.

"Why do you even start from eight anyway?"

I smiled. It really shouldn't be such a big deal when Happi engaged with me, but it happened less and less lately. We had a wall between us in more ways than one. She made me feel like a parent wanting to connect with their kid who was super embarrassed of them. If I was honest with myself, I knew that was part of the problem in our relationship. I had a tendency to be, let's say, a little…overprotective of Happi. Yeah. Let's go with that.

"Five is way too short of a countdown for me," I explained while pulling out of the driveway. "I tried it my first year of high school and *dreaded* getting up. Ten is too long. I did that as a sophomore and would kind of drift off in the middle. Eight is just right."

"But you say *four* like seventeen times."

I blinked. "Don't question the process."

Happi rolled her eyes and scrolled through her phone, her message clear. Table Scraps of a Conversation: Over. I turned up the speaker volume and pressed Play on my daily news podcast. Hoped the glib anchors would distract me with their at-times tone-deaf banter until we got to school.

"Nationwide protests continued overnight in response to the death of Jamal Coleman, an unarmed Black man in Florida killed by police in front of his children, who had the presence of mind to record..."

"I don't need a ride home," Happi said as we pulled into the student parking lot.

"All right," I said. I forced myself not to demand what she was up to. Contorted my lips into a smile to prove how cool I was with her vagueness. She stared at me defiantly, as if expecting an interrogation. When I didn't offer one, her gaze softened.

"Thanks, Kez."

She hopped out the moment the car stopped.

I took my phone off Do Not Disturb and checked my texts. When Ximena's name popped up, I smiled for real.

Morning!
Working on my game in the computer lab.
*The very empty computer lab ☺

I grabbed my bag and walked across the sprawling lawn of Thomas Edison Senior High, nodding and waving at the Bible Club kids about to pray at the flagpole and the skateboarders practicing tricks on a makeshift ramp. I wasn't popular in the way early–2000s TV shows depicted it. I didn't throw epic "ragers" or have petty rivalries with worthy adversaries. No one gossiped about my secrets on a popular website written by an unknown omniscient blogger. But I *was* student body president, likely to be valedictorian, and the older sister of one of the drama club's biggest stars, so people had definitely seen me around in one way or another over these four years.

I used to be embarrassed about how much I cared about school, how hard I had to study to get excellent grades while others seemed to coast and have near-perfect GPAs, how often I wondered if I was doing enough to get into a good college when I had no useful connections. But then, one day, something had clicked in my head, and I'd realized that I could work around feeling self-conscious about trying so hard by wearing it as a crown on my head. "Feel the fear and do it anyway" and all that.

While most people loitered outside in an effort to remain as far as possible from the classrooms they would soon be trapped in for hours, I pulled open the building doors happily, went down one hall, then another, then another. The path to the computer lab was free of students. And at first survey of the room, it looked like the lab was empty too. I walked to the last of the six rows of desktop computers. Ximena Levinson sat typing at the computer closest to the wall, absentmindedly humming to herself. I took in her slightly sagging dark wash jeans, short-sleeved snow-white button-down, and red, white, and black Adidas NMD runners. The wings of my heart beat keenly.

I closed the short distance between us. "Hey."

"Hey," she said, her resting-neutral-person-face lighting up when she saw me.

"Hey." I dropped my things in front of the seat beside hers and sat down. She leaned forward easily as I slid my hands onto her shoulders and paused to admire her face, our smiles inches apart.

"Hey," she whispered, closing in on our gap.

When we were slumming through calculus, we'd started playing this game. Find the Asymptote. But *we* were the lines on a graph sharply approaching a curve, getting eternally closer and closer but never touching. I moved in some more, admiring her long eyelashes and the curve of her forehead, her freckled nose, her chin, her lips.

Those lips.

I didn't mind losing this time.

As I brushed her lips lightly with mine, her fingers combed through the fine curls at the nape of my neck, which had a looser texture than the zigzags of the rest of my hair. I deepened our kiss, letting my hands land—

The bellows of laughter, of exhaustion, of indignation in the hallway were too loud for me to ignore now. I looked around anxiously to ensure that we were still tucked away out of the line of sight of anyone who might be peeking through the glass window of the door. Ximena noticed my quick glance, and the corners of her lips drooped slightly. Besides Happi, Ximena was the most forthright, confident, swaggy person I knew. Heads turned and followed her when she walked down the hallway, because her aura of IDGA-single-F-itude was magnetic. The boys wanted her enviable sneaker collection and impeccable undercut. The girls wanted her expressive, large brown eyes and delicate bone structure. And the way Ximena carried herself let everyone know she knew it too.

I didn't like when I did this. Made her doubt herself.

I was my truest Keziah Leah Smith self with Ximena. We had never exchanged dramatic *I love you*s in our time together, but I had yet to come up with another word or phrase that encompassed everything I felt for her. Nor had I come up with a word for the unbearable sensation that spread through the hollows of my gut when I imagined the looks of horror and disappointment on my mom's and dad's faces if I told them I was in love with my best friend. And that she was my girlfriend. I knew intellectually that it wasn't my job to make my pastor parents love me—all parts of me. I also knew it wasn't my job to worry about what the congregants of the church they led would think. But I wasn't ready to hear what they would say to me. If they would try to pray with me. If they would declare callously and with conviction that, like God, they loved the "sinner" but hated my "sin." In their eyes, I would no longer be one of the holy ones, one of the good ones. I wasn't ready for that.

Once a week on my YouTube channel, I talked about how the world was overdue for acceptance. Inclusion. Tolerance was no longer enough, because it didn't require real commitment on our parts to embrace what made us each unique. Instead, it showed that we were fine with each other's differences so long as they weren't displayed for everyone to see, tucked away and never truly celebrated outside of the safe confines of the group in which you belonged.

I knew that being your authentic self, no matter where you were or who you were with, wasn't just an act of rebellion. It was an act of self-love. It took courage to step out and live your life out loud not just for everyone to see, but for *you*, damn the consequences.

I was ashamed to admit that I wasn't there yet.

Ximena broke away from me silently.

I opened my mouth to say…well, I wasn't sure what I could say that she hadn't heard from me before.

You're the kind of girl you fight wars for.

You're the kind of girl you fight wars with.

Ximena reached into the front pouch of her backpack and pulled out a beat-up old paperback. The top corner of the book was missing, as if someone had taken a bite out of the faded cover. "My *abuelita* said that this should help with your

AP Human Geo paper. It's the copy of *The Negro Motorist Green Book* that she used way back when."

I carefully took the book from Ximena and turned it around slowly in my hands. "Wow," I breathed. "It's like holding a snapshot in time between my fingers. Holding one of these never gets old."

"You're such a nerd." A tiny smile returned to Ximena's face. "All that research you've done is impressive."

"I can't wait to show it to you." My face and heart grew warm. "You won't believe the stuff I found online through the New York Public Library's database, and the couple seconds I got to skim my dad's heirloom copy, which he won't let me take out of the house. I told him that if that book could survive the deadliest war in history, it should be able to survive me taking a peek at it once in a while, but he acted like I said I was going to burn it. Thank your grandma for me again."

"She told me to tell you that she's just paying forward the kindness someone gave to her when she first arrived in the US," she answered. "Then she told me to leave her alone so she could focus on her *novela*."

Ximena had to get her fierceness from somewhere.

"Oh, grandmas," I said. I bit my lip. "So… I got a weird message this morning."

Ximena straightened in her seat.

"Weird how? From who?"

I showed her the email, watched her face contort in confusion. Worry.

"Who is this?"

I shrugged. "They sent something once before, but I didn't think anything of it. I know psychos come out the woodwork when you're a public figure, but it kinda freaked me out."

"Did you tell your parents?"

I looked at her like *come on now.*

"Fair enough, but can you like *do* anything about this? Go to the police?"

"They would laugh me out of the station. It's fine," I said firmly. "I just wanted to share because I was a little shaken up, but now I am *fine.*"

Ximena opened her mouth—

"How's the video game going?" I asked abruptly. She was going to study Game Design at NYU. We'd opened our college decision emails together in March and then celebrated when we each got into our dream schools. Wiped tears of relief from each other's eyes when we saw that all our hard work had paid off.

I never brought up what might happen to us when she was at NYU and I was at UC Berkeley, double majoring in African American Studies and History. She didn't either.

Ximena looked at me. "Really well," she finally said as she closed her programs and shut down the computer.

I knew that, in New York, Ximena would find someone who wasn't locked in a closet. She'd leave me behind like the three-hour time difference and the thousands of miles that would be between us.

"Will I see you tomorrow for the protest?" Ximena asked.

Man. The protest. I was going without a doubt, but I hadn't told my parents yet. I knew they'd put up a fuss, and I'd been holding off on letting them know. As soon as Ximena and I got word that POCs Uniting for Justice was organizing an event, we'd known that we had to be there. We'd tried to convince our other best friend, Derek Williams, to go too, but he said something along the lines of *Hell naw! I'm not about to become another statistic out in these streets.* He sounded like my parents.

"Yeah, I'll be there," I said.

"So, uh, I've got coding."

I nodded as she gathered her things.

She left without another word.

"I'm sorry. I think I'm in love with you," I whispered, trying it out on my tongue a little too late. One of these days I'd be able to say it to her proudly. Maybe I'd pull a page out of the retro Tom Cruise handbook and hop on a desk and shout it for all of our classmates and teachers at Edison to hear. But as the bell rang and I sat alone staring blankly at the black computer screen, I admitted something else to myself.

Today was not that day.

After placing the *Green Book* Ximena had gifted me in my bag, I realized that the assignment due in my first period history class was not there. I groaned and ran out of the lab, dodging students who were also stampeding through the hall, to get to my car. I sighed in relief when I saw several sheets of paper at the foot of the passenger seat and rolled my eyes at Happi, because she *had* to have felt them under her shoes, then grabbed my work and rushed back inside.

"Wait, wait! I'm here!"

Clutching the stack of notes in my hand, I scurried to the classroom door as the bell's final warning died away.

Mr. Bamhauer let me in with a smile but pointed dramatically at the front of the room. "You know the rules, Madame President."

I contained my huff and stood before my desk in the first row. Mr. Bamhauer was a man made up of power move upon power move. If you peeled each of them away one by one, you would eventually find that they were there to cloak a tiny little gnome of fragility.

Bing Mathis jerked his head lightly at me from his seat beside mine, and I followed his gaze to Mr. Bamhauer's desk, where the assignment had already been collected. I dropped my papers on top and mouthed *thanks*. Bing had been late to class last week because his school bus had broken down and he'd had to wait for another one to pick him up. After he'd finally gotten to class and explained this, Mr. Bamhauer had nodded and said, "You know the rules, Mr. Mathis."

"Now that everyone is here..." Mr. Bamhauer began, and the din of the room silenced immediately. "We can continue where we left off in our unit on the Civil Rights Movement."

I pressed record on my phone so that I could go back and review anything I missed the first time. Mr. Bamhauer encouraged this so that we wouldn't ask him to repeat himself. He paced between rows of desks with his arms folded.

"As you know, you can't look at a calendar and point to an exact date as the start of the Civil Rights Movement. But let's say it began around 1946, when many Black soldiers returned home from World War II, through 1968, with the signing of the Fair Housing Act and the death of Dr. Martin Luther King Jr., yes? During this period, African Americans advocated for equal rights under the law, something they had been doing since the abolishment of slavery in 1865."

He paused. I shuffled on my feet. Where was he going with this?

"But even as some African Americans fought for these rights, there were others who recalled a simpler time. In fact, there were some who didn't want to be free once slavery ended. There is a fascinating oral history in the Library of Congress of a woman born into slavery in Alabama who reminisced about her master's kindness."

I gasped and felt every single gaze land on me.

Mr. Bamhauer sniffed. "Would you like to say something, Madame President?"

"Um. Yes!"

"By all means, *please* do," he huffed.

"While this one woman might have felt that way, I don't think it's an accurate connection to make about formerly enslaved people in this context. I would argue that being given freedom without any tools with which to build a life after bondage might explain why someone would wish to go back to what they'd known. For a person to long for slavery after being considered property as a human being, whipped mercilessly, and ripped away from their family? That shows trauma. What exactly would you say are the redeeming qualities of the systemic degradation of the human spirit and bodies that was the enslavement of African descendants?"

"There's no need for the pretentious language, Madame President," he said. "But I'll bite. Perhaps 'redeeming qualities' isn't the phrase to be used here, but there is something to be said about the fact that slaves weren't working around the clock and even had Christmas off. And the woman I mentioned appreciated having everything she needed for survival, especially food—poultry, fruits, veggies, milk…"

My eyes widened. He ignored me.

"Furthermore, there's no denying the negative impact the ratification of the Thirteenth Amendment had on the Southern states. In fact, their economies were completely upended."

It took everything inside of me (and then some) to not yell at the apex of my lungs that Mr. Bamhauer was wrong, wrong, *wrong*. That this history he was teaching so flippantly was more than black words written on white pages, underlined with the gray graphite of pencil. That the green money of these Southern states hid something bigger: red blood shed on brown soil, watered by the tears of Black families being broken apart, generation after generation.

How could they trust someone like this to teach the future leaders (and followers) of America? This revisionist history was unacceptable. But I couldn't say any more. Not now, anyway. Mr. Bamhauer had strict rules against students interrupting his lectures for any reason that didn't involve preventing imminent death. He'd chuck me into the hall before the words left my mouth. So, I bit my tongue, and I didn't even whimper when I tasted blood. He soon moved on to the court cases I'd reviewed this morning, and he let me sit down when he got to the subject of nonviolent protest. As though everything was fine.

As soon as class was over, I marched right to Mr. Bamhauer's desk and demanded an explanation. "Sir, were you suggesting earlier that slavery was just a wrinkle on the history of this country? Do you think it wasn't that big of a deal?"

"Why, of course slavery was bad," he said with a smug little smirk, his thick mustache twitching. "It was abolished, after all."

"But that's not what you suggested today," I pressed. "Are you going to make that clear next class?"

Mr. Bamhauer stood and started to pack up his things. He had a planning period next, and everyone knew he used it to take a smoke break. He looked at me, boredom in his eyes.

"May I offer you some advice, Miss Smith? You should consider taking a step back from all of this…activism. I know colleges say they won't penalize you for the protesting and the advocacy, but people are watching. And this moment that's happening right now with your generation? It won't last."

He liked to play devil's advocate (not that the devil needed one) for the good old days and didn't enjoy being questioned for it.

He folded his arms. "Don't you have another class to get to?"

I spun on my heel and stormed out of that room in a thunderous cloud of rage and disbelief. I had to think. My next class was AP English Lit, and we were meeting in the library, which was perfect. Ms. Crown was giving us time to work on our study outlines independently and to have small group discussions about *Brave New World*. I suspected she was just as over the semester as we were and was confident we wouldn't embarrass her when our AP test scores came back, so she left us to our own devices. An idea was already percolating in my mind, and I needed to work through what had just happened.

I ran up a flight of stairs, frantically making my way to the media center. I was doing a great job of avoiding my dawdling classmates, sidestepping students lost in conversation, until I turned a corner and smacked right into a hard chest.

"Derek! Sorry, I'm on a mission…" I said to my best friend, who looked deep in his own thoughts. He barely grunted. I followed his distracted gaze and saw Happi, wearing oversize headphones and muttering lines to herself. She sauntered past us without even a glance our way, and I rolled my eyes. I didn't have time for this.

"Oh, hey, Kez," Derek said belatedly.

I waved him away. "Gotta go!"

I walked to the library and got to work splicing together the audio I'd recorded of Mr. Bamhauer, complete with faculty picture, and then recorded a video of my reaction to the lecture. In less than a half hour, I reviewed the footage, logged into my YouTube account…and hit Upload.

4

SHAQUERIA

TUESDAY, APRIL 10—
1 WEEK BEFORE THE ARREST
LOS ANGELES, CALIFORNIA

I didn't know why I agreed to meet with her. Yeah, she was perfectly put together, dressed up all fancy in a beige maxi dress that I didn't know how she kept clean, and her high heels looked more expensive than all my possessions combined. But a social worker was a social worker, whether they were decked to the nines or were wearing an ill-fitting suit that cost $19.99 on clearance at Ross. I had moved to LA to escape…this. The pitying looks from new social workers fresh out of their practicums. The boredom from the grayed ones who were jaded and had seen it all. Twice. They tried to help—some more than others—but all the effort in the world couldn't give me a family that stuck. That cared. That wouldn't hurt me.

"What do you think of the chicken?"

So she liked to wine and dine before getting into the nitty gritty. Cool.

"It's fine." It was free, so it was better than fine, but she didn't need to know that. I was still trying to find a job that would keep me available for auditions and pay enough to afford this heinously expensive city.

She popped a cut square of syrupy waffle into her mouth and smiled. Waited. I put my fork down.

"Ms. Howard, Roscoe's is great and all, but what are we doing here?"

She wiped her mouth. I glanced at the napkin. Not a whisper of her matte lipstick had transferred to the paper.

"Oh, just Sienna is fine."

Her sister, my former drama teacher back home in Jackson, Mississippi, was the same way. She insisted we call her Ms. Priscilla and not by her last name. I'd mostly kept to myself at school, and she had respected that while pushing me to give my all in my performances. Her class was the first place that I'd ever felt like I had space to truly breathe. Stretch muscles I didn't know my body had.

"Well. Ms. Sienna—I'm sorry, it's the Southern girl in me," I said apologetically, my excuse for this insistence on keeping a distance between us. "I'm so glad Ms. Priscilla is doing well and that her baby came into the world okay."

"Me too," Sienna said. "I will say, though, that she was very sad to learn you were gone when she returned from maternity leave."

I nodded slowly. There we go.

"I know I'm preaching to the choir here, but I turned eighteen, and in the state of Mississippi—and California, for that matter—I have the right to exit the system. So I did."

She leaned forward. Tapped her manicured nails on the sticky table.

"Yes, of course. But you've seen the statistics, haven't you? Youth in foster care have a much more successful transition to independent living in adulthood if they remain in the system for as long as possible, which in California's case is twenty-one years old."

I sighed. I hadn't truly believed she was different, but a part of me had hoped to be proven wrong.

"With all due respect, Ms. Sienna, I've been a statistic my entire life. Adding one more number over my head about how I'm bound to fail won't make a difference."

Sienna's eyes widened in horror.

"Oh! Gosh, I, I didn't mean to minimize your existence—I just want the best for you."

"Why? You don't know me."

Now it was my turn to wait.

"Well." She squirmed in her seat. "Prissy says you're really talented, and I can see just from speaking with you here that you're intelligent. We've got to look after each other and there's no reason—"

"So you think I'm 'one of the good ones'? The kids that aren't *too* messed up, that you can put on your government website? And what if I wasn't a good actress, or smart, like you say?" I laughed. My words sounded hollow in my ears. I was giving her a hard time, when all she wanted to do was help. But the thing about helping was that the helpers always got tired. And I got tired of trying to be helped. I had opened my heart to strangers over and over again, felt the love stomped out of it one too many times. All that was left was scar tissue.

"No one ever thinks of me that way. No one thinks of me at all, really," I said. She opened her mouth to interject, but I shook my head. "Look. Ms. Priscilla is a really nice lady, and her class was my favorite, pretty much the only one I went to consistently. But it was time for me to go. I saved up all my cash from work at the gas station and moved to the place where I could try this acting thing out for real, for real. And when I got here, I remembered quick that the only person I can really depend on is myself. I don't want to watch my back in group homes or feel unwelcome in people's houses. My life is hard, but I been knew that. So can I live?"

After lunch, Sienna insisted on driving me back to my neighborhood, and I took her up on the offer. I didn't want to spend what little money I had on an Uber, and the thought of dealing with LA's infuriating public transportation system when I didn't have to made me want to scream. She kept the conversation light for the rest of our time together, and let Janelle Monáe trill in the background between her comments about the traffic and the most popular tourist spots in the city.

"Right here is fine," I said, pointing to a cluster of tall buildings towering just as high as the patch of palm trees beside it. I could tell the area looked nicer than Sienna had imagined.

"Roommate," I said simply. No need to go into how I needed a new one fast because my stupid ex-boyfriend left. Just like everybody else.

"Here you go," she said, stopping so I could get out of the car.

"Well. Thank you for lunch," I said. "And, uh, you're a good sister for doing this for Ms. Priscilla."

She smiled sadly. "It was nice to meet you. I can certainly pull some strings to have you re-enter foster care if you decide that's what you want to do. We have some great resources in

Los Angeles County District Attorney's Office. And—I mean this—please, *please* reach out if you need anything."

She handed me her card through the window.

I nodded and waved as she drove off.

Once she was comfortably far away, I kept walking. I actually lived a few blocks down in a crappy studio. The entire downtown area was rapidly gentrifying, and I didn't know how I was going to afford rent on my own next month. I wasn't ready to go back to Jackson just yet. I needed to stay on the go, try to outrun my racing thoughts. I'd moved here to start over. Live the life I wanted to live. The first step? Find a job. Any job.

A tourist on a scooter came barreling down the sidewalk. Practically ran my ass over. While I was able to hop out of the way just in time, I still managed to topple backwards, my pivoted body ramming into the bulletin board posted outside of a local recreation center. I yelled after the long-gone man and grumbled from my spot on the ground. I was about to pick myself up when a flyer fluttered into my lap. I reflexively started to crumple it but stopped when I saw the words OPEN CASTING CALL staring back at me. I smoothed out the page and read.

They were looking to create a new show spun as the next generation of *Gossip Girl*, but grittier. Not *too* gritty of course. The beautiful, rich teens born of the right families would never face repercussions and would be allowed to make mistakes without fear of ruining their entire lives. Not like someone in real life. Someone like me. When the characters inevitably drank too much, rebelling against what they'd view as the unattainable pressures of living up to their family legacies, and threw up onscreen, even that would be glamorous. Vomit splashing directly into a porcelain toilet. Throats unburned by bile still allowing for perfectly clear delivery of well-rehearsed lines. Hair swooped back to keep from getting sullied by their mess. Eye makeup miraculously still intact. The audience would swoon about how *real* it was and how they were just kids, growing up and figuring out life.

I was still sitting on the ground when someone stopped in front of me. "What you doin' down there, girl?" the person asked, reaching to help me up. I took the hand and said thanks.

Her name was Jaz. One moment I was lost, wondering what the hell I was doing with my life and searching unsuccessfully for HELP WANTED signs posted in restaurant windows. Desperate. The next, I'd not only stumbled across a show that I would die to be on but the opportunity to make some real money so I could stick around in LA.

My luck had finally changed.

5

HAPPI

"Are you sure
That we are awake? It seems to me
That yet we sleep, we dream."

We dream
We dream
We dream

Sometimes I like to pretend I'm asleep and my life is simply an intricate dream. Depending on my mood, I imagine I'm actually four years old and at any moment, my preschool teacher will wake me up for snack time and I'll still have my whole life ahead of me. Lately though, I'm just three months younger. That fateful Tuesday in April never comes. I am snuggled in bed, slurping up a warm bowl of my mom's spicy chili chicken noodle soup because Kezi and I have caught a mean cold and are in no state to go out. Occasionally, we don't have the sniffles but an overdue case of chickenpox, despite our vaccines. That way, Kezi can't leave. Kezi and I are cooler than cool. We stay in and slather cold layers of calamine lotion and aloe vera on each other's backs. I cornrow her hair. She wraps mine. We don't go to school that day. We don't argue in the halls. We don't walk away on terrible terms.

But I keep opening my eyes to this reality.

I am back on my bench outside the theater, not dumb enough to really slumber here, but I need to be where I was during the last moment I had some semblance of peace. Not even peace—uncomfortable neutrality. Before those faces of confusion and surprise were engraved in my memory. Before I walked away from my family, again.

Nevertheless, my mind is operating on high gear, and thoughts ricochet across the edges of my brain and cut into my reverie.

Why did you leave?

What is wrong *with you?*

Breathe.

Just breathe.

How could you?

I avoid looking at the two guys around my age across the street who are playing music from enormous speakers and engaging in a loud, vibrant conversation over the beats. The slow punctuations of trap music compete with their words. (The music is losing.)

"Hell naw!" shouts the one in an oversize Bulls jersey.

"What?" snaps his friend in silver basketball shorts.

"You 'bout to get shot down!"

"But I'm smooth, though. My swag so good it makes up for my face."

I snort in an attempt to stifle my giggle. I put on a good show, usually, but I wish I had a quarter of the confidence of this unfortunately mugged but seemingly charming guy. My dad joked in a sermon once that we all got the saying wrong—it's not that God don't like ugly. He don't like ugly souls. It makes all the difference.

"Aye, girl!"

I groan inwardly but keep my expression detached. While I was admiring their Black Boy Joy convention from afar, I never intended to join it. *Aye girls* usually end with someone pissed off. The guy feels slighted when a girl keeps walking or says she's not interested, and the attention-seeking takes a nasty turn. Suddenly, the girl isn't that cute anymore. And thinks she's too good to turn around. Uppity.

The boys stroll across the street before I say a word, taking advantage of the stopped traffic at the red light. They're closer to my bench than I am to the theater. It's darker than when I was out here earlier, but I don't want to cause a ruckus by running away. I think of one of Kezi's YouTube videos I binge-watched after she died, about how Black boys are considered more mature and dangerous when they're much younger than other kids. Maybe it's a stupid thing to do in my case, since they're guys and I'm all alone, but I stay put.

"Don't be scared," the one in the Bulls jersey says as he lowers the music's volume.

"I'm not." I cross my arms and feign boredom.

"We wanna ask you something… If my boy Titus asked you out, what would you say?" He points to his friend.

"No tha—"

"Lemme clarify, I'm not asking *you* out," Titus cuts in. "I'm asking a girl *like* you out."

My pulse slows down and I relax. "Oh! And who are 'girls like me' exactly?"

"You know." Oversize Bulls Jersey motions vaguely in my general direction. "Fancy. She contours her face and shit."

I laugh so hard I cry.

"See? Reagan would wear waterproof mascara too," Titus says. "She's smart like that."

"How do you know her?" I ask.

"Marcus—" Titus points to Bulls jersey "—used to mess around with Reagan's cousin. When she wanted to get serious and he didn't, he ghosted her."

I groan and shake my head. "I know for a *fact* that this Reagan girl thinks you're trash now."

"That's what I said! But *Marcus* is the one going around leaving people on 'Read.' He's a fuccboi. Not me," Titus whines. "All I want is a chance to show her!"

"You have any classes with her?"

He shakes his head sadly. "She goes to a prep school across town. I told you, she's smart."

"Hmm. Well, where do you get to see her?"

"I don't. Only when I'd be chilling at Marcus's and she'd come over with her cousin."

"But her birthday pool party is tonight," Marcus offers. "And you better believe we about to crash that shit."

Marcus looks at me pointedly and asks, "Where are you from anyway?"

"What do you mean?" I say.

"It's obvious you ain't from here."

"Don't worry about it."

"Well, if you're not going back to 'Don't Worry About It'

anytime soon, you should swing by the Nash Park Pool to-night. Around eleven. Bathing suit optional. Birthday suit encouraged."

I roll my eyes. "He *is* a fuccboi, isn't he?"

Now it's their turn to laugh.

"Dang. For real, Happi?"

I turn and see Genny storming toward me. She's pissed.

KEZI

Dinner at the Smith house was serious business. Even though Mom and Dad were both full-time pastors, they made it their mission to ensure that our bodies were just as nourished as our souls. Actual words spoken by my cheesy-ass parents.

I inhaled my mom's world-famous double-crust chicken pot pie as soon as I floated through the front door. I followed the delicious scents of rosemary and turmeric and made a bee-line straight to the kitchen like a greedy fish being pulled by a hook. I stood in front of the oven debating whether or not I could sneak a little piece from the bottom of the cast iron skillet without anyone noticing. I grabbed a small spoon from the utensils drawer and, just as I looked over my shoulder to check that the coast was clear, Mom entered the kitchen.

"Mmm hmm. I knew I heard you come in," she said as she walked to me and plucked the spoon from my fist. She crossed her arms, her face pulled into an exaggerated frown. "If you even *think* about cutting into that pot pie before it's done, you'll never be able to use that hand again. Which would be a shame. You have such nice hands."

"Aw, come on, Ma. You know it's one of my favorite things you make. Let me get a tiny bit," I pleaded. "I won't even break the pastry."

"You can save those puppy dog eyes for someone else," Mom said heartlessly as she took me by the shoulders and led me out of the kitchen, farther and farther from the yummy food. "Now go wash up before dinner."

I sighed loudly as I made my way upstairs. Cheerful pictures of me, Happi, and Genny lined the wall, leading to the second floor. No one ever mentioned how Happi's smile had gotten less and less bright through the years, as if the light within her had dimmed. The bathroom was the first door on the right at the top of the landing, but it was firmly shut. I could hear someone having an animated conversation inside so, of course, I pressed my ear to the door.

"Love can transpose to form and dignity:
Love looks not with the eyes, but with the mind;
And therefore is wing'd Cupid painted blind:
Nor hath Love's mind of any judgement taste;
Wings and no eyes figure unheedy haste:
And therefore—"

"Happi!" I banged on the bathroom door. "How many times do I have to tell you that you have to practice your lines in your room? You can't keep hogging the bathroom like this, girl!"

"And how many times do *I* have to tell *you* that the bathroom has the best acoustics in the house and lets me know how I'll sound onstage?!"

"I. Don't. Care! Open. Up!" I accentuated each word with a pound on the door for emphasis. "See? We got acoustics out here too!"

Happi swung open the door and rolled her eyes to the heavens as she brushed roughly past me.

"Thanks, sis," I said as sweet as dripping honey to her retreating figure. She didn't even turn around to acknowledge me.

I tossed my book bag on the bathroom floor and shut the door behind me. I had only ten minutes to wash up and head downstairs for dinner. Mom was a stickler for us eating together as a family, and we had to be on time. If I arrived a minute after 7:00 p.m. without a good excuse, I'd be in for an earful. And Mom didn't want to hear anything about Happi hogging the bathroom either.

"Figure it out and keep me out of it!" Mom had said one too many times whenever I complained about my sister's selfish ways.

At least when Genny was around, I had reinforcements to make Happi get a move on and let the next person handle their business. But Genny had her own place out in downtown LA now. I missed her all the time, especially since it seemed that Happi and I had basically nothing in common anymore. Dinnertime was particularly a point of contention for us because, even though I secretly loved it when we all got together, Happi would rather be doing anything *but* that. If it wasn't for our family dinners, I wouldn't know what was going on in her life at all, despite us attending the same school.

That was part of the reason Mom had consistently kept up these daily meetups. For as long as I could remember, my parents had gone to pastors' conferences. One year a long time ago, the conference focus was on the family unit—because *if you can't lead your flock at home how can you be trusted with the Lord's sheep?* From that moment forward, my mom became obsessed with giving us the tools to become the best possible version of our family. One moment she was reading us an excerpt of a popular Christian blogger's article that highlighted the positive impact of parents and children sharing a daily meal. The next, we were rounded up to sit around the dinner table and recite our Highs, Lows, and Lessons of the day over a plate of shrimp tacos and mango salsa.

"It's not every day that you get a second chance," Mom said that first night as we sat around the previously unused walnut dining table. She was always talking about second chances, because it was a value she had been raised with. Her grandfather Joseph was murdered when her own father, Grandpa Riley, was a child, and it had altered the trajectory of Grandpa Riley's life. When an eight-year-old boy watches his mother fall to her knees as she learns her husband is dead—when that boy grows up in a series of tiny instances after he watches the men involved in his father's lynching never be held accountable for their crimes—of course it is life-changing.

Grandpa Riley's voice sharpened into a bitter, ragged edge when he told me once, and only once, that law enforcement hadn't even bothered to go through with a sham trial that would have undoubtedly resulted in unanimous exoneration for the perpetrators. That kind of shock, heartbreak, injustice, results in a second death—that of innocence, light, and hope. That bright, joyful eight-year-old boy was gone, a shell of a child left in his place. He went down what he called "a dark path," until he had An Encounter with God as a Young

Man and became a pastor. "But the Lord has been so kind as to grant us just that. A second chance. We will not waste it."

And so began our Organized Family Fun, or as Genny, Happi, and I called it when our parents first came up with this idea, OFF. (As in: Jesus, please turn it OFF.)

This evening was no different than any other. At first. Mom was perched at one end of the table, chattering about her day visiting sick congregation members with Derek's mom, Aunt Imani, while Dad ate silently across from her, nodding his head here and there to show he was listening.

"All right, Happi," Mom said. "It's your turn. Give us your HLLs."

Happi yawned exaggeratedly. "High: the girl who was originally going to play Helena in my school's performance of *A Midsummer Night's Dream* transferred schools suddenly, so Mrs. Torres is recasting her role. Low: Kezi banging on the bathroom door like she's lost all common sense."

It was my turn to roll my eyes.

"And Lesson: I guess really learning my lines for this role, because I'm going to try out again. This time, I'm going to kill it."

"Very good," Dad said after he swallowed a large spoonful of pot pie. "What about you, Kez?"

"Well…" I started as I wiped my mouth. "I would say that my High was definitely standing up to my low-key racist history teacher, Mr. Bamhauer."

"What's that now?" Mom said putting down her hibiscus tea. "You know we don't send you to school to be making scenes—"

"He basically claimed that slavery wasn't that bad."

Dad choked on his bite of chicken.

"Don't worry, I didn't say anything crazy to him that would

get me expelled or anything," I said. I'd chosen my words carefully. And then I'd shared my thoughts online.

Mom looked at my calm face suspiciously but let it rest.

"My Low is having to deal with Happi hogging the bathroom. *Again*." I wasn't getting into the real drama I was going through with Ximena.

"Petty," Happi interrupted.

"And—" I said, raising my voice to talk over my sister "—I would say that my biggest Lesson today would be everything I read in this little book here."

"What book is that?" Happi asked, right before I pulled Ximena's gift out of my book bag.

"It's Ximena's grandmother's copy of *The Negro Motorist Green Book*," I said. "It was like a special kind of Yellow Pages. Except this one was to help Black people travel safely through the US during Jim Crow. *Abuelita* Caridad has one of the most recent editions from the sixties. They stopped publishing a few years after the Civil Rights Act was passed."

"Okay...thank you for the PBS special," Happi said. "But you could've just said that it's another version of that crusty old pamphlet Dad keeps locked up in the safe. And Ximena's hardly Black. Her granny too."

"I'm not even going to get into how problematic it is that you think Ximena isn't Black enough," I said to Happi with a look of disdain. "The *Green Book* was primarily used by African Americans, yes, but it was also used by people who were considered second-class citizens at the time. That includes Latinx, Jewish, and multiethnic and multiracial people. And for your information, Ximena's grandma happens to fall in several of those groups. I'm going to include her firsthand account of using this book in my AP Human Geography report about the Great Migration."

I glanced sideways at Dad. "The internet's great and all, but I'm so relieved I also get to work with a physical *Green Book*, since *someone* won't even let me look at their copy..."

"Hey now," Dad said defensively. "I told you that I've only got two heirlooms from my grandparents. That crumbling yellowed *Green Book* and an old letter from my grandpa to my mother. And while they're in my possession, I'm not letting anything happen to them."

Mom nodded in support while Happi rolled her eyes.

"Maybe you can compare the listings in Ximena's copy of the *Green Book* with the online database, since she has a newer version of what's included on the website," Dad suggested. "And if you don't get an A on that project, I'm going down to that school myself, because your teacher would have to be crazy. You're putting in a lot of work there, missy!"

"Yeah." I smiled. "But it doesn't even feel like it. You know how much I love this stuff. It even gave me an idea to go on a road trip to celebrate my graduation. I started putting together the itinerary and everything a few weeks ago and posted a video yesterday announcing the stops I'm making this summer. I'm going to be in Chicago already because of that award I'm accepting, so I figured we could take Route 66 back home to California. Our last *Green Book* excursion should of course be Clifton's, that restaurant we went to last year to celebrate my birthday... Grandma DeeDee said her dad's best friend Parker was one of the first Black chefs they ever hired, after he moved out west for training. Maybe I can invite the Williamses again when we get back to give everyone a recap!"

"Graduation road trip?" Happi scoffed. "That's so lame."

"I don't think so! I'm going to film it for my YouTube channel, and I'm taking Ximena and Derek with me. You might want to keep your calendar open for this 'lame' trip, because I want you and Genny to come too. It'll be a last sister-friend hoorah before I go off to college."

"Hmmm. I think I'll pass. But thanks."

Mom and Dad exchanged a glance, and Mom interrupted before I could reply.

"So, Kezi! I think that sounds like a lovely idea. And speaking of graduation, let's talk about more immediate celebrations. Like dinner tomorrow. I know the big party is going to be this weekend since your birthday falls on a Tuesday, but do you have any special requests for what you'd like me to make?"

"Honestly, Ma, whatever you cook will be fine with me. Shoot, I'd be more than happy if this pot pie was the last meal of yours that I ever ate, it's so good. And spicy!"

Mom smiled widely with pride. One of her grandmothers was Haitian, which mainly meant that Mom threw scotch bonnet peppers into anything savory she cooked to feel "connected to the island."

Wonderful. I'd put her in a good mood before I dropped the bomb that I had been sitting on since I sat down to dinner.

"Besides," I continued. "I might be a little later than seven for dinner tomorrow...since I'm headed to the protest."

"What protest?" Mom and Dad said in unison.

"You know," I said, then slowly took my last bite of food and gulped down my water, stalling for time. "The one that they've been talking about on the news these last few days."

"Which one?" Happi asked. "I'm losing count."

"You must have heard about Jamal Coleman, the father in Florida whose kids watched the police shoot him to death a week ago," I said. "I'm going."

"No. You're not." Mom spoke with such finality that I almost agreed with her. "I don't have to remind you of all people that my grandfather Joseph was *murdered* and the police were not on our side, do I? He used that special *Green Book*, tried to find a place where no white people would bother him, and they still found the man. An entire family was destroyed. The police didn't want to hear about it then, and they don't want to hear about it now, particularly when they're directly involved in all this foolishness."

"I'm with your mom on this one," Dad said, always the unified front.

I cleared my throat.

"Tomorrow, I turn eighteen, and that means that I'm officially an adult," I said.

Happi's eyebrows leapt up to her baby hairs as I stood to clear my place at the table.

"I'll be an adult who makes her own choices. Who gets to live out loud. And what I want to do is my part to make society better for us all. So that no more families are destroyed. Especially the ones that look like ours.

"So you can be with my mom on this one all you want, but I'm still going."

7

Dear Daddy,

I stopped calling you Daddy in public a long time ago because I need my street cred. Don't worry though. I know you'll always think of me as your little girl. You see, I know a lot of things. For example, I know you're nervous, wondering what type of job I can get majoring in African American Studies and History. And I know you'll be proud of me no matter what. And I of course know you'll support my dreams even if you don't always get them.

But as I sit here and contemplate all of these things I know as confidently as my own name, I realize you probably have no idea why I want to pursue this particular degree in the first place. Well, it's because I'll be able to dig into our stories. I can do my part to help pull together the threads of our past to form a better view of our historical tapestry.

When I'm delving into my research, it's like I'm a detective on a case, following a trail of clues as far as it can take me. At the end of this chase is a less opaque understanding of what we've gone through as a people. It's a call that I want to answer again and again.

Anyway, I was able to use my super sleuthing skills on something closer to home. As soon as I sat down to write my report about *The Negro Motorist Green Book* for my AP Human Geography class, I knew that I wanted to keep exploring. It made me think not just about how Black people were living during the period of the guide but specifically how our own family was navigating this country. That led me to calling up Grandma DeeDee and mapping our relatives' moves through time. And the result of that search is what you're holding in your hands right now.

It's called narrative nonfiction. Basically, I took my conversations with Grandma DeeDee and learned about our past loved ones. These pages hold the story of Great-Grandma Evelyn. I'm so proud of this, Pops! I've started talking with a POC drama troupe about maybe filming something for my YouTube page and everything. I'm even thinking of having Happi play Great-Gran Evelyn, but she doesn't know it yet. Do you think she'll say yes? It's going to be a series about how real people used the Green Book to travel through the US, told through the eyes of our family. It's my way of having her legacy live on. I think she'd be proud.

And I know I haven't mentioned the elephant in the room about you and Ma getting mad at me during dinner.

But I'm hoping that when you read through this, you'll understand why I have to go even though you don't want me to. Evelyn had to run away when trouble came knocking on her door all those years ago. But now that we have the chance to at least speak up and let ourselves be heard, I'm never going to stop fighting for that. Because it's not just for me. It's for all of us.

Love,

Kezi

8

EVELYN

SUNDAY, AUGUST 1, 1937–
80 YEARS, 8 MONTHS, 16 DAYS BEFORE THE ARREST
NEW YORK, NEW YORK

"Oh, how I miss my hair," Evelyn thought aloud wistfully as she tugged on a silky tendril.

It was all there of course. God needn't update the official count on her head. But it was gone just the same. A brief rustle of wind lifted the bangs from her face then gently guided them back down. To mock her. One small consolation was that the strange, straight strands hanging limply down to her shoulders, jet-black and shining with pomade, would not stay that way long.

Beside her, the neighbor's dog had her tongue splayed out of the corner of her pointy mouth; she was beyond panting. My, my, Evelyn's companion was *shuddering* from heat exhaustion. Evelyn leaned over to caress the animal sympathetically and laughed when the golden retriever shrugged her hand off. It was too hot for affection.

This was a warmer summer than last by several degrees. And as such, it was but a matter of time before the droplets of sweat and splashes of chlorinated pool water would find their way into Evelyn's tendrils, where they would curl and kink and knot her locks back into her preferred halo of an afro. To be clear, Evelyn liked to think that her hair would be as desperate to return to its nappy roots in the height of winter, with air as dry as a cotton ball. Ah. Cotton. Like her old hair.

No more distractions. She swiped her hair from her eyes one last time and stared at the flyer like it was the answer to all the prayers she hadn't bothered to utter this entire summer. The creases from the neat square she folded the paper into when she wasn't admiring it had rubbed off some of the ink, but it was no matter. She knew the words by heart: *Thank you for your sponsorship of Warm Springs. We welcome you to...*

"Is that *Evelyn Hayes*?" said a dull-witted voice.

Evelyn cringed. Antonin Cerny was a stereotype, unfortunately. Each dimpled cheek, sharp angle of chiseled jaw, and gorgeous hole of nostril seemed to correspond with the loss of an IQ point. He was very, very handsome. Like his daddy, Mrs. Cerny liked to say. Emphatically. But Antonin Sr. had been nowhere to be found for fourteen years now. So Evelyn wouldn't know.

"Yes, Antonin," Evelyn replied as she slipped the paper into her pocket. "I changed my hair, not my face. Or my address."

Perched atop her family stoop on West 122nd Street was where she felt most regal. If Evelyn sat at the highest step of the staircase, with her back pin straight, it didn't matter that she was missing the scepter and crown. Residents of their thriving Harlem neighborhood would stop by, pay their respects. Never mind it was just to find out if Mrs. Hayes was taking new customers, or ask about Mr. Hayes's shoulder, or check in on Calvin at Morehouse. *I still can't believe that boy went all the way down to Atlanta. I wish my son would fix his mouth to tell me he was going to Georgia! Like the white folks in the North aren't bad enough. Well, anyway, tell your ma I stopped by...*

Church had been over for hours, but Antonin was still dressed in his blue slacks and white button-down shirt. His growth spurt had finally kicked in this summer, but his wardrobe hadn't caught up. He liked the way girls looked at his growing chest and his ripening forearms. This was not conjecture. The boy had been dumb enough to tell Evelyn that one lazy afternoon two weeks ago. Then he'd asked her if *she* ever looked at him that way, and Evelyn had pushed Antonin from her throne, all the way down, down, down to the sidewalk, just as two friends from school were walking by. Of *course* she had looked. He had turned his head and grinned as he let the girls help brush him off and usher him away.

But here he was again, leaning on the iron railing like he rented the place. (Not owned.) His feet were planted firmly on the sidewalk, but he still looked at Evelyn in thinly muffled, enraptured fear. She pretended not to notice.

"So what emotional turmoil are you currently enduring, Miss Evelyn?"

"What are you talking about, boy?" She crossed her arms to underscore her words.

"I don't claim to know everything, but I do know women." He chuckled to himself. The dog almost lifted her furry head to see what was so funny, but seemed to realize she didn't care. "And what fifteen years with my mother as my mother has taught me is that when a woman changes her hair in such a drastic manner, we all better watch out."

Not bad.

"And what do you think I'm...enduring?"

Antonin considered her thoughtfully, even biting his thumbnail in that way he did when he was thinking hard.

"By the looks of it..." he said as he sat down beside her. Their elbows kissed. He didn't move. (She didn't either.) "A broken heart."

"*Of course* you would go straight to—"

"But not regular heartbreak," he said, speaking louder. "Whatever you're dealing with has poked a giant hole through your soul."

Hmm.

Maybe there was something going on underneath that bed of waves of a head after all.

Nevertheless.

"I was supposed to go somewhere with my daddy, but I changed my mind and didn't want to anymore," she said. There. A change in subject.

"But you're a girl. Aren't you supposed to do everything they tell you?" He meant it in the nicest way possible.

Evelyn glared at Antonin, cocking her head so that the daggers she was shooting at him would lodge firmly in his pitch-brown irises.

He put his hands up in surrender. "Hey, I don't make the rules. And if I did, I wouldn't make them that way."

"Well, my family doesn't live by 'the rules' much," she said. "My mama probably makes way more money sewing clothes than my daddy does at the post office, for one."

"How is Mrs. Hayes? I haven't seen her at church lately. My mother wanted to show her how she styled the new dress she made her."

The electricity between their bones, piercing through skin easily, fizzled at the mention of Evelyn's mother. She pulled her arm away (okay, reluctantly) and embraced herself.

"Do you ever fear you and your mother are too close?"

Antonin chuckled. "Never. It's been me and her my whole life. I'd be more afraid if we weren't close."

He looked at her with an eyebrow raised. He'd made the sharpest of points.

"Mr. Cerny, I hope you listened hard to Pastor's sermon this morning!" Evelyn's father's voice boomed as he rounded the corner and approached the stoop. People on the block liked to say Mr. Hayes had a preternatural sense of awareness. That he could tell who was near his daughter at all times with just a sniff of the air.

"Yessir," Antonin said, leaping to his feet. He held out his hand in greeting as Mr. Hayes walked up the steps. Her father ignored it.

"James 1 verse 15," Mr. Hayes bellowed. He paused, waiting for Antonin or Evelyn to recite. When they continued to stare at him blankly, he shook his head as if to say, had they not been at the same service he'd attended this morning?

"...after desire has conceived, it gives birth to sin; and sin, when it is full-grown, gives birth to *death*." Mr. Hayes looked meaningfully—no, menacingly—at Antonin as he ended on *death*. No need to spell it out more explicitly than that.

Antonin's burgeoning little Adam's apple, a few months ago just a seed against his throat, bobbed up and down as he gulped.

Before Evelyn could offer up a bit of snark to calm her father, the front door creaked open slowly.

"Walker Hayes! Is that you harassing Evelyn's friends again? If you don't get in here..." Mrs. Elsa Hayes stood at the threshold with her arms crossed. She wore a magenta housecoat speckled with tiny white lilies. The dress, which would typically skim her slim body, puckered in the middle, revealing her waist. After the sudden weight loss, Mrs. Hayes had taken to altering all her clothing. When she had the strength.

As she frequently said, even before all of...*this*, life was much too short to wear anything unflattering.

"Mama! What are you doing up?" Evelyn raced to her mother's side and took her arm. "Where are your crutches? Do you need any help?"

"I'm fine, I'm fine," Mrs. Hayes said. "I have polio—I'm not buried in a coffin. Besides, I wanted to get a feel of what I was working with now."

She waved her daughter's concerns away and cracked open the door wider. "Antonin? Well I'm glad *somebody* had a good vacation! Come here so I can admire you better."

Antonin smirked at Evelyn as he bounded up the steps and presented himself before Mrs. Hayes. His eyes betrayed no surprise at seeing the woman's thin arms and legs, a sliver of what they'd been just a few months ago. Evelyn's mother had spent most of the summer doing what her doctors called "recovering" in a hospital. Evelyn never said it out loud, but what she was really doing was wasting away.

"Would you like to stay for dinner?"

Evelyn's eyes widened as she shook her head vigorously at her mother.

"I would absolutely *love* to," Antonin said as he smiled that outrageous smile.

"Perfect. I'll take that help now!" Mrs. Hayes laughed at the frowns on her husband's and daughter's faces.

"Alma sends her best, dear," Mr. Hayes mentioned as he folded a napkin neatly across his lap. He nodded gratefully at Evelyn as she put his favorite silver fork in front of him.

"Oh, I'm sure she missed me distracting her from all that boring mailman talk you and Victor are always doing," Mrs. Hayes said ruefully. "But tell me, did the new copies come?"

"They sure did!" Mr. Hayes said. He pushed himself out of his chair and took wide steps to the coffee table, where the leather Bible case Mrs. Hayes had bought him last Christmas sat. He pulled out a crisp but skinny book. The curved black lines on the green cover emphasized its bold title: *The Negro Motorist Green Book*. Mr. Hayes handed it triumphantly to his wife and dropped a brief kiss on the top of her head. They had always been affectionate, but even more so lately.

"Oh, Walker, it's beautiful!" Mrs. Hayes breathed. "They must be so thrilled."

"What's that?" Evelyn asked as she finished passing out the cups and utensils and finally took her seat. Antonin had set the dishes on their place mats without asking her if she wanted help. They'd laid the collards, the corn bread, the roast beef, the macaroni and cheese on the table together. She pretended to ignore him as he slid into her older brother Calvin's seat, grinning pleasantly at her parents' exchange.

"Last year, my colleague Mr. Green and his wife Alma, along with a fellow named George Smith, began publishing a little book of safe places Negroes in need of services can go to in New York," her father explained. "It got so popular that he published it again this year and even expanded the locations."

Evelyn took the book from her mother and slid her fingers over the boxes of auto repair shop addresses on the second page. Her gaze fell on a line at the top of the following page, an old adage she'd learned in school long ago: "An ounce of prevention is worth more than a pound of cure." The quote was a setup to explain the value of car tune-ups before arduous road trips, but Evelyn's mind skipped a few paces beyond that, to what a lack of preparation would mean to a Negro motorist whose car stalled on the wrong side of town. Ben

Franklin had not been thinking of the likes of them when he'd penned that famous line.

"That is a genius idea," Antonin said. "Mother is always a little shaken up before she has to go on the road for a gig... you're never sure what you might run into." Mrs. Cerny was a lounge singer. Some people at church didn't approve of her "lifestyle," but she did, and that was the only thing that mattered. She was out of town performing in Washington, DC that weekend, which partly explained Antonin's quick acceptance to dinner. (The other reason being that he loved to do anything that got a rise out of Evelyn.)

"Does that mean they think people will have money to spend, going out on the open road and stopping at restaurants and hotels?" Evelyn asked her parents.

The country was slowly recovering from the worst economic downturn in more than a generation. People had been hungry. Empty. They were still angry. Just when life had seemed to finally be getting back to a tentative normal, a new wave of recession had hit a few months ago and knocked everyone back off their feet. Grown folks on the block argued about a fresh deal, a new deal, flip-flopping on whether President Roosevelt had hurt or helped in the long run.

Somehow, through it all, the Hayeses had kept standing. By now, Mrs. Hayes's stitching and styling were celebrated enough that the people who were so rich that the winds of the economy didn't sway them this way or that (because they were the ones blowing) were loyal customers. As for Evelyn's daddy, well, he was a postal worker, and that old creed held true: neither snow, nor rain, nor heat, nor gloom of night, nor a great depression would stop the mail from being delivered. A few other neighbors counted themselves blessed not to belong to that ever-inclusive unemployment club. The Donaldsons next door, the

Washingtons the house over, the Fletchers across the street. No Rockefellers here, but they were doing okay.

This block was special. Beyond special. Mr. Hayes called it unction, a holy anointing. Evelyn felt blessed that, when her stomach growled, she had enough food to sop up the acids bubbling within her. However, the idea of God sprinkling favor on her family and friends but withholding it from others who were just as pious and worthy made her uncomfortable. Even the ones who weren't pious or worthy—did they deserve to starve? To freeze? To lose everything? She knew it made her father uneasy too, because the one time she'd asked him about it, he'd ordered her to hush. And if *she* was thinking about the disparity, *they* must be as well.

All that to say, Evelyn wasn't particularly surprised when a frantic *BANG BANG BANG* cut into their dinner just as she pierced her fork into her final morsel of roast beef. Her pulse quickened as her father walked to the door. She sucked in a breath when he turned the knob after recognizing the silhouette in the peephole.

"Th-the Kress on 125th!"

Brother Draymond poured himself into the foyer, not bothering to wipe his sweaty brow or remove his hat. He was the owner of the dog that Evelyn had been looking after and, like much of the neighborhood, he attended First Baptist, where he served as a deacon with Evelyn's daddy.

"What? Slow down, Draymond!" Mr. Hayes commanded.

Mrs. Hayes looked at the disheveled man across the room in alarm. "Come in, come in, have a seat," she said. "Evelyn, fetch him some water."

Evelyn was up, with Antonin on her heel. She walked slowly to the kitchen, hoping to catch more of Brother Draymond's frenzied words.

"The city's gonna burn to the ground! They got a new owner down at the five-and-dime, and the man claimed a Negro boy came in and stole a knife worth ten cents."

Evelyn stopped what she was doing. Antonin had been over enough times in search of free food to know where they kept their glasses. He brought one down from the pantry and scooped a few ice cubes into the cup before filling it with water from the pitcher in the refrigerator. She nodded at him gratefully as they walked back to the dining room, where Brother Draymond now sat staring blankly at his hands.

"The boy denied everything…but the white folks shopping in the store swarmed him and demanded he put the knife back. They brought in an officer who was patrolling out front and shouted 'arrest him, arrest him,'" he said hopelessly. "The boy wasn't much taller than Cerny here was a few weeks ago."

Evelyn's and Antonin's eyes met across the table. She rubbed her hands over the goose bumps that sprang up on her arms.

"They dragged that young man outside with him crying 'I didn't do it, I didn't do it' the whole way. Some other folks got into it and started throwing rocks, and another man had a gun and shot it in the air. Last I heard was some white men were going to round up their people and weapons to light up the neighborhood."

"This unlawful arrest was just an excuse," Evelyn said in realization.

Brother Draymond looked at her in surprise.

"There's been talk about putting us in our place for a while now," she said slowly. "To prove there was nothing special about us, to show there was no reason this neighborhood got to keep our jobs when they'd lost theirs."

"That is an astute observation, young lady," he said. "And now they mean to set our world on fire. Thank you for the water. I just came to collect my dog here for protection, and I got more folks to warn. A few of us are knocking on doors so everyone is aware."

Mr. Hayes cleared his throat. "I'll join—"

For the first time, Brother Draymond took in Mrs. Hayes's frail body, noticed the legs that did not really move, the sturdy sticks propped up on the wall behind her.

"Take care of yours, Hayes."

The air froze for just an instant. Their minds came up with every possible scenario of what could happen if they stayed in that house, if they guarded what was theirs. Evelyn sensed the smoke already. Felt the heat on her skin, anticipated a pain much deeper than the brief singe on her neck from the hot comb that morning. The terrible words that would be hurled at them like rocks. The physical pain that would reach their bodies. Her parents whispered urgently between themselves for a moment before her father hurried upstairs to grab the folder of birth certificates and the like that they kept in a drawer in their bedroom.

They filed into the car in a trance, no question that Antonin would be coming along, looking up at the darkening sky clouding with gray and black and licks of yellow-red. Mr. Hayes muttered a prayer and turned on the car. The shouts of the rioters were getting louder.

Evelyn didn't think. She jumped out and ran back into the house.

Elsa and Walker Hayes had never felt terror the way it exploded in their chests when their only daughter left the relative safety of their automobile. The relief that slowly crept in when they saw her appear seconds later waving a green book over her head could never make up for that fear.

To the untrained eye and mind, leaving a percolating race riot in the northeast and heading into the heart of the South was…unwise. At least Jonah had been running *away* from Nineveh when he was swallowed up by the giant fish. But Mrs. Hayes was desperate to make sure her baby boy Calvin was fine. She needed to confirm with her own eyes that the current horrors of Harlem hadn't somehow oozed their way to him by a sixth sense of knowing that he was from their block. A glance at the map Mr. Hayes begrudgingly kept in his glove compartment had shown Georgia was just as close (or far) as their relatives in Illinois. So they were going to Georgia. Evelyn blinked back tears of happiness and patted her pocket.

"Evelyn, did you bring a comb with you?"

Evelyn grunted an *of course not.*

"What a surprise," Mrs. Hayes said. "Luckily, I always carry one in my purse. You have to wrap your hair if you want it to last."

Evelyn took her mother's comb and started guiding the strands (just a tad frizzier than they'd been earlier that day… the scalp sweat from the sheer nerves of escaping an impending attack by white people intent on burning the world to the ground would do that to anyone) around her head. She let her hair fall like a curtain over her face when she caught Antonin staring at her. "What?"

"Don't you think Evelyn's hair is so beautiful?" Mrs. Hayes interjected.

"It sure is, ma'am." Antonin grinned.

Mr. Hayes *harumph*ed from the front seat. "Careful."

"Doing my hair is my own special ritual, but lately I've avoided it, what with it falling out from stress," Mrs. Hayes explained, turning in her seat to face Antonin. "Never mind that—" She waved her hand, to advance to the part of the story she really wanted to share. "I mentioned to Evelyn how I liked pressing my hair because it allowed me to focus on one task for a while, and that it gave me time to think. And how the smell reminded me of my own mama...then Evelyn asked me to press *her* hair this morning. Isn't that thoughtful?"

"That sounds like something our Evelyn would do all right," Antonin said.

Evelyn bit the inside of her cheek to stop from smiling.

9

HAPPI

THURSDAY, JULY 26—
3 MONTHS, 9 DAYS SINCE THE ARREST
CHICAGO, ILLINOIS

I knew Genny would make her way to my bench. I think I was subconsciously waiting for her to drag me back to the real world. To the sadness.

"Who's happy? I don't see no smiles," Marcus says to Genny.

He chuckles at his joke but stops abruptly when he sees the disappointment on my sister's face. She doesn't need to say excuse me or elbow her way closer to me. The boys just fall away to give her room.

"Your mom breaks down in front of I don't know how many people in the middle of a speech about *your dead sister*, and you walk out to talk to a bunch of random *dudes*? For real? You need attention that badly?"

Her words are a slap.

I get up before she tells me to, suddenly self-conscious about how I'm coming off to these strangers.

"Talk about what interests her," I mumble to Titus as I hitch my purse onto my shoulder.

I walk quickly away before Genny says anything else.

"Oh shit! I knew she looked familiar," I hear Titus whisper. "I think they're related to that girl who died out in LA a few months back."

"Sorry to ruin your group date," Genny sneers as she follows me.

My face burns and my eyes sting as I blink back tears.

Her certainty is what frustrates me most. She really believes I was flirting instead of trying to escape my frenzied thoughts and the panic that has invaded my body since April. That's the type of person I am to her.

Well. She doesn't deserve to see that part of me. The truth.

"I needed to take a break and get away from everything," I say in my most apathetic tone, sliding my mask back in place. "I can't act like I'm perfect all day like you can."

"What is wrong with you?"

I stop walking.

When Kezi first died, there was a brief moment when I thought things would change between me and Genny. For essentially my entire life, we've been superglue and sandpaper in a toolbox. Stuck together but only by happenstance. At first glance, someone might say it was the almost ten-year age gap, but that wasn't the case for her and our middle sister. It was just *our* problem. Mom and Dad were obsessed with each other and growing the church. And even though Kezi always tried to reach out to me... I wasn't the most receptive. She and Genny meshed. They had things to talk about. Follow-up questions to ask. Lunch. But that didn't happen with us.

"This isn't about looking perfect, Happi. What kind of perfect family travels around reminding people the police killed their kid? What sounds perfect about that?"

"You're twisting my words and you know it."

"I'm not twisting anything. But we're about to have dinner with our parents, and I need you to not do anything to stress out Ma any more than you already have."

I wipe my eyes with the back of my hand and adjust my face, but instead of entering the theater again, Genny walks purposefully toward the back of the building, where a few cars are still parked. She unlocks the door of a lemon-yellow Mustang convertible. The car is decorated with enormous plastic sunflowers and red, yellow, white, and pink tulips. Black power fist decals and 3-D peace signs are studded along the bumper and body.

I refuse to ask where it came from and pretend to be unimpressed as I slide into the back seat.

"You better get in the front. I'm not your Uber driver."

I stare at her in the rearview mirror, ready to argue. Dinner with my family is the last thing I want anyway.

As though she can sense it, Genny sucks her teeth loudly and rolls her eyes as she pulls out of the parking spot. "For someone who tries to act so grown all the damn time, you're being real immature."

I ignore her and glance down at my phone. Nothing.

The ride is as silent and charged as you would expect it to be. Genny has one of her annoying meditation session apps playing, which I try to drown out with my earbuds. I don't need another person to tell me how to inhale and exhale. Nothing can push this weight off my chest.

Genny doesn't say a word as we pull up to the hotel. She hands her keys to the valet in the driveway and smiles like her car is the most average-looking vehicle ever and then heads inside. She doesn't look back to see if I follow, or watch the valet circle the car in bewilderment.

The hotel floor is bustling with bellhops and people checking in while others stumble to and from the bar. The restaurant a few steps away is just as popping, but I spot my parents immediately, at a table tucked in a dimly lit corner.

Mom and Dad are the type of people who have always had eyes on them. Mom has flawless skin and short, wavy hair she keeps in a pixie cut. Dad's got a thick fade haircut, a dimple in his right cheek, and no dad-bod. They're captivating together. Basically two Beyoncés. Even before what happened with Kezi, people came up to them just to chat because they seemed like they were having so much darn fun. The women are always surprised when they learn Ma is the mother of two teenagers and one fully-grown adult. Dad plays the good husband when they get to that part of the exchange, because he'll politely let my mother have her moment even though her spiel clearly makes him uncomfortable.

As we get closer to the table, I notice an older couple leaning in to listen better to whatever Mom is in the middle of explaining.

"Thank you! I hope I look like you when I hit seventy-six!" Mom says.

"Honey, if this is you at forty-four, then I'm sure you'll be just fine," the woman replies.

"You know, I truly, truly believe it is a blessing from the Lord. Like I said, we used to live in sin and had our first girl in our teens," Mom says as easily as discussing the menu Dad was pretending to be engrossed in. "That was a shock. What did an eighteen- and nineteen-year-old know about raising God-fearing babies?"

The older woman's husband pulls out his phone to read an imaginary text message.

"But my God is a God of second chances, He is! Malcolm and I got married straightaway and even eventually heard the call to go to the seminary, and we pastor a growing church back in LA."

"Amen!" The woman waves her hand gently in the air. I can see the feathered fan she undoubtedly uses on Sundays so clearly in my mind.

"I like to think my family is like Job's. I even named my daughters after the children he had once the plagues and sickness and death stopped," Ma continues.

"Speak of the devil! Guess who's here?" Dad says.

"Were your ears burning, ladies?" Mom jokes when we approach them awkwardly. "Mrs. Loretta and Mr. Billy, this is our eldest, Jemima Genesis, and the youngest, Keren Happuch."

"Genny," my sister clarifies as she shakes their hands.

I wave listlessly and sit down. They can call me whatever they like. I'm never going to see them again.

"You know, Kezi—Keziah Leah—we liked to call her our 'doing it the right way baby.'"

Dad grunts.

"And—and *of course*, Happi was our beautiful bonus baby. We got to finish our little trinity of names. Granted, by then, I thought we had moved into the second act of Job's life when the bad stuff already stopped happening… But it's God's will."

For the first time, I notice the three and a half empty wineglasses on the table in front of my mother.

Dad clears his throat and smiles tightly. "Well, it was very, very nice to meet y'all. And thank you so much for the support. We're about to tuck in to some dinner, just the family, and be off to bed. Long day, you understand."

"Jesus! Look at us, monopolizing your time," Mrs. Loretta says as she swats her husband's chest. "I told you not to let me talk too much. You have a wonderful evening, you hear?"

Mr. Billy shakes Dad's hand, and Mrs. Loretta gives Mom a firm hug before walking away.

"That was…a lot," I say. I decided in the car to act like the scene in the theater didn't happen. Take my direction from the audience, if you will. Maybe if I'm more pleasant at dinner than I usually am, they'll leave me alone.

Before I even have a chance to determine what my fate is for the night, Genny grabs one of the empty glasses and taps the rim gently with her fork.

"Ahem. So now that we're alone… I have an announcement to make," she says. "As you know, Kezi would've graduated this past May at the top of her class, and she wanted to take a road trip to celebrate." Genny rests her purse on the table and pulls out a tattered green pamphlet. "More specifically, she was going to explore old Route 66 and its nearby roads with the help of *The Negro Motorist Green Book* so she could investigate what life was like for people like us back then."

"Yeah…" Dad says, leaning forward with a slight frown.

"I want to take the trip in her honor and vlog about it on her YouTube page! I could even somehow tackle the web series she planned to do using her narrative nonfiction. With Happi," she adds hastily. "We would cancel the meet-and-greets she set up with her followers of course. I don't think we're ready for that kind of interaction… Ooh and I've already gotten my principal investigator's blessing at the lab. It will be our way of commemorating Kezi's life and upholding her legacy."

Mom sobers up real quick and puts down the piece of bread she'd been buttering. "No," she says simply.

Genny's chuckle is free of any humor. "I'm not exactly asking y'all for permission. I was hoping you'd be supportive, after everything we've been through these few months."

"Everything we've *been* through? You must be out your damn mind if you think a road trip across the American heartland is what you need to be doing right now," Mom says.

"You're like the new face of social justice! How can you say no when in your own speech today you talked about Kezi's—"

"Malcolm, speak some wisdom into your daughter," my mother says tiredly.

My dad drums his index fingers on the table and is silent for a moment, unquestionably experiencing the wave of déjà vu washing over him like it is with me. With Kezi. Then, "Gen, this country is dangerous. You know that. I'm not too comfortable with the idea of my two little girls—"

"Number one. I'm not a little girl," Genny whispers. "Number two. You have three daughters. *Three.* And what one of them wanted was to celebrate the next chapter in her life." He opens his mouth, but she plows through. "But there are no more chapters. I have to do this one last thing for her."

"I don't need history to repeat itself!" Dad slams his fist on the table. A man and woman sitting a few tables over jump in surprise at the noise and point at us. "Look what happened in California. And you want to go hunting for this madness out in *Missouri* and *Oklahoma*?" The only other time I really saw him lose his cool was when we were going to Kezi's funeral. His eyes had the same look of dazed disbelief.

"Hey there, I'm back and yay, the rest of your party's arrived! Are you four ready to order?" The waiter looks around my age and must lack the ability to read a room or even a closet. He lifts his pen dramatically over his pad of paper, then tucks a loose dreadlock behind his ear and waits.

I close my mouth, which had been hanging open during the verbal tennis match between the two most soft-spoken members of the Smith clan. I didn't think it was Job's first daughter who would be getting ripped into tonight.

"Sorry. Make that three instead," Genny hisses, pushing herself out of her seat. She pulls out two folded pieces of paper from the *Green Book* and slams them on the table. I recognize the assured round lines of Kezi's handwriting before the sheet flutters closed again, and my throat catches as I read the first line of the first page.

To Daddy...

It's like she never left.

"I'm hitting the road tomorrow, with or without your blessing."

10

KEZI

I didn't even pretend to pay attention to the presentation about cellular respiration in second period AP Biology. Yes, it was my birthday, but my mind was focused on the rally. I was itching for class to come to an end. My teacher must've noticed how uncharacteristically spaced out I appeared, so when she asked me something about the citric acid cycle, she looked just as surprised as I was when I said the correct answer. (Tip: when in doubt, it's always mitochondria.) We were about to break for lunch, which meant that in a few short hours, I would be on my way to the protest for Jamal Coleman. My nerves had been on ten all day as I thought about what it would be like to take my digital activism offline to my first in-person protest. Even if it meant my parents weren't speaking to me. That was okay. I'd win them over again.

"Don't forget, everyone." The shout rang over my class-mates as they loudly got ready to leave. "Your assignment on oxidative phosphorylation and the electron transport chain is due this Friday at the beginning of class. I won't take it from you if you try to sneak it in at the end!"

My peers finished packing up their belongings, and I quickly did the same. I had one thing on my mind, and that was to get to the cafeteria as fast as possible. I was meeting Ximena and Derek for lunch, which was something I did every day, but the anticipatory buzz I felt in the pit of my gut was new. I hoped Ximena and I would be able to convince Derek to join us, but I wasn't holding my breath. If anything, he would help me and Ximena figure out the best ways to maximize our presence at the march. We would mostly just be walking in tandem with the surrounding protestors, shouting as one. But we wanted to come up with a chant that was clever enough to get the whole crowd to join in and foster a greater sense of unity. So far, all the ideas we'd come up with were trash.

I wound my way through the crowd of students, avoiding people as they ran through the halls or stopped in the middle of the walkway to chat. I noticed a few kids staring at me in-tently, whispering as I walked past. Strange.

Just as I was turning into the cafeteria, I made out a famil-iar neon-pink book bag bobbing closer and closer to the exit.

Now where does that girl think she's going? I thought as I watched my younger sister attempt to sneak off of campus. Well, she wasn't really trying...or sneaking. She was more so daring anyone to stop her. The first time I'd heard the phrase, "Ask for forgiveness, not permission," I'd immediately pictured Happi, simply being herself. It was her life's motto, whether she knew it or not. And attached right beside her was her human parasite of a boyfriend.

There was no denying that Santiago Garcia was objectively attractive, if there was such a thing. Tan olive skin, dark curly hair, and the stubble of a fledgling beard that lined his sharp jaw and directed your eyes right back up to his striking hazel ones. Happi was head over heels for this fool…and so were the rest of the girls in her grade. Even a few of the seniors would joke about wanting to rob the cradle for a piece of him. And some of them had successfully done so too, Happi be damned.

I quickened my pace to catch up to the two truants and grabbed Happi by the arm a few feet before she reached the door to freedom.

"What the hell?" Happi yelled as she spun around to see who was holding on to her. Santiago turned with her, ready to step in, but stopped as soon as he realized it was me.

"Aw damn," he said, gaze hopping back and forth between me and Happi. "I'm gonna wait for you outside, babe."

Santiago didn't even pause to hear if Happi had any objections and slipped out of the building. He knew that he was on my ain't-shit-list ever since his trifling ways became known to me and the entire school. He had never even tried to get back into my good graces either. (Maybe because such a place didn't exist for him.) Especially since I had pulled him aside to read him for filth at Russell Stewart's party a few months ago after I found him cozying up to some girl from another school that nobody even knew. Happi had seen me whispering at him furiously and had started shouting at *me* for getting on his case. And I had just stared at her, wondering how she could be such a dummy.

"Where do you think you're going, Happi? You don't think you've missed enough school this semester?"

"First of all, *all* of my absences have been excused." Happi counted on her fingers. "And second of all, you need to mind your business."

"Well lucky for you, little sister, you *are* my business."

A shadow of annoyance flickered across Happi's face. She hated whenever I asked her any question at all. Showed that I cared. And she always made sure to point out that Genny was never on my case like I was on hers... I'm certain she thought I was babying her, but I only checked in because I wanted to know she was okay. And if I didn't, who knew what could go down? I was usually good at not mentioning the glaring fact that I didn't really do much to warrant our older sister worrying about me.

"You think just because you're a year ahead of me and have your little YouTube followers and a random viral moment you can tell me what to do?"

"I didn't say that, Happi," I said. "And furthermore... Wait... Viral moment? What are you talking about?"

"Have you even looked at your phone since you posted that video of you roasting Mr. Bamhauer? Everyone's talking about it."

I pulled my cell out of my pocket and looked down. I had what looked like hundreds if not thousands of comments on my YouTube channel. Whoa. A major youth activist had posted it on his social media pages. It had blown. All. The. Way. Up.

This is someone who's in charge of KIDS? Oh hell no!

Thank you so much for posting this. We need to get this man out of that school!

Mesmerizing. Smart. Articulate. You're so special, Kezi. Do you know that? Just tell me what you want to do about this guy and I can take care of it.

"I'm gonna go, Kezi," Happi said, snapping my attention back to her. I really wanted to read through all of the comments and block any weirdos, but my rebellious sister needed a voice of reason to keep her out of trouble. I tucked my phone back into my pocket. I was a little worried about whether or not Mr. Bamhauer would find a way to turn this on me and get *me* in trouble for calling him out. I'd really have to put up a fight then. But those thoughts would have to wait.

"Look," I said, my attention squarely focused on Happi. "I'm just trying to make sure you don't get yourself into trouble with that waste of space. Besides, I know you haven't told anybody where you're slinking off to. And God forbid something happens to you...we need to know where to look first."

Happi sighed exaggeratedly. "Again, I'm gonna go. I have an audition to get to. Okay? Cool. Bye."

"Nuh uh," I said pulling my sister's arm again as she turned to leave. "What are you auditioning for that would take place in the middle of a school day? Pregnant teen?"

I regretted it as soon as the words escaped my mouth. I heard my mother in my voice. The worst part of her. Our mom had started warning us against messing around with "fast boys" the moment we could pronounce three-syllable words like pu·ber·ty. At least she'd included guys in her slut-shaming. Mom didn't want any of us to end up "with child" early like her, especially while we were living under her roof. *"I'm not about to be watching over anybody's kids!"*

What she really meant was that she wasn't about to have us embarrass her in front of the church, walking around with basketball bellies one month and bawling babies the next. The possibility of having a daughter who had no interest in boys, fast or slow, never crossed her mind.

"How *progressive* of you, Kezi," Happi said. "Did I say it right? Pro-Gress-Ive?"

"Look, I'm sorry. That came out wrong."

"I don't even know why you're acting like you give a damn," Happi continued. "And not that it matters, but I'm going to audition for a TV show. Sometimes they're on school days. Santiago is auditioning too. If I'm lucky, I'll get the role and be able to film somewhere far away from you. Let's shoot for Atlanta."

This was going worse than I anticipated.

Happi paused and looked up, as if waiting for her next words to float down from the ceiling.

"You're not better than me," she said finally, body angled more toward the exit.

"I never—"

"You've never said it, but you've always thought it. I may not have the most book smarts out of the Stupendous Smith Sisters, but I have emotional intelligence."

"Of course you're smart. I didn't mean to make you feel like I don't think you are. I just think that you should make better deci—"

"Look. Leave me alone," Happi said slowly. "The only thing we have in common is our parents. Allegedly. And that's fine. You're not responsible for me, and I don't need you to be."

"But I *want* to be, Happi!"

"How about this? *I* don't want you to be."

The final twist into my heart. There was once a time that, if I shut my eyes and thought back really, really hard to when we were kids, I'd come up with memories of Happi following my every move. If I got a cowboy hat, she got a cowboy hat. If I read the most books in second grade, then she would try to do the same in first. That period in our childhoods hadn't lasted long. But I still think about it a lot.

"You're the one who's going to be in major trouble for going to that stupid protest you have no business going to. Especially since our folks told you no. And now that you've got this video floating around, you know you're going to be called down to talk to the principal any second now. Worry about yourself."

I tugged on the straps of my bag in frustration. There was some truth to what she was saying. But I'd never admit that.

"How can you be so willfully ignorant?" I said to my sister as she walked away. Again. "It's our job to speak up when things aren't right, Happi. Just because something hasn't happened to you directly doesn't mean that it can't one day. We all have to stick together. Stop being so...self-centered."

"*I'm* the self-centered one? Don't act like you didn't calculate how all this shit you do looked for your college applications. Stop pretending like you don't live for Mom's praise and for those hypocrites at church to give you a pat on the head." She enunciated each word. "I am not like you. I am not living my life for people. I am living it for me. It's not my fault you can't."

I didn't know when she'd developed the capacity to be so cruel. I couldn't figure out how much of this was my fault.

"You don't know anything, Happi," I whispered.

My baby sister turned on her heels. "Stop lecturing me!" she shouted, loud enough for all the kids around us to hear and fall silent. "You don't get tired of always being so woke? Go take a nap sometime, damn!"

I gave up. I would not—could not—stop her as she flung open the double doors and stalked out, leaving me behind with only the teasing laughter of our fellow students to mock me.

11

SHAQUERIA

TUESDAY, APRIL 17–
THE DAY OF THE ARREST
LOS ANGELES, CALIFORNIA

It wasn't always this way, but for so long, my life has been about belonging to someone else.

First as a ward of the state of Mississippi.

Then as a foster child of all the women and men who said I could call them Mom and Dad, so long as the checks from the government didn't bounce.

Now it's to Darius. If you let him tell it, I was one of his ladies starting today.

But no matter who I belonged to, I always did something to mess it up.

I looked down at the script I held and saw the splotches of tears dancing all over the pages in my trembling hands. My asthma was flaring up from my nerves and making me shake.

All I had to do was nod, just like Jaz told me, but I still managed to get it wrong. Why had I mentioned the audition? Did he look like the type of guy who would be understanding about a girl having her own ambitions? I couldn't believe I had opened myself up like that. Again. I must've thought I was one of those characters I tried out for all the time but could never land. Headstrong. Smart. Beautiful.

I had met Jaz just a week ago, but we understood each other. She'd seen a girl sitting on the sidewalk looking broke and miserable. Vulnerable. I'd seen a girl who looked hard but was dripping in a pair of gold gladiator sandals and an outfit that looked more expensive than the one that social worker I'd had lunch with had been wearing that day. I wasn't dumb. I knew Darius probably paid her well to prey on girls "like me." Castaways. The ones society liked to pretend didn't exist until our bodies ended up in an alley somewhere and no one came to claim us. I knew it was a risk to work for a guy like him. But I promised myself I wouldn't stay in this world for long. I would make my money and then get out before anything happened.

"Man, shut yo' dumb ass up!" Darius shouted at me right before smacking me so hard across the side of my face that the inside of my mouth split and filled with blood. Like a lever had been pulled to open a dam. But even I wasn't foolish enough to spit it out on the floor. Not on Darius's pretty white carpet. Even if all I wanted to do was empty my mouth and suck on my rescue inhaler. I breathed in deeply through my nose, tried to calm myself down. "I don't give a damn what you have to do today. That's not what I pay you for."

Darius was right. He didn't pay me to talk back to him. He didn't pay me to have auditions on days that coincided with his deliveries. And he sure as hell didn't pay me to have plans for a future. So I shut my mouth like I should've done in the first place and took the brick he put in my hand.

I was going to give this to his buddy Tyler. A white boy at USC who had somehow gotten himself indebted to Darius and was now his go-to guy on campus. Jaz said that working with Tyler was always easy because he was just a stupid kid. All he wanted to do was finish his four years in college, graduate, and never have to deal with Darius again. He didn't want to be a part of this any more than any of us ladies, so our exchanges with him would always be quick. Not like how I heard it was with some of the other fellas that I would one day have to meet up with.

But this was my first delivery, and Jaz had somehow convinced Darius to go easy on me. Start me off small with Tyler. I had to thank her for looking out for me, when I got the chance.

I stuffed the package into my backpack for Darius to see, and as soon as I was out of the house, I pulled out my inhaler and took two deep puffs. I was okay. I threw my lifeline back into my bag, set an alarm to remind me when to leave for the delivery and got moving. I hadn't loosened my grip on the script though. It helped remind me who I was.

How funny was it that acting like other people helped me feel more like me? Maybe it was because I've always been an actress in a way, with a cast of strangers walking onto the stage and through the revolving door that was my life. Everyone knew that, in a good story, every character needed to *want* something. And God as my playwright didn't disappoint. Each member of the show wanted something from me. Good behavior. Money. Obedience.

I hastened my steps as I made my way to the audition I had been prepping for in stolen moments yesterday. I knew

Darius had just said that he didn't pay me to do anything but make his deliveries, but he wouldn't even know I had gone if I played my cards right. I'd just head to my audition, say my lines, and go meet Tyler right after. I would have plenty of time to do what I'd come all the way to LA to do *and* my new job. As long as I wasn't late, Darius would be none the wiser, and I'd be one step closer to fulfilling my dreams.

Besides, I couldn't miss this. Not when fate had practically shouted my name, telling me to come to this audition.

I pulled out my phone to check the time just as I walked up to the location of the tryouts. It was a little after noon. *I've got this*, I told myself as I entered the shiny office building. It was half reminder to myself and half prayer to the universe. I made my way to a short, frazzled blonde woman. She was walking around purposefully, clipboard in one hand and black pen that she *click, click, click*ed in the other.

"Hi. I'm here for my audition for *Thatcher Academy*. I was told to arrive at 12:30 p.m."

The woman asked for my information and flipped through the papers in her hand. She came across my name and put a check mark beside it. But I was already Sloane, the frosty loner of Thatcher Academy who had been burned one too many times.

It wasn't too far from my truth.

"We'll call you when we're ready," the woman said and started to walk away.

"Do you know how long it will take?" I asked before she could leave.

She looked back at me with a smirk on her face. "You've got someplace more important to be?"

I didn't answer, and she sighed.

"There are quite a few people ahead of you, but it shouldn't be more than an hour," she offered before turning away to deal with some major casting crisis that I wasn't privy to.

I grabbed a seat among the dozens of acting hopefuls but didn't sit there for too long. It was always the wait that got to me. As I stood up to search for a bathroom where I could practice some breathing exercises and calm my nerves in private, an overhead system crackled to life. My pulse galloped as my thoughts turned to the drugs in my bag. *Was that the police?*

Nope. Just the name of the next person being called in for their audition. My heart slowly settled down as I realized no one was checking for me like that. I wiped my palms on the side of my pants. I needed to relax. I found the women's restroom easily, but there was a couple standing right in front of the door. A short Black girl with perfectly pressed hair and a Spanish boy who was too fine for his own good. They were clearly having an argument but trying their hardest to not let everyone be all up in their business. I squeezed past them without saying excuse me and stepped into the bathroom. I could still hear them through the closed door as I pulled off my book bag and shuffled through for my inhaler. It was a nervous habit, but I always had to check that it wasn't far from reach. Just in case my jitters got the best of me and took my breath away. The brick that Darius said was "worth ten" of me sat in the folds of my sweater. I covered the taped-up package further and tried to put the drugs in a place far, far away in my mind.

"Why do you always have to start with her like that though?" I could hear the guy saying.

"You don't get it. She's always judging me!" The girl had thrown out all attempts to keep her voice down now.

"She's looking out for you! She's your sister. And every

time you try to pick a fight with her when I'm around, she thinks *I'm* the one who's a bad influence."

"Oh, so does that mean that *I'm* the bad influence?! You know what. Table this." She was hissing at him again, apparently finally aware of how loud they were being. "I'm not about to look crazy in front of these white people."

The bathroom door swung open as the girl stormed in and slammed her neon pink backpack on the bathroom counter. I quickly zipped up my bag and tried not to appear guilty. She didn't look at me as she rummaged through her stuff, but she was clearly crying. Her face was scrunched in anger but even so, it was apparent she was a pretty girl.

There were mostly white teens waiting outside to audition, but just enough folks with melanin present that critics would praise the future cast for its supposed diversity and inclusion. She was a contender. Big, expressive brown eyes. Full lips tugged down at the corners as she pulled herself together. She was a bit shorter than me, but I could actually see my face in hers. We could be sisters. But I didn't have any family to speak of. I had no one.

"Guys suck," I said with a small shake of my head. I grabbed a few paper towels from the fancy weaved basket next to me and handed them to her.

The girl took them from me and dabbed at her eyes, trying to smile. "Thank you," she said, her voice still wobbly with tears.

"Forget about him and focus on why you came all this way," I said. "I actually snuck in here to practice some breathing exercises, if you want to do them with me?"

She looked at me strangely but didn't answer.

"There aren't many of us here," I said with a shrug. "We've gotta stick together, you know?"

This time she grinned for real. "Okay."

We stood there, the both of us pulling in deep breaths through our noses, our stomachs inflating like balloons full to bursting only to let the air escape slowly through our mouths, the tension slipping out with it.

In…three…two…one.

Hold…two…one.

Out…four…three…two…one.

"Thank you for doing that," the girl said after she'd retouched her makeup to erase any sign of crying. She was ready now. "I'm—"

"Happi Smith?" The same voice from earlier blared over the intercom system. "Please head to the audition area. Happi Smith. Please head to the audition area."

"That's me," the girl explained, already making her way to the door.

"Good luck!" I said. "Oops—I mean, break a leg!"

She smiled at me one last time and left. I just knew deep down she was the kind of girl they wanted for this show. The casting directors would take one look at her and sense she was one of the good ones.

I hoped there was enough luck left for me.

12

HAPPI

"If I can recommend anything for the table, it would *definitely* be the sesame crusted calamari." Our waiter picks up right where he left off before Genny stormed away.

He must be an improv performer. *The show must go on.*

"What do you think about the fried lobster mac and cheese balls?" I ask politely. It feels strange to be on this side of a family explosion. Genny does not blow up. She sighs and meditates and thinks through all her potential actions and choices until it doesn't matter what decision she makes. She tries to talk me out of pursuing acting for the sake of practicality. She does not dramatically leave meals and declare loudly that she will disobey her parents.

In public, at that.

I do. I am the dynamite. But not tonight. Dad is silently fuming, and the puffy bags under Mom's eyes are begging for a cold compress.

In the past, whenever I'd leave dinner in a huff, the continued clinking of glasses and scraping of plates would make me want to scream. It was as if they hadn't realized I'd gone. My blood would run hot if I heard Kezi tell a joke that made our parents laugh while I was upstairs fuming. Like they couldn't care less about how I was feeling. But sitting here in their company, I suddenly understand the need to keep the wheels moving, just for a sense of normalcy. It's not as if we're going to rehash what just transpired and bare our souls in front of this complete stranger anyway.

"Well, personally, I avoid all dairy because I'm tragically lactose intolerant, so I can't really say...but it's one of our most popular—"

"I can't do this," Mom cuts in. Glass number four is now empty too. She opens her purse and clumsily sifts through its contents before giving up in irritation. "Malcolm, please—"

My dad whips out his wallet and leaves a few bills on the table before pulling out my mother's chair. She grabs his hand gratefully and heaves herself up from the seat.

"You know what, we're actually going to head to our room instead. Thank you so much for your hospitality, young man," Dad says. "Happi, you can go ahead and eat here or order room service if you'd like. We'll see you in the morning."

His lips curve up for less than a millisecond then shoot back down, as though his face needed a moment to register that he's given up trying to smile.

"Let me know if you need anything," I offer weakly.

He nods. My mother looks straight ahead and says nothing. She has a right to be upset with me. It hasn't been that long since I walked out on her in front of a live audience, after all. I wish I could reach over and hug her tightly. But I have cultivated our relationship to be one that exists on as little love and light as possible.

The waiter's unflappable armor finally cracks, and he grimaces at my parents' backs as they walk out the restaurant.

I gaze at the three empty seats around me.

"Yeah...uh...did you still want those appetizers?"

I shake my head slowly.

"No, thanks. I don't even like cheese. I wanted to get them for my mom. But she left."

"So you *do* exist!"

"Excuse me?"

"My boyfriend absolutely abhors cheese, and he's always claiming that there are more people like him out there, lurking in the shadows of society, pretending to be normal. But you're the first I've met."

I chuckle. "We indeed exist. Our organization meets every Wednesday at four a.m. while everyone's still asleep and digesting all that lactose."

"You're a clever one, aren't you?"

I sigh. "That's usually reserved for my older sister."

"Wait. Was that the one who was about to flip over the table when I came over?"

I lift an eyebrow at him in warning. "She's been through a lot. I'm surprised it took her this long to...express herself." I have serious beef with Genny, but that's between me and her.

The waiter considers me slowly, wrapping a thin dreadlock around his finger thoughtfully. "You're making me real sad."

Okay. It's time to go.

"Imagine how I feel," I say, scraping my chair loudly against the floor. "Tip's on the table. Bye."

"Wait a minute!"

I pause.

"I didn't mean, 'you're making me sad, please go away.' I was just stating a fact," he explains. "Listen, I'm going to check on my other tables, but take a look at the menu. Okay?"

I'm not ready to be by myself. I nod.

My phone buzzes and I look down.

Sorry was busy

Santiago's text message burns like a pot of boiling acid. I get that he was busy, especially since he actually won a role on that teen soap opera we both skipped school and auditioned for the day Kezi died. "Javier" is the brooding new boy in town with a full ride to the show's elite private school and has plenty of secrets up his tattooed sleeves. The showrunners (and Santiago himself) are convinced he's going to be a fan favorite. In between me preparing for Kezi's funeral and traveling for Mom's speeches and Santiago's filming and media training, we haven't seen much of each other over these past few months. The only thing left to do is say goodbye. But I am too much of a coward and not ready to have one more thing change in my life. And Santiago doesn't want to be the guy who dumped the girl with the dead sister.

My fingers speed type my gut response and press Send.

Why did you even bother answering?

In our chat box, the dot dot dot of a reply appears, then disappears.

I grimace and exit my texts, and as I'm about to switch my screen to black, I get a notification from Instagram. One new follower. One new direct message. The profile picture of this KingggMarcusIV is familiar. One of the boys from the bench.

> I was so happi when I found your IG…
> My invitation still stands btw.
> Stop by Nash Pool Park if you wanna chill. Or talk.
> Or swim. Jk I don't want to mess up my hair.
> -Marcus

As I'm deciding what to do, the waiter returns and taps on the table.

"Ah. You're still here! Ready to eat your feelings away? Or are you more of an avoider? Because I'm going to a party tonight when I get off work in a few. And you look like you need to escape your life for a little bit."

Escape. I've needed to escape my life for a lot longer than he could possibly know. I've needed to escape the whispers. The nudges. The sorrowful looks from people who can't fathom what my family's been through. Yet at the same time, the past three months have felt like I've been observing someone else's existence, as an unwanted guest in their body.

Some poor girl lost her sister, and I have had a front row seat through it all. She had to watch as they stuck her sister's ashes in a wall much taller than that girl ever was. She had nothing to contribute to the girl's only remaining sister's absurd plan to drive around the country as a reminder of what had been lost. Who had been lost. She saw that poor mother fall apart because she couldn't put her broken heart back together again one last time. She couldn't blame that mom for not being able to look that coward girl in the eye. So she was alone.

I am utterly alone.

Come on. I know what it looks like, to even contemplate

going anywhere with a total stranger, albeit a harmless–looking one. I am lonely, not stupid.

But I am so, so lonely.

I don't even expect anyone to identify with me anymore... but when I am surrounded in a pit of strangers, I can lose myself. In the music. In the smoke. In the heat. And because that's what parties are for—to lose yourself—I don't feel as alone then.

I hesitate.

"If you want to go sulk in your room, that's okay too," he says simply.

"I'll come."

The waiter's face brightens at my words.

"Yay! Um. It's a pool party but...I guess you could wear that..."

I look down at my church clothes and wince.

"I didn't really bring any party clothes... I have my airport outfit. I'll change into that," I say. Sweats suggest not caring; my flouncy blouse and slim black pants suggest confusion.

"Cool, I'll be closing out. Meet in the lobby in ten?"

I rummage through my purse in search of my room key and find it just as the elevators open to my floor. Once I'm in my room, I step over the piles of business casual clothing strewn about that I had packed for the events we've attended in Chicago the past couple of days. Mom's speech at a Black sorority's national conference. A tour of a brand-new community center. A stop at an inner-city summer school. A blur of moments when I shut off my brain in order to feel a little bit sane.

I avoid looking at the unmade bed. Kezi (and makeover shows galore) always said that your bedroom was a visual representation of how you felt internally. I guess the empty Reese's Cups wrappers and balled-up socks and underwear would say, *Anxious insomniac is dead inside and feels guilty for being a jerk to anyone and everyone close to her.*

In the bathroom I pull out the magnifying vanity mirror and examine my face. The foundation from earlier is not as flawless as it was a few hours ago, but it's holding up well enough. I switched to waterproof eyeliner because I got tired of trying to fix it up after crying. I quickly dab some vitamin E and mint lip balm over my lips to soften them before applying my go-to nude lipstick. Genny might think I obsess over my appearance because I'm boy-crazy or something else equally as wrong and ignorant. The truth is, if I'm going to be forced to live in this world and interact with people, I refuse to give them any ammo. Despite what they've read in the papers or seen on the news, they don't know me, and they don't need to know about the messy bedroom inside me.

My black flats slide off and my busted high-top Vans come on, and then I'm headed back to the lobby to meet Jalen, the waiter, whose name I made sure to ask for before splitting up to get ready. I let the door click shut behind me and do a cursory jiggle of the knob to make sure it's locked.

"Where are you going?"

Genny is walking down the hall in full head scarf and footie pajamas. She's carrying a mini tube of toothpaste, which I imagine she just got from the front desk downstairs.

"Out."

"That's a real good one you know, Happi," she says as she reaches my door and crosses her arms.

"Genny. I get that you're my older sister, but you don't have to do all this. I have a mom. And a dad. They're not checking for me the way you are, so you can just chill. Get a life even."

The retort slides smoothly from my mouth, but the hairs on my neck stand up, because I think of that last conversation I had with Kezi. The one I've been playing over and over for the past few months. Despite everything, these words still come effortlessly. The look my sister gives me is not one of surprise, but I have clearly stung her, as I knew I would. I want to turn off the autopilot but… It's easier for me to hurt my family than deal with…everything.

"Whatever," she says as she opens her door. "Just be up in time for the picnic tomorrow."

I grunt and leave her standing outside.

Nash Park Pool. Not too far. Won't be gone long.

I draft a text to Genny as I wait for my Lyft to roll up. It's a weak peace offering. An olive branch with dried-up leaves and all the olives plucked off, but it's something.

I hesitate before pressing Send, contemplating whether I will receive a reply lecturing me about all the terrible choices I'm making in life. Truthfully, I wouldn't mind if she did respond with that. I always wonder whether the last time I say something slick to my remaining sister will be the last time I say anything to her at all. Whether one day the pain in her eyes will scar over to indifference.

"Elevating athleisure to another level, I see," Jalen sings, taking long strides to where I sit in the lobby. His stuffy vest has been replaced with blue-and-white-striped short shorts and an American flag tank.

"Yep, that's exactly what I was going for," I joke.

"Is the pimpmobile almost here?"

A quick glance at my phone tells me that our ride is arriving any minute, so we step out to the driveway. My one stip-

ulation to going to this party with him was that I would get
the car so I could be sure he wasn't a kidnapper. Teennapper.
I felt slightly comforted that he was going to the same party
those boys invited me to earlier. Chicago was big. But it was
small too. Like LA.

A car matching the description of our ride stops in front
of us. I tilt my head to check the license plate is the same as
what's in the app and then slide inside. The driver has Toni
Braxton's "He Wasn't Man Enough" blasting loud enough
to suggest that she is working out some emotions in her head
and wants no interaction, which is fine by me.

"This song is exactly what we need right now!" Jalen says,
swaying to the deep timbre of Ms. Braxton.

"And why is that?" I ask.

"We're not going to a regular pool party. It's a nineties soi-
ree. Excuse me, dancery. The DJ isn't budging past 2002."

"You do realize that's beyond the nineties, right?"

"Yeah, but you have to account for those songs you think
are part of the decade but creeped past it... Ashanti's 'Foolish.' Any of Usher's *8701* stuff," he explains.

"Isn't that all a little before your time? You're like, what,
nineteen?"

Jalen gasps.

"I am a spry eighteen years old! I just like music. Love it
so much I'm majoring in it at Loyola, actually."

Kezi used to blast her nineties playlist from the speakers in
her room with the door open. I'd pretend it bothered me, but
I was secretly inhaling all the lyrics, the background vocals,
the soul. It was the soundtrack to her life. And mine.

"I get it. Brandy and TLC get me in my feelings every
time," I offer. "And I knew you were in the arts! The way

you kept going at dinner...you looked like there was nothing you hadn't seen before."

"Oh, that's because it's true." He winks. "We've all got our drama, right?"

I smile at this kind stranger gratefully, more at ease with him than I am with my own family.

"This is it, thanks," Jalen says to the driver when we arrive.

I drop a pin of my exact location to Genny.

In case anything happens. I am always thinking about if something Happens. In the back of your mind, you know that anytime you leave your house, get in a car, stand outside for some fresh air, think too much...something can Happen. I just never believed that it would happen to me. Or someone as close to me as a sister. Even though Mom isn't speaking to me at the moment, I can't let anything Happen. She couldn't take it.

We emerge from the car, and Jalen motions for me to follow him. There are a few people milling about at the entrance, but we walk past them to where the real party is. Some guests are playing in the pool. I catch one girl sneakily pulling down her blindfold to orient herself in the direction of her prey before screaming out, "Marco!" Even more people are standing on the sides, eating hot dogs and gulping from red plastic cups.

"Jalen!" A girl in a neon yellow bikini runs up to my companion and throws her arms around him and squeezes. "You made it!"

I stand to the side awkwardly.

"Of course! I wasn't going to miss my favorite cousin's first grown birthday party. You only turn eighteen once. Happi, this is my cousin Reagan. Reagan, Happi. We go way back. Like, almost an hour."

Her skin is glistening like she just came from the water, but her hair is still impeccable—head *and* lashes. I gasp.

"Do you know a guy named…" I shut my eyes trying to remember. "Titus! He's friends with this guy named Marcus who thinks he's funnier than he is?"

"Yes…" She looks at me strangely.

"He's in love with you," I blurt out.

Jalen gives me a double take before guiding me away from his stunned cousin.

"I don't know if I can take you places anymore if you do that again," he quips.

I explain my chance meeting with Reagan's admirer while we grab hot dogs cradled in poppy-seed buns and towering with pickles, tomatoes, relish, onions, mustard, and celery salt then move to wait in line for our drinks. When we get to the front, I head straight for the frozen margaritas.

I feel the music in my marrow. The rhythms leap down my arms and legs, swirl in my hips. I pick up my dancing right where I'd left it, at its peak. I have never been shy about per-forming. The sensation of eyes on me is rejuvenating when I actually want it there. I control what they see, what I want them to perceive. But tonight, I am not reciting a monologue or executing complicated choreography. I am losing myself. In myself. And I don't want to be found.

"Are you Happi to see me?"

Without looking at his face, I can tell that it's Marcus. And he's smirking.

I turn around, unimpressed.

"Do you have any idea how often I've heard that joke?" I say, hand on my hip.

"I know it's the first time you've heard it from a fine boy from Chi-Town."

I burst out laughing and so does he.

"So you *are* happy to see me."

"Where's your boy?"

"Titus? He's definitely following Reagan around like a lost puppy. I got really glamorous friends," he says with a grin.

"I saw her," I say. "I get the allure."

I take a sip of my drink and chew on the more solid bits of slushie.

"Ow," he says, cringing.

"I like the cold," I say simply. No need to get into explaining how ice jolts my senses awake and stops me from being numb for a moment. I start to move again, to signal I'm here to dance, not talk.

"I don't bump with Tevin no more," Marcus declares. I have finally stopped to take a breath, but my head keeps spinning. Around and around it goes. We're standing near the entrance, where it isn't so congested but the music can still be heard.

"You better take that back!"

He shakes his head. "You know that song, 'Can We Talk?'"

"Of course I do."

"He gave a generation of guys the balls to step up to these girls, made it sound real romantic and smooth, and then when you try it yourself, you get shot down."

"Dude. You can't be blaming one random R&B singer for your lack of swag."

"Hey, I'm not talking about me! But imagine someone running after a girl asking her for her name over and over again like he does at the end of the song."

"Yeah," I chuckle. Everything seems funnier right now. "That would be harassment. These songs are more like... A fantasy." I glance at him. "You know, when I saw you earlier today, I thought you and your friend were trying to get at me."

Marcus cackles.

"And I was not here for it!" I say loudly over his laughs.

"Yelling at pretty girls across the street isn't exactly my style," he says, moving toward me. "I walk up to them and speak softly."

I wonder if he can feel how warm my face is. I wonder how much of that is from nerves and how much is from the tequila.

"How does that work out for you usually?" I whisper breathlessly.

"Well, they have to get close enough to hear me right."

Santiago crosses my mind. The weak laces that hold us together, the ones we are both too craven to cut ourselves, are untied in this moment. I lean in to Marcus and place a hand on his bare chest. I sense his heart beneath my palm. It's beating much faster than the chill expression on his face suggests it would be. I like having an effect on people. Sometimes I forget that at the end of the day we are all just guts and hearts and bones pretending that we're more than.

He is so near that I smell the frozen margarita on his tongue. He's still too innocent to think of getting a Henny and Coke or something "manly" at a party. It makes me smile.

I feel myself floating up to meet his smooth light brown face. Peer into his deep brown eyes. My lips part of their own volition, and then my stomach lurches as the butterflies it contains bat their wings mercilessly...

I vomit all over his Boost 350s.

"My *Yeezys*!"

13

KEZI

Ximena beamed as I settled on the bench across from where she and Derek were seated in the cafeteria, but her grin quickly disappeared once she got a better look at me. My face was still hot from Happi's verbal assault.

"What's wrong, Kezi?" Ximena reached her hand across the blue linoleum table to hold mine. "Are you okay? You shouldn't be walking around looking so sad on your birthday."

"Yeah, I'm fine," I replied as I unlaced our fingers. Even in the aftermath of my sisterly showdown, I had to keep up appearances. I kept the tulips that Ximena gave me on our first date pressed in the pages of my diary. But I wouldn't hold her hand in public. Maybe Happi was right after all.

"You don't look fine, birthday girl," Derek said, eyebrow raised high in question.

"Ugh. Okay, okay," I said, caving. "I just got into it with my lovely younger sister. Happi literally hates everything about me. But honestly, what else is new?"

Derek opened his mouth to speak again, but I interrupted. "And don't ask me for details either. I'm sure you'll soon be caught up to speed by one of our many classmates who happened to hear when she very loudly told me off."

"Dang. Y'all really don't like each other," Ximena said, and popped a french fry into her mouth.

"It's nuts," Derek said. "Remember how close we used to be when we were younger? That seems like light-years ago."

Our families had been in each other's lives for decades now. When our great-granddads met in the Army during World War II, they created the ties that would graft together the roots and buds of our family trees for generations. They made plans for their futures, even though they knew there might come a day when they would be expected to lay down their lives for their country. A country that tried its hardest to prevent them from feeling like they belonged.

My great-grandpa died overseas, but Derek's great-grandpa Parker remembered the evenings they had spent talking about their big dreams and all they wanted to accomplish after the war. Their friendship had grown over dinners at barbecue joints they'd found in the *Green Book* they had to use even when making deliveries for the military. When he'd finally been discharged from the army, Parker had found my great-grandpa Antonin's widow, *my* great-grandma Evelyn, and convinced her to move to California with him in 1946 to start over, that same *Green Book* that my father now guarded with his life guiding their way. They'd formed a bond through grief, but had become fast friends, and Evelyn was even best woman at Parker's wedding when he got married a few years after they settled in LA. Our families have been tight ever since.

And the bond between Derek and Happi was forged as children in the same Pre-K program. The running joke was that D and Happi's bond was solidified over a single pair of clown shoes in the dramatic play section of the classroom. (All the other kids were terrified of clowns, like all well-adjusted people should be.) From that point on, you wouldn't find one without the other far behind, both wearing just one shoe, running after their classmates while honking big red noses. They did everything together: eat, dance, read, wash their hands. There was even one time when they were having a playdate at our house and they snuck out with the car keys. They almost made it down the street in the Camry before Ma yanked open the driver's door and ended their joyride.

While Happi did well enough in school, her interests were focused on activities she could do outside of class. Still, she had always made a point of bragging about how smart her best friend was. That was, until those smarts landed him in sixth grade in what was supposed to be their fifth-grade year. She was crushed, even though she'd tried not to let on. Before long, Derek was spending all of his free time attempting to make friends with the kids in his new middle school. He tried everything he could to fit in and seem more mature. But nobody was buying it. Luckily for him, I had taken pity on his little self and pulled him under my wing. I'd thought it would make Happi glad to see that I was helping her BFF get acclimated to his new surroundings, but I quickly learned that I was wrong. Not long after that, Happi wouldn't even glance Derek's way when he came over after school to do homework. Although the two of them had been going through it for years now, I just knew they would find their way back to each other. The roots ran too deep.

"Maybe it's just a phase and she'll grow out of it?" Ximena suggested halfheartedly.

"Maybe," I replied. "Anyway, we're not here to talk about Happi. We need to prep for the rally later today. Are you sure you don't want to go with us, Derek?"

"Uh, yeah. I'm positive." Derek stole another of Ximena's fries before she could swat his hand away. "The last thing I need is to bring my Black ass out there and get arrested. Then one thing leads to another, and *I'm* the one you're marching for next. I'm good."

"You sound almost like Happi. That's exactly the reason you *should* be marching, Derek!"

The look on his face told me that he wasn't going to change his mind. I rolled my eyes and turned to the next item on my list. "We need to come up with a good chant. Can you at least help out with that?"

Derek smirked. And with that, the three of us set out to create a bomb rallying call...but failed miserably. After almost twenty minutes of terrible suggestions *(Hey hey! Ho ho! Kez, we ain't got ideas no mo'!)* we decided to call it quits and just stick to following along with what the other protestors came up with.

"It's our first rally, Kezi," Ximena said as we packed up to head to our respective classes. "We're there to support. Don't worry about taking the lead for this one."

I anticipated the rest of the day would drag on, but it rocketed forward, thanks to my video of Mr. Bamhauer.

In AP Bio, we once learned about viruses and how they replicated and moved through organisms. During the lysogenic cycle, the virus lies low and just makes hella copies of itself through the infected cell's machinery. But then, it reaches a point called the lytic cycle, where the cell is absolutely stuffed, and it bursts. Then *those* viruses go off and infect other cells.

This wasn't my first viral video. I had a substantial subscriber list. But I had never had a clip spread like this one had. It had reached its own lytic stage, and this was the moment the cell ruptured.

My peers were riled up. They shared, retweeted, and reposted as soon as they saw the video, spreading the word about Thomas Edison Senior High's incompetent history teacher who needed to be removed from his position—effective immediately.

As my classmates and I waited for Spanish class to begin, pods of conversation sprang up around the room.

A pencil tapped on my desk. "Yo that video…" said the girl seated beside me.

"Oh my *God*, I was just about to say!" said the guy in the desk behind us. "I've let…weird comments of Mr. B's slide because I thought I couldn't do anything about it."

"You know he told me he thought political correctness was the worst part of our society? I didn't even ask him about that!" She shook her head. "*Some*body needed to say something."

I tried to nod sagely but, on the real? It was one of my proudest moments ever.

When the last bell finally rang, I was lightning, bolting out of class before anyone had even finished gathering their things. I'm not usually one of those students who starts packing up before the teacher completes their last thought, but today I had to make an exception. The eagerness to be at a real-live protest had made it impossible to stay focused. I raced through the halls and arrived at my locker, then tossed my human geography and biology books inside. I slammed the door shut and very narrowly missed the fingers of the girl who owned the locker next to mine. She gave me a squinty glare as I raced away.

"Sorry!" I shouted back to her as I zigged and zagged, bobbed and weaved through the crowd, making my way to the student parking lot.

Ximena was already waiting for me, like I'd known she would be. She leaned casually against her cherry-red Prius, arms folded, black aviator sunglasses perched on her nose. She tipped them down to meet my eyes. Tilted her head slightly as she smiled. Goose bumps danced up and down my arms.

"Honestly, you should have a Mustang if you really want to pull off this too-cool-for-school look you've got going on," I said with a smirk as I slid into the passenger seat.

"And unnecessarily expand my carbon footprint? I thought you knew me better than that, Kez."

I was a tightly wound ball of nerves as Ximena drove down Angeles Vista and Leimert Boulevards. Houses, cars, and people blurred into one like the strokes of a leaky watercolor painting as we zoomed along. (With intermittent stopping, of course, because this was Los Angeles traffic after all.) I searched endlessly for a song to listen to on the radio to give my hands something to do, until finally Ximena reached over and placed her hand on my lap, palm side up. I smiled, and this time I held on, her fingers warming my own as I finally started to relax.

"Why are you so anxious?" Ximena asked. Her eyes widened. "Wait, you didn't get another one of those emails, did you, because you have t—"

I shook my head. *Thank God.* "No, no," I replied. "I wish I could tell you. I'm just feeling…strange."

"Maybe it's because this is the first time you're taking your activism on the road," Ximena mused. "You'll be fine. I'm right here."

"Yeah." I gave her hand a little squeeze. "I should channel this energy into a video for my YouTube."

I reached into my book bag and pulled out my DSLR. It was a Canon EOS 5D Mark III and my most expensive purchase ever. I'd paid for this camera with the money I earned from the ads that play before, during, or after my videos. It marked the moment when my parents started to realize my "little YouTube hobby" was pretty special. I placed it carefully on the dashboard of Ximena's car and cleared my throat a few times before I began speaking.

"Hey YouTube! It's your girl Kezi. I'm with my friend Ximena." I turned the camera toward her so she could wave, and then repositioned it in front of me. "We're heading to the protest for Jamal Coleman in South Los Angeles. I wanted to hop on and make a quick video to explain why I'm participating in this rally today. I think it's so important for us to speak up for those who can't, and to join in the chorus of people who are already raising their voices. It's vital to post our grievances online and let the world know that we won't stand for injustice anymore. But we've also gotta show up in real life. A trending topic is easy for us all to hop on. But organizing, making signs, petitioning for changes in legislation, marching? That takes dedication. And it shows we're willing to come together when it counts."

"You're such a natural," Ximena said as I closed my camera and placed it back in my bag. She glanced at me, the right corner of her lip tilting up in the way it does when she's about to say something slick. "Friend."

"Shut up," I said with no heat behind my words. "Everybody doesn't need to know my business like that."

"Mmm hmm."

It was funny. Before we were dating, before we were even friends, we were enemies. I'd dramatically called her my nemesis at dinner after the first day of high school and everything. She was always raising her hand in class. Seemed like a huge know-it-all. And she glided through the halls like she knew how fine she was. Then Mr. Scholls, our English teacher, made us partners to complete a group assignment on *Pride and Prejudice* (I know, I know). We hated each other so much that we made competing presentations and met with him after school a few weeks later to beg him to allow us to be graded separately. Didn't work. In fact, he threatened to fail us both if we didn't "stop with the bullshit."

I went over to her house the next day and we called a truce, because neither of us played about our GPAs. I fell in love with her grandma first though. Ximena and I were barely speaking at her table when *Abuelita* Caridad nearly floated into the room and gasped.

"And what is this? Is the war over, *mija*?"

Ah. So she talked about me too.

I could hear my mother growling, *If you don't get up and show you have some home training and sense…*in my head and got out of my seat to greet the older woman. She hugged me then pulled away to examine my face.

"There's no war," Ximena had grumbled.

"Of course not," *Abuelita* Caridad had declared. "She's the kind of girl you fight wars *for*, not against."

We were still about ten minutes out from Expo Park, the

home base of the march. The music on the radio trilled softly in the background as I tapped my phone. Genny had texted me earlier today, but I hadn't gotten back to her. It was right around when Happi was fussing me out. Genny's sister senses must've been tingling. I opened my texts to reply and then decided to just give her a call.

"Hi there! You have reached Genny Smith, as you can see, um, hear, I'm not here right now. Please leave a message after the beep!"

"Hey, sis! It's me, Kezi. I'm on my way to the rally with Ximena." Ximena waved wildly from her seat. "She says hi. Sorry I didn't text you back earlier. I was too busy getting chewed, gargled, and spit out by our lovely baby sister. I'll tell you all about it at lunch tomorrow. That girl is something else. Anyway, I'm feeling a little nervous for some reason. Maybe it's because I'm finally going against the 'rents and they're giving me the silent treatment for it? I don't know how Happi handles being on this side of the law all the time… But yeah. I was just calling to say what's up. Wish me luck!" And then at the last second I added, "Love you."

"That was sweet," Ximena said, looking at me from the corner of her eye.

"You're sweet," I answered, and reached for her again, kissing the back of her hand.

We rode the rest of the way in silence, my face frozen into a goofy smile that only Ximena could elicit.

Tension fizzed in the air and filtered into the car, even with the windows shut. Hundreds of people were making their way up South Figueroa Street toward the epicenter of the rally. Some were wearing shirts with a picture of Jamal's face blown up on the front below the words *Rest in Paradise*. Others wore black tees, names of the many, many fallen listed in white font like a morbid credits scene at the end of a movie: Martin, Bland, Garner, Brown, Taylor, Floyd, No More.

"Wow. It is hot!" Ximena exclaimed once we'd found a parking spot and hopped out of her Prius.

"Seriously. I hope my camera won't get messed up as I record." Marbles of sweat had already sprouted on my forehead. We were parked quite a ways away from where we needed to be, but it was the best we could do on a Tuesday at almost 4:00 p.m. in the city. I pulled my camera out of my backpack and wrapped the strap across my body before safely tucking the bag into the trunk of the car, and then handed Ximena the poster that we'd worked on over the weekend. STOP POLICE BRUTALITY was written in large crimson letters, paint dripping down the page like drops of blood.

We joined the flow of protesters, a river of people guiding the way as their cries washed over the ears of everyone who would listen. Local news stations lined the streets, their big white vans and their too-tall antennas acting as beacons, competing with the palm trees to reach the sun as we drew closer to Exposition Park Drive. We were mere paces from the Natural History Museum of Los Angeles, the California African American Museum, and the LA Memorial Coliseum, spots I'd visited in amazement since I was four years old. Now I was eighteen and hoping to make that same little girl proud, the one who once swayed before the might of the dinosaurs and stood in awe of the dignity of her people's history. My camera was rolling, ready to capture it all.

Finally, we were at the center of the rally. Police stood around with riot gear, their polycarbonate shields smeared with spit and sweat as people chanted about injustice. Even through their helmets, I noticed that some of the officers looked bored. Another day of senseless shouting, in their eyes.

"Hi, everyone. Diane again. Can we all please take five steps back?" blared a voice over a megaphone. I turned to see a short light-skinned woman wearing one of the Rest in Paradise shirts standing on a small platform. "We can make ourselves heard without crowding. Remember. This is a *peaceful* protest. Now, let's welcome a very special speaker. Mrs. Monique Coleman, Jamal's mother, is here with us today."

Diane stepped down from the platform. Mrs. Coleman was a tall woman, thin. She had a full head of hair that at one point must've been jet-black. Definitely a #1 in the kanekalon pack. But now, her hairline was streaked with gray.

I remembered the first time that I had seen Mrs. Coleman on the news. She'd used every bit of her height to help project her voice, over the heads of people in a crowd but still straight through their hearts. Today, she was a shell of her former self. A once majestic willow tree, withered.

Mrs. Coleman took the mic and spoke. "I am tired."

The crowd murmured their agreement.

"I'm tired of hearing statistics about our likelihood of being stopped by law enforcement. I'm tired of civilians believing they have the right to put their hands on us and their bullets through us. I'm tired of speaking to politicians when all the promises they make are empty. I'm tired of how the police continue to disrespect our children. Beat them. Kill them. I am tired that our fellow Americans don't understand why this would anger us. But even though I'm tired, I know you are all here to help raise me up."

Everyone cheered in unison. Their shouts seemed to give Mrs. Coleman a little bit of strength.

"One day, when I have decided to put down this mic and

let someone else pick up this burden, I hope you'll remember my boy. He was kind. He was a dreamer. He was my son. But more than that, he was a person. And I hope that you'll remember his name—Jamal Coleman. Because if we should forget, it won't be too long until they do this to another one of our babies. If it's done to one of us and we don't say 'no more,' it will only be a matter of time before they come for the rest of us."

Mrs. Coleman carefully stepped down from the stage and handed the microphone back to Diane.

"Thank you so much, Mrs. Coleman, for your powerful words." But she was already gone, making her way through the crowd with her family surrounding her, ready to be done with the day.

"Hey," Ximena said, turning to me. "Maybe we should try to catch her. It would be awesome if you could get her to say a few words on camera for your channel."

I watched Mrs. Coleman's retreating back, the way her shoulders drooped in exhaustion. "I dunno. I don't want to bother her."

"Come on," Ximena said, pulling my arm.

We had just started to navigate the throng of people when we heard someone shout.

"It's done to one, it's done to all. Don't forget his name—Jamal!"

We turned to see a line of protesters positioned directly across from the police officers. They continued to repeat the chant, the solitary voice now amplified by at least twenty others, a domino effect of resistance. And with each repetition, more joined in.

I raised my camera up to make sure that I was capturing this moment and focused on a man in a black tracksuit staring down a policeman. I walked toward him without realizing what I was doing. He was chanting along with the rest of the protestors, but his eyes remained laser focused on the officer.

"Step back!" the officer shouted.

The man stopped chanting. "I'm five steps away from you, just as the organizer requested."

Ximena shot me a wary look. The energy between the two men was mounting, an electric charge waiting for some unfortunate soul to come along, touch it, and be fried to a crisp.

"I said step back!" the policeman said, raising his shield.

"We have more than enough space between—"

Before the man could finish his sentence, the officer charged forward and collided with him.

"Hey!" I shouted reflexively. "He didn't do anything wrong!"

I didn't know what to do. I wanted to step in, intervene somehow. So I did the next best thing. I pulled out my phone and went live on my Instagram page.

"I am currently at the rally for Jamal Coleman at Expo Park," I said trying to keep the shakes out of my voice. "This man was exercising his First Amendment right to peacefully assemble when he was attacked by one of the officers present."

Viewers jumped onto my livestream immediately, and comments skittered across my screen.

Hell yeah

You look especially beautiful today

Be careful out there!

"Ma'am. I'm going to need you to stop recording." In my haste to go live, I hadn't even noticed that an officer was now standing two feet from me.

"It's her right to record!" Ximena yelled, stepping forward.

The officer ignored her. "I'm asking you to put your phone away, or I'll have to take it from you."

"For what?" Ximena's face was red, her eyes narrowed in anger.

"Ximena, it's okay," I said, moving to put my phone in my pocket, though I left it streaming.

"No!" she shouted, pulling my phone back up. "We will not be intimidated!"

"Ma'am." The officer moved closer, motioning to hand over my phone.

"Sir, with all due respect. I'm not doing anything wrong. We're at a protest. We're allowed to record," I said slowly, in what I hoped was a nonthreatening tone. My heart rapped at my chest. I didn't want this exchange to go any further than it already had.

"If you don't follow my instructions, I'm going to have to take you in."

Ximena lost it. "Take her in? Take her *in*?! For what? She's *not* doing anything *wrong*. You just don't want there to be any footage of your buddy assaulting an innocent person."

"Ximena, it's really not—"

"Of all the people here, you decided to harass a teenager?"

"Ximena—"

"Okay. That's enough. Hand it over," the officer said.

"No! She's not going to do that! You need to back off and—"

"Shut up!" I shouted. "It's not that serious. I just want to go—"

"Did you just tell me to shut up? You're coming with me." The officer reached forward and grabbed me forcefully by the arm. My phone fell from my hand to the concrete, and the screen cracked, a spiderweb of fractures appearing at the point where it hit the ground. I could see the messages on my live stream continuing to flood in.

Ximena grabbed my phone and held it up in the officer's face. "I want the world to see the face of this coward officer as he takes my girl away. His badge number is—"

The policeman plucked my phone from Ximena's hands and slammed it to the ground again. This time, the screen went dark.

14

SHAQUERIA

TUESDAY, APRIL 17—
THE DAY OF THE ARREST
LOS ANGELES, CALIFORNIA

My name is called. Sha-kweer-ee-uh instead of Sha-keer-ee-uh. They messed up the pronunciation like I expected them to, but I didn't dwell on it. It was a bit comforting, actually, knowing that these people with the power to change my life could make the same type of annoying mistake as just about everyone else on earth.

The room was spacious but sparse. Three expensive-looking casting directors, a woman in the center with a man flanking her on each side, sat at a wide table littered with scripts, laptops, and coffee. I placed my backpack on the chair directly in front of their table and briefly wondered what was worth more, their outfits and electronic gadgets, or the brick in my bag. Jesus, what had I gotten myself into?

"You're auditioning for the role of Sloane, correct?" the woman said briskly. She took a quick sip of her drink and then tensed her face as if it burned. She was too busy to blow.

I nodded in terror. Blinked a few times to pump the fear out of my eyes. Stared blankly into the camera's little red dot.

"Whenever you're ready," she said, meaning at that very moment.

I coughed. Exhaled. Started.

These words were old friends by now. I had studied them over and over and over until I saw them in my dreams. But for some reason, the flame that lit the emotion beneath them had been doused. Although my nerves were trying to get the best of me, I fought back. And with each uttering of a line, I felt a little more of Sloane shining through. The pure joy of playing someone else was returning. Yes, thank God, the rush was back—

Too late.

Their eyes told me everything I needed to know. They were uninspired by this performance. Their hands were confirmation. Papers shuffling, a peer into a smart watch's tiny screen, a pen tapping on the table softly.

We decided I was a No at the same time.

"Thank you for your time," the woman said. Dismissed.

No. No. I couldn't have come all this way to fail before I even had a chance to fly.

"I really, really want this," I croaked. "I can do this. Please—I can show you—"

The man with the glasses squirmed in his seat, uncomfortable. The woman glanced at her watch again impatiently but said nothing. I grabbed that silence. Didn't let go.

Paused.

"Let's make one thing clear, Javier," I hissed. "Those girls?

Those girls will take one bite out of you, maybe two. Crunch your bones down to dust. Savor how new and sweet your blood tastes."

I chuckled bitterly.

"But then they'll lick their fingers. They'll get bored. And you don't want to see the students at Thatcher Academy when they're bored."

The man with the rolled-up sleeves leaned forward, his hand scrawling a quick note as he read Javier's line again. "What are you saying?"

I glared at him with every atom of contempt I held in my body, for all the boys who assumed I owed them something, for all the adults who should've loved me, for all the lives I'd had to live to find the one that would stick.

"You think you can show up here, throw an arm over my shoulder, kiss me a few times, and *know* me? Do you really believe you deserve to keep my secrets?"

"I—"

"Let me answer for you," I said raising my voice just slightly and adding a touch of a quiver. "You don't. No one here does. And that sure as hell includes the new guy."

They all exchanged loaded looks across their row of power. The dude who read for Javier even clapped a little.

I did it.

"Thank you so much," the woman said, with a smile. "You really woke us up. Who did you say your agent was again?"

I bit my lip.

"I don't have one at the moment but—"

"No worries," she interrupted quickly. "This audition is open to everyone for this very reason. To find the diamonds in the rough."

"And you…" the bespectacled man said, shaking his head. In awe? "Well, we will be in touch."

I nodded slowly, reminding myself to breathe. "Thank you for this opportunity."

I floated out of the room and through the waiting area. I stepped outside and spread my arms wide, soaking up all the sun. I was alive. They didn't hate me. I might just make it. The thought electrified my body, shot sparks through my limbs. But I had to keep it moving.

A man stirred on the bus bench right outside the building. My—

My heart thudded to the sidewalk.

Darius smiled, and my cheek tingled from the memory of his hand colliding with my face earlier. He had been waiting.

15

HAPPI

FRIDAY, JULY 27—
3 MONTHS, 10 DAYS SINCE THE ARREST
CHICAGO, ILLINOIS

Everything hurts. My brain. Stomach. Pride. My eyes creak open in protest at the stream of sunlight aimed right at my face. I bolt forward in the bed when I realize my hotel room window was slightly smaller than the one I see now. This isn't my room. My head spins at the quick motion and settles again as last night's details drift lazily into my mind. So many drinks. Dancing by myself. Entertaining that boy's advances. Getting close enough to…

I shut my eyes and sink back into the bed.

"Oh no you don't!" Genny glides into the room, much too awake and unnecessarily loud.

I growl and slide the white comforter over my head.

"Sorry, Happi. I let you sleep as long as possible, but it's time to get up," Genny says as she gently tugs at my pillow. When I turn over in an effort to ignore her, she whips off the linen in one yank. I'm still in yesterday's outfit.

I drag my head to the side of the bed where the alarm sits on the nightstand. The clock claims it is 11:00 a.m., but my body swears it is about six hours earlier.

"I thought the picnic was at noon," I grumble.

"It is!" Genny says perkily. "But Dad sent a text this morning saying that they want to have breakfast together. I was able to push it back to a quick brunch before heading to the park."

"Wait—*Dad*?"

Our father is a man of few words, verbal or written. The only way we know our texts get to him is because he's one of those monsters who keeps his Read receipts on.

"I know," Genny replies. She begins to untwist her long, medium box braids from the jumbo flexi rods she had wrapped them in. She runs her fingers through the bouncy curls but then bends her head over to guide the braids into a tight topknot, her default style. I've always thought that she wears her hair like that because she doesn't want any of her secrets to escape.

I heave myself up and swing my feet to the floor. My shoes are lined up nicely, waiting for me to slip them on. Genny's doing. I grab my bag, which was resting on the coffee table, and drag myself to the door. She hands me a bottle of coconut water and smiles.

"Thanks." I pause, anticipating the disappointed admonishment that is coming.

Silence.

I shut the door and take the few steps to my room. Everything is as untidy as I left it the night before. My messy room of an inside is even messier.

I know I shouldn't, but I roll onto my bed. My body aches, and my brain is foggier than the bathroom mirror used to be after Kezi would do steam treatments on her hair. Last night wasn't the first time I drank. Before I stopped taking communion, I used to sip wine from the tiny little cups at church one Sunday a month. There would be pilfered beer at the drama club after-parties too, but I would usually just hold on to the one cup all night. Yesterday was a new experience.

I will be at your door in 10, k?

I glance down at my cell phone and send a quick thumbs-up to Genny. The last message I sent her had been slightly longer than a single emoji and much more in distress:

Plz gt me

My mind goes back to the party, and I remember feeling my middle clench, and then doubling over on Marcus's shoes. Looking up in groggy horror as he screamed. Having party-goers rush over in confusion, then disgust.

I heard the whispers.

Can't hold her liquor.

Messy.

Out of control.

I took in Jalen's wide eyes as he reached me, and his cousin Reagan's look of mortification.

"I'm sorry," I croaked. My throat burned and my voice gave out, so it sounded like *I'm sore.* Same difference. Marcus looked torn. He probably wanted to be a good guy and not drop the girl who'd just unloaded on him. It was the type of story that made for a funny toast at a wedding. But we were not there. He hadn't signed up for this.

"Just go," I whispered. "Please."

He bit his lip, and I waved him off. I balled up the rest of my pride. Threw it away. Sent my sister a frantic text.

"Are you okay?" Jalen said. "Oh God, I should've been watching you."

"We're barely a year apart, if that," I choked out. "You're not my chaperone. It's fine. I'm fine."

"Do we need to go…to the hospital?" he asked nervously. I could see his silent prayer, *Please say no, please say no, please say no*, zooming straight to God's omnipresent ears.

"Nope, I'm good," I said.

"Maybe I should call a—"

"No worries. My sister's on her way to pick me up."

I pressed my phone's home screen. No message. I blinked back tears.

She's finally done with me.

"I'm actually gonna go to the bathroom while I'm waiting," I said. "She's almost here."

"Okay…" Jalen said dubiously.

I stumbled to the clubhouse, stepping gingerly over the towels, pool chairs, and scowls. When I'd locked myself into the biggest stall, I couldn't believe it, but I giggled. Kezi's ghost was loud and clear: *Do you* really *need to use the wheelchair accessible bathroom? You can cop a squat in smaller quarters, Happi!* The giggle moved to a chuckle, and the chuckle, a full laugh. I grabbed my sides to stop the aching as my body shook.

"How am I doing without you, Kezi?"

The laughs stopped, of course. Because shouting at the phantom of my sister did not make me feel better. She should still be here. Alive. She *must* be. The tears I'd held back escaped and found their way down my nose, past my neck, and into my shirt. I tried to breathe in between the sobs, exhale as I coughed away the bitterness that had nestled itself deep in my throat. I would just stay there forever. Perhaps I'd consider moving after I was all dried out from bawling and was just a pillar of salt, like Lot's wife.

Buzz.

Here.

My self-pity party ended abruptly, like this night out. I rose to wash my hands in the sink before splashing cold water on my face to wake myself up. The rough brown paper towel I used to pat my skin dry was blotched with makeup and tears. When I stepped through the door, it would just be me and my eyeliner.

The party was still raging when I gathered the nerve to leave the bathroom. I nearly ran into a hard body. Marcus was standing right outside the clubhouse as though waiting for someone. When he realized it was me, he sighed in relief and held up a water bottle, then silently offered it to me.

"I'm good," I said. I raced to the gates and didn't look back (unlike Lot's wife). I didn't even groan at the whacky exterior of the car that had distracted the revelers from their conversations and grinding. Jalen was outside too, leaning into the driver's window to hear what Genny was saying. I climbed in and shut the door. Jalen waved goodbye, and I lifted my hand halfheartedly. We peeled away slowly.

I waited:

What is wrong with you?

What did you expect to happen?

That's what you get.

Instead:

"Who wears sneakers to a pool party?" Genny said.

My sister and I reach the hotel restaurant before our parents. The host leads us to a table, and we take the menus he hands us but don't open them. There are a few businesspeople sipping cups of coffee and dining alone, but it's pretty quiet. Genny and I sit in silence as well. She thumbs through her phone and I stare into space, wondering what the hell I'm doing with my life. I glance at her screen and spy a map.

When the storm in my head finally gets too loud, I take out my own phone as a distraction. I scroll through Instagram lazily but stop and zoom in on a post from KingggMarcusIV:

Yoooo what should their couple name be? Teagan or Ritus? Oh and shout out to the cupid who got them together 😊

Above his caption is a grainy photo of Titus and Reagan sharing a long floating noodle in the pool while looking deep into each other's eyes and grinning shyly. I can't help but smile. At least someone had a good night. I'm still too mortified to even Like the picture though and put my phone away instead.

"Take your sunglasses off," Genny mutters.

"Huh?"

"It's more obvious that you're trying to hide something when you've got sunglasses on indoors. Especially since you know better than to do that."

"Right this way, sir." I look up and see Mom and Dad being led to our table.

"Your server will be with you shortly," the host says once they've sat down.

Dad used to play the piano when he was younger. When he gets nervous, he taps out the scales on whatever surface is in front of him. I watch his fingers glide across the tablecloth, *C, D, E, F, G, A, B, C, C, B, A, G, F, E, D*—

"So," he says abruptly. Mom adjusts the shades she has on. Genny raises her eyebrows at me.

"We are scared. No, terrified," Dad continues. "It's always been terrifying to be Black in America. But that's all I've ever been. Your mother and I thought that if we kept our heads down, raised you gir—women right—" he looks pointedly at Genny "—you would be safe. But that…that didn't pan out."

"It's not fair," Mom says. She whips off her sunglasses and stares at me and Genny plainly. Her eyes are still bloodshot, but they aren't as severely red as they were at dinner last night. "It's not fair that our children are killed just because of who they are or what they look like."

"And we stayed up talking until late," Dad chimes in. "We read the letters Kezi wrote for us the day before her…birthday. The ones you left on the table. She told us in her own words why she had to move forward despite our reservations. And God spoke to us plainly too. He 'has not given us a spirit of fear, but of power and of love and of a sound mind.'"

A dull ache thuds into my head as I follow where his words are leading us.

"We got on our knees and prayed about this a long time," Mom says. "And the Lord my God said that Abraham was scared to leave Ur. David was frightened of Goliath. Mary worried about the whispers of the community when she was called to carry Jesus."

Genny leans forward in her seat. I shake my head slowly.

Dad continues. "But their fear was the start of their journey. It was never the end. My grandmother Evelyn used the

Green Book to rebuild her family and start over in a new place. My mother met my father in California because of it. And here are Naomi and I, the parents of women who want to honor that bravery and power. So though we are still *terrified...*" He pauses. "We give you our blessing. Go do what you have to do."

We do not stay for brunch. By the time they are done rattling off Bible verses and blessings, we all decide that we should just head to the picnic. The event will definitely have food, but Mom is one of those people who likes to nibble on something at home (or a hotel) before going elsewhere to eat. ("You never know what you'll find!") Since Genny has that ridiculous rented car, we all pile into it and head to the park.

"You have to be vigilant, of course," Mom says. They have not stopped talking about the road trip since they announced their change of heart. Their excitement seeps into Genny's spirit, lifting it higher and higher until it reaches the ceiling of the car and hovers there. Her determination is present too, no doubt. Genny was taking this trip regardless of what our parents said. Like how Kezi went to that rally. But rebellion isn't Genny's way. She's glad to be home in the lush garden of our parents' good graces.

"Of course," Genny says cheerfully.

"Do you know the route you two are going to take?" Dad asks.

"Sure do," Genny replies. "Old Route 66 and the new interstates, like I-40. I wasn't playing when I said Kezi planned everything already. This trip will be like...driving by numbers. We're just connecting the dots for her."

They all nod their heads solemnly.

I slide my eyes to the left and the right. Mom is looking

out the window. Dad is staring straight ahead in the passenger seat attempting not to be the back-seat driver that is in his nature. Genny hums along to the sounds of the rain forest playlist she has on. It is a melody that makes sense only to her.

I do not want to be here.

I do not want to go on this trip.

I do not want to be trapped in this car any longer than I must.

I am not ready to be caught up in the sadness, to be drowned in the memory of Kezi over and over and over and over. I loved my sister. I am certain she did not know that. And that truth suffocates me. Taking steps she will never walk herself flicks a broken switch in my brain and makes me insane.

I can't do this.

"No one has once asked me if I want to go," I say. "You've all had your tantrums…no, stay put, but oh, wait, we changed our minds, please go! And not one of you bothered to get my opinion on this trip."

Genny exhales. "Well, Happi—"

I cut her off.

"Let me make this easy for you. I'm not going."

As I make my pronouncement, we arrive at the park. Genny and Mom lock eyes with Dad in the rearview mirror, the Smith Family signal for An Impending Discussion.

I hop out of the car and walk straight toward the food table.

The buffet before me of potato chips, potato salad, hamburgers, coleslaw, and baked beans looks innocuous enough. But when the scent of sweet relish and dill pickle claws into my nose and reminds me of last night, I decide to fix a light plate for later. I cover my meal with a napkin to ward off flies then focus on filling up a paper cone with cherry and lemon snow cone slush. Sweet and sour, like Kezi and me.

As I find a place to sit, I ignore the glances of the families mingling amongst themselves. They are fractured mirrors of us. They are the grieving widows, mothers, widowers, sisters, brothers, fathers, cousins, friends, lovers of the people whose bodies have been desecrated, whose faces get printed on shirts in veneration, and whose names trend online when another person joins their ranks. There goes the uncle of a pregnant woman who had been beaten so hard, she lost her baby. Beside him is the grandfather of a man shot and killed while standing on his own property. A few kids chase each other under the tables and through the jungle gym, not yet aware that the cherished memories of their loved ones will fade with each inch they grow.

"Hi!"

I close my eyes slowly, sending a rare prayer to ask for this human mosquito to leave me alone. All I want is to sit in silence. Soothe my frenetic heart into beating at a more reasonable pace.

I feel the girl scoot onto the bench of the picnic table where I'm sitting. Yet another unanswered prayer.

"I'm Asia Coleman. I wish I could tell your sister thank you." When my eyes fly open, the most put-together preteen I've ever seen in my life sticks out her hand and shakes mine firmly.

I gasp. "Jamal..." is all I say, and she nods. Her father was the man slain by police a few months ago in Florida. The man Kezi went to march for.

I absorb her pressed top. The crease in her jean shorts. Her hair, perfectly smoothed into a straight bun. Asia had a growing social media following, cultivated after her father was killed. The moment she opened her mouth to express her grief at the first press conference after Jamal's death, the media and folks online couldn't get over how "articulate" she was—*"and in the face of such tragedy at that!"*

They deemed her One of the Good Ones. Sometimes the phrasing was different—A Nice Kid, A Child with Promise— but the intent was always the same: this little girl was worth listening to *because look at how composed she was*! If we read her report card, we would see all As. If we spoke to any of her teachers, they'd call her a star student. Her father, Jamal Coleman, immortalized on the internet, if not in the history books, took her to church every Sunday. The cognitive dissonance of it all was something I couldn't take. If I had been the one to die that day in the hands of police instead of my sister— what would they have said about me? I skipped school like I was allergic to desks? I got messy drunk at parties? I could have been a better sibling and daughter? And though that was all true, should those facts have any bearing on whether the world was livid at the injustice of my death or mourned for me? For Jamal Coleman? For Kezi? All the rest?

When she is called to the witness stand to shred her heart apart in front of a supposedly impartial jury of those officers' peers, maybe they'll listen to her instead of whispering about her weight or how sculpted her hair is or the syntax of her English. Maybe they'll just see a girl, robbed of her father. I doubt it though.

I had noticed her speaking with a group of adults while I people-watched after deciding to take a risk and eat something from the plate I made earlier to quell my grumbling stomach. They held on to her every word. Their gazes followed her hands as they moved animatedly throughout her story. She spoke with the confidence of someone who had recited the words often, while somehow retaining all the emotion. She was a family spokesperson, like Mom.

That's an impossible job for an actual grown-up. But she's a kid.

"How do you do this?" I ask, keeping my eyes straight ahead. I pick at my barbecued chicken. Tear a piece off with my fork and dip it in my potato salad.

"I was angry," Asia says quietly. "I still am."

I find her gaze, swim in the deep brown of her eyes.

"Why do you keep going then?" I ask. "How do you not let it eat you up?"

"Sometimes it does," she says thoughtfully. "There are days when I tell my mom that I can't deal with everything and I just stay home from school and watch TV."

After the shock and funeral planning and back-to-back events died down, there were days I couldn't move from my bed. The act of lifting my head from my pillow, dragging my body to the bathroom, and having to see Kezi's door was too unbearable. I started sleeping on the couch downstairs just so I could avoid being so close to her room.

"But that's only sometimes," she says. "I know enough now that, at the end of the day, or my life, I want to feel like I did the best I could to make the world better for other people. So other kids don't feel like I feel."

I consider this preteen, with her calm demeanor, faint smile, and sense of justice… I am not there.

"Hey. What did you mean by thank you? Were you a fan of Kezi's?"

She brightens. Kind of. "I was in my civics class and my teacher showed one of your sister's explainer videos. It was about your rights when a police officer gets in your face," she says. "That was the day my daddy was killed."

Whoa. I had no idea Kezi's videos were part of curriculums. That schools trusted her words enough to share them with students. That they internalized them enough to use her tips in life-or-death moments.

"How old are you?" I ask.

"Just turned thirteen. But I feel fifty." Asia grins as she says it, but there is an emotional maturity about her. The kind of mental aging that comes with loss and growing up too fast.

"So you're telling me, when that cop came up to your dad's car, you thought to record because of Kezi?" I remember that video clearly.

I have a right to do this. Speak calmly.

"Yeah. My voice was trembling just as much as my hand was while I recorded," she says, looking down at her fingers. "Even though Daddy died... I wanted people to know the real story."

I don't think. I take her hands in mine.

"Because of you, we know what happened," I say. "I'm glad you saw her video. 'Lost' body cam or not...we know the truth because of you."

Yes, we're crying. I pull out the thin napkin in the plastic utensils packet and hand it to her as she gives me hers. We laugh.

"I'm sorry you lost a sister. I don't know if it makes a difference to tell you...but you can leave here knowing she helped a lot of people."

It helps. A little. But *I* didn't know Kezi. Not the way a sister should.

I wish...

Then I realize.

I have to find Genny.

16

KEZI

I could hear Ximena's shouts as the police van drove away. I was in the back of the vehicle, seated on a long, narrow bench and farthest from the door. As the officers had urged me forward, I'd noticed thick black block letters printed on the inner doors and groaned softly. The mocking words echoed in my mind, bouncing down my tense neck muscles to my restrained hands as we pulled out: HOLD ON TIGHT, IT MIGHT GET A LIL BUMPY. There were three other people with me. Two women sat beside me, one of them much older and the other about my age. The man in the black tracksuit was alone on the other side, a metal partition separating him from us. As we sat quietly, I couldn't help but replay what had just occurred. One second I was listening to Mrs. Coleman's speech about her son, and the next, I was being force-fully dragged into the back of a cop car.

Ximena had followed along, screaming about wrongful arrests and other theoretical concepts she had learned about in social studies, but the officer had paid her no mind. There was even one point when she'd grabbed my right arm and the officer had pulled on my left, leaving me in the middle about to be split in two. During the tug-of-war, my camera strap broke, and Ximena bent down to pick up my most prized possession. The officer used her moment of distraction to pull my arms behind my back and slide a zip tie decisively over my wrists.

"Cut it out, Ximena!" I screamed when she reached for me again. "You've done enough!"

Ximena jumped back as quickly as if she had touched a flame. Her face was flushed with rage, and confusion danced across her features.

"I know you're trying to help but you're only making it worse. Just go call Genny!"

"I'm calling your parents!" Ximena still followed, this time leaving more distance between herself and the officer, her shout a little quieter than before.

"Hey. I saw what you did out there, kid." The man with the black tracksuit was speaking to me through the divider, his deep voice pulling me from my thoughts. "Thank you for standing up for me."

"Oh. Yeah. It was nothing," I said reluctantly, certain that the officers could hear us from where they were seated. "I wasn't trying to be a hero or anything."

"That's what makes it even more impressive," he said, a smile in his voice. "True heroes are the people who do something simply because they know it's the right thing to do."

"Yeah, well. It still sucks that we got arrested for it."

"A small price to pay," he said.

"I'm—"

The police van took a sharp turn and we all lurched to the right. I tried to use my hands to keep my balance, but since they were held in place behind me, there was nothing I could do to stop my head from banging into the side of the car.

"Hey! You have people back here you know!" the older woman shouted.

Something warm trickled down the side of my face. I didn't need my hands free to know that it was blood. Suddenly, the car veered again, and I slammed into the girl next to me.

"I'm sorry!" I said to her, trying to straighten myself in my seat.

"It's…okay…" she said through labored breaths.

"Are you all right?" I asked.

"My…asthma…"

We were seated so close that I felt each breath she took rattle through her chest.

"Hey. Let's breathe together, okay? In and out, real easy."

She nodded and followed my lead, matching each inhale and exhale. Her pressed hair was matted to her forehead, glued down by sweat. I probably looked exactly the same, since I'd straightened my hair that morning to switch it up for my birthday. Her long lashes finally fluttered open once her breathing returned to normal.

Just as I opened my mouth to ask the girl her name, the tires squealed, and each of us slid haphazardly across the back seat of the van.

"Yo. They're doing this shit on purpose!" the man said, raising his voice.

The rest of the ride was a pinball game, the four of us

bouncing off the walls and each other. My stomach flipped with anxiety at each sharp turn. I prayed that Ximena had called my mom and dad. I didn't want to give my parents a reason to yell at me and say *I told you so,* but I would take them fussing me out for all eternity if it meant not being in this van. I needed them.

My head was whirling when we finally came to a stop. I heard the heavy footsteps of one of the officers sauntering to the back of the van. The doors swung open and sunlight flooded in. My stomach jumped to my throat, and I threw up at my feet.

A small group of people crowded around a man giving a speech as the officers led us through the precinct. Two balloons with the words *Happy Retirement* on them floated around him, lost souls in search of peace. The man didn't look old enough to be retiring, his sandy brown hair just starting to gray at the temples.

As if to explain, his voice floated above the crowd. "I am truly going to miss you all. And while I'm heading to Oklahoma to be closer to my dad, just know that you all are like family to me too."

Our eyes locked as they maneuvered us prisoners past the group. Even from across the room, I sensed the intensity of the man's gaze following us, probably irked that we'd distracted his colleagues from fully listening to his speech. Shivers pranced down my spine, and I looked away. How odd was it that in the same day, life could proceed normally—calmly—for others while your own went up in a ball of flames?

The girl from the police van marched hesitantly in front of me as we wove through the precinct. I followed close behind her, although we hadn't spoken again since leaving the van.

It was a strange comfort to have her near. But that feeling of familiarity was cut short by the officer who processed us for booking. She took one look at the both of us and separated us without saying a word. I watched them lead her away, the feeling of panic that I'd been trying to keep in check fighting desperately to claw to the surface. The girl turned around to look at me. I smiled at her in encouragement as she turned a corner. And then she was gone.

An hour later, I was still sitting in a holding cell with thirty other women when my name was finally called.

"Kez-EYE-uh Smith?"

"It's KEH-zee-uh," I corrected.

"Right. Well it's time for your phone call."

I followed the officer and almost cried with relief at the sight of the phone. I drew in a shaky breath and dialed my mom's number. She picked up after the first ring.

"Keziah!" The panic in her voice oozed through the receiver. "Oh my God. Thank the Lord! We are stuck in traffic but on our way. Are you okay?"

"Yes, Ma. I'm fine," I replied. "Just a little banged up."

"Banged up? What do you mean banged up?"

"It's fine," I said carefully, aware of the police officer sitting nearby. "When will you be able to get me out of here?"

"We're working on it, Kezi, and have called an attorney but it's not that simple. This isn't detention. You're in jail!"

"Trust me, I know!"

"Do you? You should've just listened to me and your father and not gone to this damn protest!"

"Are you serious right now? You're going to take the short time that we have for this phone call to yell at me?"

"Well, maybe you'll actually listen. Ximena called me in tears talking about how you interrupted an officer while he was making an arrest. Now, the only way that would make any sense to me is if you momentarily lost your mind."

"Mom, you weren't there!" I said raising my voice. "They were arresting a man who did *nothing* wrong. You didn't raise me to not speak—!"

"No! We raised you to be smart, and that was far from it. You put yourself in real danger, Kezi. There's nothing wrong with what you do online, but you have to understand that things are different in real life. This isn't some little video that you just fire out and go about your business. What you do in the real world can change the course of your whole life."

"Little video? For real? I don't care what you say. I was doing the right thing and I would do it again. HE DID NOTHING WRONG!"

I had spent the last hour trying to keep my cool, keeping my head bowed when talking to officers, making sure to not raise my voice too much when I spoke. But the dam that was safely storing all of my raging emotions had finally broken and everything was rushing out, engulfing me in despair, drowning me.

"Kezi, you need to keep your voice down!"

The fear and regret in my mother's voice was palpable.

Like clockwork, the officer who had taken me to make my phone call was now standing right beside me. "You're going to have to get off the phone."

"Officer. Please. I'll keep it down. I've just had a very stressful day and I want to finish this conversation with my mother," I said.

"Well you should've thought about that before you started shouting. Now hang up so that I can take you back to the holding cell."

"Please, sir. I'm a minor. I'll be quick. I just need to know when they're coming to get me."

"Kezi, just listen to the officer," my mother said in my ear. Her voice was strained as if she was trying to hold back a scream.

"According to your ID, you are an adult. I'm sure your mother will be getting you soon, but your time on the phone is up."

He was right. I had completely forgotten what today being my birthday meant. The very reason that I was able to go to the rally without my parents' permission in the first place was now why I could no longer speak to them.

"Please," I said weakly to the officer. My eyes burned from the tears I held back.

The policeman reached forward, ignoring me, and wrapped his hand around the phone. I was still holding on and reflexively tightened my fingers. This was the second time in one day that a policeman was taking a phone from me. The second time that I was being silenced.

"Mom!" I yelled into the phone, the tears that I had been trying to contain now racing down my face, each drop falling freely as I cried for my mother again and again. I heard her shouting back, but I couldn't make out what she was saying over the sobs that racked my body.

Another officer made his way to me. He was bigger than his colleague. I felt myself deflate, my chest caving. Each step he took was a pinprick in the balloon that was my resistance.

"I'm sorry, Ma," I said. And even as I let the phone fall from my hand, I knew my mom must have still been screaming, an anguished echo as she repeated my name.

The second officer slammed the phone into the receiver before turning to me. I was sitting as calmly as I could in my seat, gulping back tears, trying my hardest not to move from the fear that coursed through my body as the first officer reinforced his grip on my shoulder.

Within seconds, I was on the floor. The second policeman slammed me down as easily as a rag doll. My forehead made a sickening crack as it met concrete.

"Stop resisting!" they shouted. Even though I lay as still as a body of water on a cold winter day, as death. I didn't fight as they dug their knees into my back, as they pushed my head down, as they broke my spirit. All I could do was cry, the noise that erupted from my body an ancient sound, one of pain, loss, hopelessness.

Finally, the handcuffs were on my wrists, my arms locked in place behind me. Tears continued to stream down my face, and my shoulders shook with silent sobs. Should I bother to tell them that I was afraid? That it was fear that had me holding on to the phone? That I was scared for my life? Certainly they knew. But did they even care?

The officers dragged me past the first holding cell, parading me in front of the other people locked away in their confinement. A warning of what happens when you don't immediately obey orders. We arrived in front of an empty cell, and as soon as the first officer opened the door, his partner removed the restraints from my hands and tossed me inside like discarded garbage.

And then I was alone. Their job of putting me in my place complete. It took everything inside me to prevent the wail building at my core from bubbling up and spilling out like lava, magma destroying everything in its path. Instead, I became small. I was a wounded bird lying on the side of the road, not quite dead but wishing it were so after having its wings clipped.

I lay on the floor a long while, shivering against the concrete, unable to muster the strength to lift myself onto the hard box of a bed. The world tilted beneath me as my vision swam in and out of focus.

How many times had I bashed my head today? I needed to stay awake. But the more I tried to keep my eyes open, the dizzier I became... It wouldn't hurt to close my eyes for a second would it?

When the smell of smoke reached my nostrils, I was at the precipice of alertness. A tightrope walker hovering between wakefulness and sleep. Was this ringing in my ears a sign of a concussion? No... It was an alarm, the blaring alert repeating its call to action. If I listened closely, I could just make out the sound of many people walking—no, running, their steps like beating drums, each stride reverberating in my head.

What was going on? I tried to use my arms to lift my body from the jail floor but found that they were jelly. It was a sign...surely it would be all right for me to sleep for just a moment...to close my eyes for less than an instant and snuggle down into the sudden heat that was invading my bones from where I lay on the floor.

Soon I was drifting, consciousness slipping from my grasp as the room dimmed around me. Peace was near, hovering coyly outside of my touch. I reached for it and shuddered when the muffled noise of shouts faded away into barely there whispers. At last, my arms opened wide, and I slid into the welcome embrace of rest.

PART II

"12 When they saw him from a distance,
they could hardly recognize him; they
began to weep aloud, and they tore their
robes and sprinkled dust on their heads."

—JOB 2:12

NEW INTERNATIONAL VERSION

17

HAPPI

Genny and I are standing beside her tricked-out car with our parents, listening quietly as they list their demands for this road trip.

"You'll call us at least twice a day. First thing in the morning and last thing before bed."

"We need a midday text in between these calls to make sure everything is okay."

"No speeding."

"No drinking and driving."

"If you get pulled over—"

"Ma! I think we got this," Genny says, interrupting our parents. At this rate, they'll be rescinding their blessing before we even stick the key in the ignition. Or we'll spend the two weeks of this trip nodding as they spout rules for the road instead of getting a move on. "You really don't have to worry. We'll be perfectly okay. We'll call and text a lot if it makes you feel better, but we're also going to update Kezi's YouTube page as a tribute to her so her followers can get some closure too. I think she would've liked for us to do that." Genny clears her throat, possibly trying to distract herself from the tears that now well in her eyes.

"Yes. She would," Dad says softly, pulling Genny into an embrace.

Even in the seconds that are meant to be light, feelings of loss weigh heavily on our shoulders. It's a thick blanket that we can't muster the strength to throw off, suffocating one second and all too familiar the next. But just like that, the moment is gone. Genny pulls back from Dad's arms to show him and Mom how to turn on alerts for new uploads to Kezi's channel.

As Genny assists our parents, I think about what happened after my conversation with Asia Coleman. I had done my best to collect myself and then tracked down Genny. I found her filling her plate with plain potato chips and mustard-covered hot dogs. The smile on my sister's face when I told her that I now wanted to come along was almost comical.

"I knew you'd come around," Genny said as she drenched a chip in the spicy yellow condiment. "Why else do you think I brought that big-ass suitcase with me?"

Turns out Genny knew me better than I knew myself. Or at the very least, she hoped that I would change my mind and had preemptively packed some of my clothes for this adventure when she stopped by our house to pick up the *Green Book* Kezi got from Ximena. That was also when Genny found the letters our sister had addressed to Mom and Dad when she had been upset about their lack of support over attending the rally. It was like Kezi led her to them. When I asked Genny what she would've done had I not come along, she waved away the question.

"Yo, when are we heading out?" I ask her once Mom has finally gotten a grasp on how to leave a comment.

"In just a little bit," Genny answers, glancing distractedly toward the front entrance of the hotel.

I start to demand to know what she's waiting for, and then my mouth hangs open, because my answer is staring right back at me. Or rather, two answers. Derek Williams and Ximena Levinson emerge from the hotel with their suitcases in tow, the wheels rolling loudly across the gravel parking lot.

The last time I saw either of them for longer than a minute was at Kezi's funeral. It was so strange to observe them all dressed up in their Sunday finest to mourn the loss of my sister. I had felt like I was the one intruding on their grief, once I finally gave in to my mother and went over to thank them for coming. Ximena's face was frozen in a permanent state of anguish, and when she hugged me, her sadness seeped into my bones, mingling with my own desperate melancholy. I couldn't even *look* Derek's way. Once upon an incredibly distant time ago, he would've been the person that I ran to, to regain some semblance of normalcy. But now all I had was Santiago, who only retreated further and further from me each time I attempted to talk about how I was feeling.

It was easy to avoid seeing either of my sister's best friends since that day. Everyone decided it was most suitable for me to stay home for the rest of the school year. I had been honest with my parents for once and told them that I would skip each and every class if they forced me out of the house before I was ready. All my teachers agreed to send my remaining assignments through email, and I ended the academic year barely passing. When Ximena and Derek stopped by the house to check on my mom, I mastered how to prevent all interaction with them. Because the sight of my sister's companions poked at a wound in my soul that was nowhere near healed. At all times, the footage of Kezi's arrest replayed over and over in my mind. It was part of me now, fused into my joints and sockets. Even the quickest glance at Ximena was a reminder that my sister was gone. And I would be lying if I didn't admit that I frequently wondered what would've happened if Ximena hadn't carried on the way she did that day, based on the footage I'd later seen on Kezi's Instagram. If my sister would be...the thought feels too cruel for me to complete.

Genny waves the duo over. They approach, each step bringing me closer to the realization that there's no getting out of this trip now. But I can't resist the urge to ask anyway. "Do I still have to go?"

"Yes," Genny says firmly.

"Hmm. And why are they here?"

"Ximena and D are coming with us."

D? I try not to let Genny's use of Kezi's nickname for my once-best friend get on my nerves. "And why did you fail to mention this?"

"Because I thought you would just use it as another reason to back out."

The tone of exasperated annoyance that Genny usually takes with me worms its way into our conversation. I'm slightly relieved. It has been a while.

"Well, you would've thought right, Genny. If I knew that you were going to have two other people with you, I wouldn't have felt so bad about staying behind."

Our parents are suspiciously silent throughout this exchange.

"Wait a minute," I say. "Did you all know about this too?"

They glance wordlessly at each other, and I receive my answer.

"Hey, Aunt Mimi and Uncle Malcolm," Derek greets Mom and Dad as he rolls to a stop in front of us.

"Hi, you two. How are you?" Mom says, giving Derek a kiss on the cheek and then one to Ximena.

"We're okay," Ximena answers with a shy smile. She turns to me. "We're very grateful to Happi for thinking of us. Genny mentioned that it was her idea to have the two of us come along on this road trip, and I just—"

Ximena is a gale of emotions. She is looking at me with such gratitude, and it takes everything in me to not hiss at Genny. It's one thing to spring them on me unannounced but a whole other to make it seem like I had suggested this. I could just as quickly end the charade and let Ximena and Derek know exactly what I think about them being here. But one peek at Derek's face has me swallowing my words.

"We mean it. Thank you for thinking of us, Happi," Derek says. "We loved her too."

I let out a deep, slow exhale and incline my head in acquiescence. I can practically feel the tension sliding off of my parents and sister. I try not to let it land on my head.

As Dad crams the surprisingly roomy trunk with the additional luggage, Derek and Ximena admire our Mustang's decoration.

"This has Kezi scribbled all the way over it," Derek says as he knocks on a black power fist sticker.

"And these tulips…" Ximena finds Genny's eyes. Nods.

"One weekend we were bored at my place and drew up our dream cars," Genny explains. "I wanted a Tesla. Kez showed me this… I didn't think about how tight it would be for four people when I rented it though."

"Or how bad for the environment," Ximena adds.

"This one, solitary car is the least of the world's worries," I say irritably.

Genny rolls her eyes.

Soon, we're all buckled up. I'm sitting in the back seat with Derek and Ximena rides shotgun while Genny has the first shift at the wheel. All of our bags are carefully stowed now, but Genny has one up in the front with her. Kezi's camera is in there, and Genny wants to keep it close.

"All right. Be safe, kids… Young people," my dad corrects himself as he taps the roof of the car.

Genny shifts the car into Drive, and my mom waves a hand to stop her before she pulls off.

"Last rule. Don't hurt each other."

The car is uncomfortably silent as we make our way to I-55 South, even with the radio murmuring in the background. You would think that we were complete strangers. But I suppose that is true in a sense. Derek and I haven't spoken, like *really* spoken, in years; Ximena and I have nothing to talk about, and Genny…well. She's Genny.

The music continues softly in the background, and I stare out the window. *This is going to be a long two weeks.*

"So…where are we headed on this road trip again?" Derek asks. He never could stand awkward silences.

Genny replies almost too eagerly. "We'll be stopping in six different states before we make it back to California. Ximena, would you mind reading from the first page of that booklet in the glove compartment?"

Ximena does as she's asked and pulls out a journal.

"Listed here we have each of the states that we'll be visiting on our trip," Ximena says. "First up is Illinois, duh, then Missouri, Oklahoma, Texas, New Mexico, Arizona, and then we're back in California."

"Wow," I say still peering out the window. "Places that have literally *never* been on my must-see list."

"Come on now. We're going to be doing some cool stuff along the way. We're stopping at an amusement park, a few museums, going camping!" Genny tries to convince me.

"Yay. Fun," I say under my breath.

"Kezi was really looking forward to seeing the Grand Canyon," Ximena says, not hearing my snarkiness. Or ignoring it. "I wanted to help her put the trip together, but she was really set on doing the whole thing herself. She'd been planning for ages! Even before I gave her the hard copy of the *Green Book*, she was using the versions the New York Public Library had scanned online. It won't be the same experiencing all of this without her."

"It won't be," Genny says, giving Ximena a small smile. "But at least we can do this together in her memory."

Genny and Ximena continue chatting amongst themselves, swapping stories about Kezi like trading cards. That time she made kombucha explode out of a teacher's nose. When she clapped back at the trolls on her YouTube page. How she could have you nursing your hurt feelings for an entire week just from an epic side-eye. Ximena laughs loudly at Genny's jokes, clearly trying her hardest to come off as likeable to the only sister she's deemed worthy enough to impress.

Ximena loved Kezi. I see it in the way she beams from only the memory of her. And though nothing can compare to Kezi and Genny's bond—they were two halves of a whole—there's something about how Ximena speaks about Kezi that I can't quite place my finger on. Something I hadn't noticed before. It's reinforced by the way Genny takes special care to comfort my sister's friend.

Derek clears his throat beside me. He's obviously trying to get my attention, but I'm not having any of that. I pull my earphones out of my book bag and plug them into my phone. I crush the buds into my ears as if I'm jamming to music, but I'm wearing them to not be bothered. Just because I'm trapped in this car doesn't mean I have to converse with him the entire time. And this way, I can listen to what anyone says in case they talk about me. I don't even need Kezi's ghost to tell me how cynical I'm being. I can't help it.

I unlock my phone to send Santiago a text and let him know that I'm going to be out of town for a while longer. If he cares.

My phone buzzes five seconds later, and my hopes soar. Until I look down and see: Cool. Safe trip. I immediately start typing away, ready to give him a piece of my mind. That's all he has to say to me? After everything I've been through? My fingers are flying across my screen, the wall of text growing larger and larger with each swipe. And then I notice Derek, tilted ever so slightly in his seat to see what I've written. I want to be angry at him for being nosy, but I can't. If I saw someone writing a novel like that beside me, I'd cringe and sneak a few peeks too.

I delete the entire message and place my phone facedown in my lap. My eyes start to flutter closed until I notice Derek doing a terrible job of faking a yawn as he leans back over to his side of the car. Are all guys losers or is it just the ones at my school?

I remember the first time I discovered Santiago. My second drama club meeting at the beginning of sophomore year.

He was overly confident. A big show-off who did everything in his power to keep the attention on himself at all times. I usually paid him no mind and did my best to not get lost in his hazel eyes. But as soon as he stepped on the stage, he was a flame drawing the audience in like fireflies. And I buzzed louder than the rest. We were paired off as co-leads to star in our school's rendition of *Aida,* and I fell for him a little more each time we practiced our lines. Dominoes in a chain reaction had nothing on me. When he finally asked me to be his girlfriend, I was ecstatic. I wasn't naive enough to think that he liked me as much as I liked him. But he'd mentioned more than once that I was his match. That we could be a power couple in the "acting world." What a joke.

"You're going to miss it all," Derek says quietly, snapping me out of my reverie.

"What?" I ask.

"Your eyes have been shut nearly the entire ride, and we've just left. You're going to miss the whole trip if you keep that up."

I look out the window and see cars whizzing past. Trees line the street here and there like uniformed soldiers stationed a few feet from one another. There's not much else.

"How'd you know my earphones aren't on?" I ask Derek.

"Oh. Well. Your homeroom was right next to mine this year. You'd always sit on the floor waiting for your teacher to get there before class started and talk with your classmates with those big headphones you've got over your ears. But as soon as that guy Quincy would sit down next to you and try to get your attention, your music was suddenly too loud for you to hear anything he said. Besides. You're always observing. It's the actress in you."

I say nothing but try not to smile. I'm surprised he noticed.

★ ★ ★

A few hours later, we're nearing our exit and Genny tells us that we'll be arriving at our first place soon. She's chattering excitedly about nothing, and I can tell she's anxious. It's one thing to be driving along I-55, but a whole other to get to the inaugural stop on Kezi's list. We are *really* doing this.

My own palms are sweating now. All these weeks and months without my sister have passed so slowly, each day dragging along as time stretches further and further away from the last moment I saw her, spoke to her. Will I one day forget the sound of her voice? Will I be able to remember the sparkling sound of her laughter only when I'm secretly tuned in to her now-dormant YouTube page, crying alone in my bedroom?

Genny exits the highway, and we see a sign that says Welcome to Springfield, Illinois. Soon the car is slowing, and we have finally arrived. I look out the window to see a modestly sized motel with its windows boarded up. The pale pink paint that once covered the establishment has chipped into a million tiny splinters of neglect.

We all pile out of the car and stand in front of the building. A faded sign on what appears to be the front door reads *Ms. Ebony's Bed & Breakfast*.

"Are you sure we've got the right place?" Derek asks as he looks up at the building, using his hand to shield the sun from his eyes.

"That's what Kezi has here on the list," Ximena says, double-checking the journal in her hand.

Genny opens up the small backpack that she brought with her on the trip. She rustles around in it and finally pulls out a familiar light green colored paperback, the *Green Book*. The pamphlet is filled with oversized sticky notes, and Genny flips to a pink one with a big number one scrawled in the top right-hand corner. My heart flutters at the sight of Kezi's handwriting, and I feel my throat close up. As I look away to collect myself, I admit that a tinge of jealousy has washed over me.

Why does Genny get to hold on to some of the last written notes that Kezi left behind? I know I was reluctant about joining this road trip but, now that I'm here, I'm being forced to come to terms with the fact that my relationship with Kezi was even worse than I thought. All this time, our bond had been stretched so tight that it was at the brink of snapping altogether, and I never once stopped to acknowledge that, to do my part to keep it intact. And it was my fault. Whenever Kezi mentioned her birthday or graduation plans, I would brush them aside, because I didn't think we had anything in common. Deep down I always hoped that maybe when we were older we would really get to know each other. That we would have more time. But as we stand staring at this decrepit building, I realize that I have unwittingly signed myself up to feel guilty over and over again by coming on this trip. My punishment for being a terrible sister.

Genny clears her throat, and I'm forced to look at her. Kezi's favorite sibling.

"Don't forget to record," Genny says to me. I stare at her for a few seconds and then remember that we are supposed to be chronicling our trip on Kezi's YouTube page. Genny, Ximena, and Derek wait as I walk back to the car and retrieve Kezi's old camera. I hold it gingerly in my hands, remembering how she'd worked so hard to be able to buy it. Soon, I'm standing beside them again with the camera ready to go.

Genny looks down at the sticky note in her hand and reads aloud. "All right y'all. We are standing in front of Ms. Ebony's Bed & Breakfast. This used to be the go-to motel for any

Black person stopping in Springfield during the Jim Crow Era. Victor Hugo Green, the creator of the *Green Book*, wrote that it was his hope that someday his guidebook would no longer have to be published because Black patrons would be welcome everywhere. And once the Civil Rights Act was signed in 1964, things started to change. Unfortunately, many of the businesses that were once thriving beacons in the community shut down, since their patrons were now able to frequent the once whites-only establishments. Less than five percent of the businesses in the *Green Book* remain open today."

"So…if this place is out of business, where are we gonna stay?" I ask.

"Clearly not here, Happi," Genny says. "It's a history lesson."

"Yup. Kezi definitely organized this road trip," Ximena says with a tiny grin. Derek nods silently beside her.

"No doubt about that," Genny replies. "The hotel we're actually staying at isn't too far. I recommend we all get a full night's rest, because we're going to head out pretty early tomorrow morning. We have to make a quick stop before we continue on our trip."

"Quick stop where?" I ask. I do not want this little excursion lasting any longer than it needs to.

"Mom wants us to visit Aunt Leslie and Uncle Clyde on behalf of her and Dad before we get to St. Louis."

"Uncle Clyde. Uncle Clyde. Why does that name sound familiar?" Derek asks.

"He's the uncle with that super hardcore church Kezi told us about," Ximena reminds Derek. "He's married to her mom's younger sister."

"Yeah. He's pretty…conservative," Genny says.

I snort. "That's a nice way to put it."

"Look, it's not my idea, believe me. I tried everything to

get us out of it, but Mom wouldn't change her mind," Genny says. "I've consoled myself by thinking about Aunt Leslie's cooking though. You know how good her peach cobbler is! We'll just have to put up with Uncle Clyde for a few hours and then we can eat some delicious food. It'll be our prize for dealing with his ass."

I look at Genny skeptically. I hope she has enough snacks in her bag for all of us, because we're going to be sitting in those pews for *at least* four hours. Once Uncle Clyde gets up on the pulpit, nothing short of Jesus Himself can take that man down. People could start passing out from hunger, and he would say that it was the Holy Ghost manifesting since he was doing the Lord's work. I hate Uncle Clyde's church. I hate Uncle Clyde.

But I keep my thoughts to myself as we all climb back into the car. I turn around in my seat and watch as Ms. Ebony's Bed & Breakfast shrinks farther and farther away. It's hard to imagine it as a once prosperous guest house. But as I continue to watch it fade into the distance, I think about what it must've been like. Families pulling up to the front steps with their bags after spending hours on the road. Ms. Ebony coming out to greet her guests and whipping them up a warm bite to eat. How did they feel, when she or her descendants closed her doors for the last time once business slowly trickled away and then dried up?

I sigh and face forward. I nestle my headphones into my ears, but this time I let the music play, hoping the sounds will drown out the whispers of Ms. Ebony's hopes and dreams that are now nothing more than lingering ghosts haunting the cobweb-filled halls of her legacy.

18

HAPPI

We're going to be in and out.

That's what Derek said when we entered Mount Zion Baptist Church this morning. But that was three hours earlier, and we're nowhere even *close* to being "out." Even Genny, who is normally the spokesperson of good behavior, is fidgeting in her seat.

"Dang this man can talk," I grumble as I scroll furtively through my phone. I have been glued to the comments popping up on the first video we uploaded, from our stop in Springfield on this ragtag adventure.

Wow, what a terrible way to start a road trip

You can do it I guess?

RIP

Good luck y'all

Kezi'll love this; can't wait to see you on the road

RIP

What's the point of visiting all these spots if none of them still exist

Kezi's videos were better

Genny leans forward to look at me pointedly, but I don't care. This is just disrespectful at this point. I can't believe people come here every Sunday to have their time wasted like this. Well… I guess it's not really wasting time, since there's not much else to do in Jasperilla, Missouri.

"And that's why we *have* to listen to the Lord!" Uncle Clyde booms particularly loudly, I'm sure to wake up the members of the assembly who are now slouching in the pews. "Because when we don't, we fall into temptation."

The chapel is stiflingly hot this Sunday; the room almost wiggles seductively like a mirage. The men shift in their suits, pulling at collars and neckties for any sort of reprieve. But the congregation is largely women, like most churches around the country, who depend on the stalwarts to pay their tithes and keep the lights on. The handheld paper fans flap in front of the faces of the older ladies in the audience, a stand-in for the hands that are normally in the air waving hallelujah. Sweat drips from beneath the brims of their violet, aquamarine, goldenrod hats. But it's too warm to focus on the sermon, let alone enthusiastically praise the Lord.

Derek is sitting to the right of me. He's been facing forward silently for the last thirty minutes, but I'm fairly certain he's sleeping with his eyes open. Ximena is on my left with her cell phone in her hand, flipping it over and over in her palm. She doesn't turn it on though. The elderly lady behind us already tapped her on the shoulder once to tell her to "put it up" after catching Ximena checking the clock on her home screen for the fifth time. (Ximena didn't have the years of honing her reflex skills to hide toys in church like a PK—a preacher's kid—like me.)

"Now, sexual sin is a sin against the *soul!*" Uncle Clyde bellows directly into the mic. "Just look at the youth of today."

Oh *hell* no.

Ximena freezes in her seat and stops fidgeting with her phone so suddenly that I instinctively reach forward to catch it because I think it's about to fall. But the phone isn't making its way to the floor. Instead, Ximena's fingers are curled over its edges like a Venus flytrap ensnaring some unlucky insect. Her knuckles are bulging from how tightly she's holding on to the device, her skin stretched so far that it looks a stark white.

"All this LGBT-alphabet-soup is the Enemy's doing. And as stewards of Christ, we must help them to find the light, to bring them back to the natural order of things."

I'm used to people dumping all types of garbage like this. It's customary to have at least one guest pastor a month come through my parents' services and meditate on the right and wrong way to live. How to raise your kids. Who to vote for. Why wives should submit to their husbands. They range from the insidious preachers imploring believers to "hate the sin but not the sinner" and the more militant screamers promising hellfire and suffering for those who don't "live right before the eyes of God."

Back in the day, these evangelists had free rein to speak on whatever they wanted and would often fall on the subject of sex—when to have it, who to have it with. But lately, my parents had heavily "encouraged" their guests to discuss less divisive topics instead. They didn't think such negativity would be good for business in a major metropolitan city with lots of young people to convert. Whether they saw it that way or not, they had rent to attend to and salaries to pay. The speakers might have shifted in appearance from wearing suits and pocket squares to ripped jeans and leather jackets, but it was the same message. The same beliefs lived in the shadows and dictated church politics. Rumors of the choir director moving in with his boyfriend, for example, led to him being replaced, quick.

I don't care for anybody to tell me what I can and can't do with my life, or where I'll be headed when it's all over. But I'm ashamed to say I've kept my thoughts to myself when I've sat in these pews. Their admonishments feel *wrong* deep in my very core. Yet I've never stood up and denounced the hate they spread on Sundays. As Ximena shifts in her seat beside me, I realize how my silence hurts too. How it shouldn't have taken *this* for me to understand that.

Ximena shakes, not from fear or being on the verge of passing out from this heat. It's from anger. She didn't sign up for this, and I hate that this guy is related to me, even if it's by marriage. Genny's hand is pressed on Ximena's knee, squeezing it almost as tightly as Ximena is gripping her cell. Even Derek is awake now. He's squirming around like a little kid who has to use the bathroom. He leans forward to look past me at Ximena, who is feverishly whispering with Genny and, again, I have the feeling that there's something I'm missing.

"If we love our children the way that we say we do, then we have to speak to them plainly. It's our responsibility as parents and as Christians to save their souls from eternal damnation!"

Ximena is a spring that's been wound too tight and catapults to her feet. In one smooth motion, she slides past Genny and steps into the center aisle of the church. There's nothing and no one who can stop her as she makes her way to escape. It's like all the heat in the building has been channeled into Ximena. And then she's at the exit, loudly swinging open the doors of the church, letting them fly until they've collided against the wall with a BANG as she leaves. More than a few congregants turn in their seats to watch her go. I already hear the whispers rippling through the audience, a rustling of wagging tongues and flapping lips at the girl with the short hair who couldn't take what they believe to be the truth.

"We're leaving. Let's go," my sister says, leaning over to me and Derek. But I am already on my feet, been ready to peace out. It shouldn't have taken me witnessing someone I know be attacked to stand up against this. Genny practically trips over herself to chase after Ximena.

"There isn't a speck of doubt in my mind that my parents are going to hear about this," I say to Derek. He nods. "And I don't care," I add.

We grab our things and dash after them.

We are silent for a long while as we sit in the car with the A/C blasting its cold air over us. To cool us off. Bring back the humanity they tried to strip away. I see the outline of Ximena's teeth as she works her jaw, her nostrils flaring with each deep inhale and exhale.

"I'm so sorry," Genny says finally. Her voice is too loud in the quiet car, too big.

"It's not your fault," Ximena says.

"No, but he's family. And I feel responsible. I should've just told Ma we couldn't make a stop at Uncle Clyde's church."

"Look. It's fine. It's not the first time I've heard something like that, and it won't be the last. But being around that shit doesn't get easier."

The look on Genny's face is understandably fury. There's something she wants to say, but she's stopping herself. Maybe it's because I'm in the car. We're practically strangers after all.

Just as Genny is about to start speaking again, the phone rings. Or more like blares—the volume is still on the highest setting from our very secular singalong when we were on the way to church this morning. We collectively jump. Genny quickly answers to stop the commotion.

"Hello?" Genny says, motioning for us to be quiet. *It's Mom,* she mouths.

"Jemima Genesis Smith, what the hell has gotten into you?!" Mom's voice booms louder than the trap beats we were playing earlier.

"Damn, word travels fast," Derek whispers to me in the back seat, and I nod in agreement.

"Mom, you weren't there. We had to go."

"Had to go? For what reason? I told Leslie that y'all were going to attend the service and then go over to her and Clyde's place to have dinner afterwards. How do you expect to go there now after barging out of church like that?"

"Ma," Genny says warily glancing at Ximena. "Can we please talk about this later? You're on—"

"No! We're going to talk about this right now. I need you to explain to me why you would leave like that in the middle of Clyde's sermon. Do you know how disrespectful that is? And I don't need anybody saying that I ain't raised you all the right way."

"Look, if it makes you feel better, we aren't going over to Uncle Clyde's house anymore anyway. We don't want to. And we're already running behind because the sermon was so long."

"That's not going to cut it, Genny. You need to have a proper excuse for why you all left the church the way you did, because—"

"*I* left!" Ximena says raising her voice over my mother's.

You could hear a pin drop in the car right now. No one raises their voice like that to Naomi Palmer Smith and lives to tell the tale.

"I tried to stay, Mrs. Smith. I really did. But I couldn't just sit there and listen to him say all those hateful things!" Ximena's still screaming at my mom as she wipes furiously at her face, like she's trying to shove the traitorous tears that stream down her cheeks back into her eyes.

"Hateful?" Mom says slowly over the phone. She's trying the word out on her tongue as if it's the first time she's ever heard it.

"Yes, hateful! The only reason we even stopped here today is because you insisted we visit this church in the first place, even when Genny tried to get us out of it. And then he's up there saying all that trash… Did he know what Kezi was to me? That we loved each other?"

"We all loved her!" my mom shouts back at Ximena. "How dare you, little girl? Now I don't know how you speak to your mama but *my* children—"

"Kezi was gay!" Ximena's voice cracks into so many tiny

pieces, fragments that no one can collect. Her voice is a whisper. "She was my girlfriend."

A gasp races out of my mouth. I don't know what I thought Ximena was going to say, but it wasn't that. Kezi was gay? Since when? How come I'm just finding out? Why didn't she *tell* me?

I glance between Genny and Derek, and they look away... because they already knew. Because they don't want to watch the shock that is etched into my face. Derek stares down at his lap while Genny clenches Ximena's hand, offering strength after her candor.

My mother is still on the phone, breathing hard. She sounds like she's gotten the wind knocked out of her. There's a rustling over the speakers, and then my dad's voice.

"Hey. Um. Mom needs a minute... Let's talk about this another time."

"Why can't we talk about it now?" Genny says. She's staring at the radio console like it's our father's face. "Don't you think it's terrible that your own child was afraid to share this with you?"

I've never heard my parents so silent before. Genny takes a deep breath and continues, "I don't agree with Ximena shouting all crazy like that at Ma, but I agree with what she's saying. We're on this trip because of Kezi. For Kezi. What sense would it have made for us to sit through and listen to Uncle Clyde say that stuff? Jesus. Even if Kezi *wasn't* gay. I know it's a lot for you to process, but this is who Kezi was. If we can't accept this part of her, then we don't accept *any* part of her."

"But...we didn't raise you all to be..." Mom says. I can hear her choking back her tears.

I know that my parents aren't going to just accept this, right here, right now. Not the way we were brought up. And the way they were brought up. But Kezi isn't here anymore. There's no trying to pray this away, fixing it with a plane ticket to some torture camp. Or pushing it aside as simply a phase to be ignored. This version of Kezi is the last version of her to exist. More than that, it's the true version. And while I try to imagine how my parents must be feeling, my thoughts turn, more importantly, to Kezi. How she had to sit through all those sermons made by pastors emphatically shouting that people like her would go to hell. How she must've felt, hiding this from Mom and Dad. From me... How could I have been left out of the loop? Again? But this is more than the loop. This is the world. Kezi's world. And I'm so far out of its gravitational pull that it's too late to bring me back.

"So what, Mom? You think Kezi's in hell now?" I ask.

Silence stretches for longer than it should, as wide as the distance from Jasperilla, Missouri, to Los Angeles, California. It's the saddest silence in the world.

"We need time to process," my dad says with finality. "We'll talk to you all later."

No one says goodbye.

19

EVELYN

Warm Springs smelled like a miracle. Evelyn had read and im-
printed in her mind how much President Roosevelt credited
the camp with his own physical rehabilitation. Now he stood
tall when he addressed the country and Congress. And if he
could get better, who was to say Mama couldn't? As they entered Georgia, Evelyn tried to temper her excitement, put her
hope on simmer. The chances that Warm Springs would be
like the pool at Bethesda, where "the blind, the lame, the paralyzed" used to go for respite…the chances that just a dip would
mean salvation…well, the chances of that were essentially none.

But her daddy agreeing to make this stop at all, choosing to
drive an hour beyond their actual destination of Atlanta, was
proof enough that divine intervention was at play. Or maybe

it was the desperate efforts of a man willing to do anything to help his ailing wife. Both? Both.

By the time Mr. Hayes pulled up to the Roosevelt Warm Springs Institute for Rehabilitation, it was early evening the next day. The stress of the impromptu trip had him agitated, and he kept rubbing his hands over his thickening stubble that had slowly grayed with time and life's stress. He couldn't sleep, not when it was so clear he couldn't protect his wife and daughter the way he wanted to as the man of the house. He didn't think too long about what state their house must be in back home, because it made his vision blur. So he focused on what he had the capacity to control and kept on driving and driving and driving and didn't stop until he'd somehow moved through five or six states, only pausing for gas and snacks at *Green Book*-vetted stations. Now they'd arrived at Georgia Hall.

Antonin leapt out of the car and opened the door for Mrs. Hayes. Mr. Hayes grunted in acknowledgement as she giggled. Evelyn grabbed the crutches from the back seat and handed them to her mother. She gasped when she looked up at the imposing building, took in its four thick white columns that jutted the brick house forward so that it met up with the sea of green grass surrounding it. The man from the Bible had been paralyzed thirty-eight years, and his pool had been bordered with five colonnades…and Mrs. Hayes had been battling this sickness for only a couple of months…but this moment right here still felt holy.

They had barely made it through the door when a woman carrying a stack of papers almost ran into their group. She looked up in masked aggravation.

"Can I help you?" Her question's intonation suggested that the answer better be no.

"Yes, where do we check in so that my wife may use the services provided here?" Mr. Hayes asked. He smiled politely, a fruitless attempt to disarm white strangers into looking beyond his massive frame. (It never worked.)

"Oh, that won't be possible," the woman said simply.

"…we can pay whatever the—"

She sighed heavily, clearly frustrated that this inconveniencing man was not understanding her.

"Negroes aren't known to have polio," she said slowly. "The primitive natur—"

"Ma'am—" Mr. Hayes tried again in his most deferential tone, squashing the distress Evelyn knew her father must have been feeling.

"My physician diagnosed me with polio," Mrs. Hayes interrupted crisply. "He said I was a textbook example of post-polio syndrome. I had polio as a child, and these symptoms have returned after—"

"Be that as it may," the woman said, eyeing Elsa's crutches warily, as though expecting her to lash out with one at any moment. "The policy of Warm Springs is that we are an all-white institution. An all-white *patient* institution." She corrected herself hastily as an older Black woman pushing a little white boy in his wheelchair walked by. "This is, after all, a very sensitive, hygienic environment. Why, President Roosevelt himself—"

"But we donated to President Roosevelt's Birthday Ball fund-raiser for this place," Evelyn broke in, waving her crumpled flyer in the air. "My parents *voted* for him—"

"Evelyn!" Her mother whispered her name, but it echoed louder than a shout in an empty coffee can. Antonin squeezed her shoulder in warning.

Evelyn was shocked she had any tongue left, the number of times she was forced to bite it.

Back in the car, on the way to Atlanta and to Calvin:

"You know what, Mama?"

"Hmm."

"You remember that man from the Bible? He never made it to the pool either. Jesus went up to him special and healed him himself."

"'Get up! Pick up your mat and walk,'" Mr. Hayes recited. "John 5 verse—"

"That's enough, Walker."

Mrs. Hayes was lying right beyond that door. Mr. Hayes was drawing her a bath, and she would soon be swirling in the dirt of Georgia, in the filth of Warm Springs's hypocrisy and denial. Evelyn had been debating with herself for the past several minutes. Leave her be? Console her? Mrs. Hayes typically got her energy from being with others, hearing them laugh as she took their measurements for a new piece. But since the polio, she'd retreated a bit within herself, to the only person around who completely understood how she was feeling.

They'd picked up Calvin and had dinner at Mrs. Suttons Cafe, a lovely *Green Book* establishment just a few minutes from his dormitory. Evelyn's brother ate steadily but quickly the entire night, prompting Evelyn to ask him when the last time was that he'd eaten.

"A couple hours ago," he'd said, looking at her strangely before biting into his meat loaf.

Mrs. Hayes was happy to bask in the glow of her son, but her smile dimmed when they reached the Negro-friendly hotel nearest Mrs. Suttons: the Roosevelt. She'd gone into her

and Mr. Hayes's room the night they checked in and hadn't
left it for the rest of the evening.

"There you are," Antonin said, sneaking up behind Evelyn
as she stood in front of the door that next morning.

"What do you want?" Evelyn said listlessly. She stopped
pacing.

Antonin shuffled on the balls of his feet and handed her a
heavy paper bag.

"I know it's nowhere near the same..." he began nervously.

Evelyn pulled out an enormous navy blue box, with a little girl carrying an umbrella printed on the front. She sucked
in a breath.

Handed him the bag back and—

Antonin's face fell.

"I'm sorry, Evelyn, I thought I'd get a few things from the
store for your mother—I didn't mean to—"

She shook her head and pointed to her own bag, sitting in
front of the hotel room door. Evelyn picked it up and pulled
out the box of salt, tipped the bag's opening to reveal the
leaves and a few big rocks from the little garden out front,
sticks of chalk, and a large bottle of soda water hidden inside.

"Daddy and I went shopping and foraging this morning
too," she whispered. "We'll make our own damned spring."

"What are you two doing dallying outside my room?" Mrs.
Hayes's voice rang out clear and startled them both.

"Sorry, ma'am! I'm moving as we speak," Antonin called
out as he walked away, leaving his bag behind. He spun to
face Evelyn while he rounded the corner. Grinned that grin.

She smiled back and knocked on the door.

HAPPI

MONDAY, JULY 30—
3 MONTHS, 13 DAYS SINCE THE ARREST
ST. LOUIS, MISSOURI

Go take a nap sometime, damn!

In the moment, when I'd screamed those words at my sister, the laughs from our peers standing in the hallway had given me a morbid satisfaction. Of course, I hadn't known that our interaction that day would be our last...but even though I had felt judged, attacked, and misunderstood, the way I'd retaliated was unfair. If I had known that was to be our final conversation, what would I have said? How do you prepare your closing monologue to someone you never really said true first words to?

I love you?
All of you.
I'm sorry for everything.
I forgive what you said.

I was jealous, but you must already know that.
You and Genny were perfect, and I was—
I'm going to miss you.
You stole a piece of my spirit when you—
Happy birthday.

To die on the day that you're born seems impossible. Birth is all about the potential, the opportunity, the big, bad world unfolding before you to share its infinite secrets. Even parents staring at their new infants through the sanitized glass of a NICU window keep faith by dwelling on tomorrow, on hope, on the belief that life will blossom for their baby. They just got here, my God!

And from that day on, a birthday is a rebirth. It's the extra life in a video game, the squeeze that gets your legs moving after a charley horse. We do not think about deathdays. Not at seventeen years old. Eighteen. Not when everyone looked at my sister and saw greatness, smelled her future doused all over her.

The Saturday after Kezi's birthday, after what became her deathday, we had a gathering at our house. It wasn't the official funeral repast, just the friends Kezi had planned on inviting over that weekend to cut cake with her. Student council members. Speech and debate clubbers. Derek. Ximena...

I almost tripped going down the stairs when I heard voices coming from Kezi's room after I'd left the bathroom. I saw red. Who would *dare* go in there? The creak from someone sitting on her bed was unmistakable. The choked-back sob of what sounded like a female voice made me pause.

"Shh. Shh. I know," Derek's deep, gentle voice whispered.

"She was my girl." That was all I could make out, but I knew it was Ximena.

Kezi was their North Star, whether they acknowledged it or

not. She was the friend in their trio who had the strongest ties to the other points of the triangle. At first, I was surprised to learn that Derek hadn't been with them at the rally, but then I remembered how cautious he was, even in grade school.

I left them alone. They were grieving too. And Ximena's words, murmured in confidence behind closed doors, had remained unspoken for. Until now.

We are so, so high.

Six hundred and thirty feet in the sky to be exact.

The Gateway Arch in St. Louis is, according to Kezi's meticulous notes, the tallest monument in America. It's over twice the height of the Statue of Liberty. But while the patina coppered liberty goddess evokes an eternal call to freedom and supposed hope and rest for weary immigrants, the gateway arch is all business.

It's my turn to handle the camera, and I do my best to steady the video without a tripod but almost drop it a few times. I focus on the view from a wide window, where the city with its dotting of trees, parks, and sharp buildings looks up at me. I train the lens on Derek, who has cleared his throat and is skimming a piece of paper from Kezi's magical notebook.

"Yeah. June 20, 1803. From Thomas Jefferson to Meriwether Lewis… *'The object of your mission is to explore the Missouri river; & such principal stream of it, as by its course & communication with the waters of the Pacific ocean, may offer the most direct & practicable water communication across this continent, for the purpose of commerce.'*"

Fellow visitors of the arch stop as he speaks, probably curious about what the dark-skinned boy in the high-top fade and quivering voice is getting at.

"Translation?" Ximena says. She has been more subdued

since the phone call in Jasperilla. I mean…who could attempt to blame her?

"Basically, Thomas Jefferson wanted to discover what was out there to the west, to grow the United States in stature and finances."

Genny, Derek, and Ximena snap their heads in my direction, and I capture their (insultingly) shocked faces on tape. I stare right back in defiance, refusing to concede that it is a little…off brand…for me to know a fact like that.

Not that I owe anyone an explanation, but I couldn't sleep last night. Like most nights. I tossed and turned, unable to stop thinking about how my parents had clearly lost their damn minds. And that I knew even less about Kezi than I'd thought. But why was I surprised? Each time she'd tried to reveal bits of herself to me, I took the pieces that she handed over and threw them right back. Of course she hadn't told me she and Ximena were a couple. It was my fault.

Eventually, when I gave up all hope of sleep finding me, I pulled my laptop into bed and researched our location. I was up until the wee hours of the morning, self-enrolled in a crash course to learn all the things Kezi would've known. I tried to imagine what my sister would have been drawn to when she was putting together our trip, what she wanted us to learn. The more I read, the closer I felt to her. This would be my way of competing with all the secrets and stories those closest to Kezi had to share.

Genny recovers fastest.

"Something a lot of folks don't know is how the US was even able to go through with the Louisiana Purchase in the first place," she says.

But I know.

"The slaves in Haiti revolted and, thanks to their clutch

guerilla warfare and yellow fever, the French military sent to contain them lost. Badly. Eventually, Napoleon decided to give up his ideas of making a French empire in the New World. And since he already had a potential war with England to deal with, he sold almost nine hundred thousand square miles west of the Mississippi for a cool fifteen mill."

I glare pointedly in their direction at the end of my speech, daring them to say something. Ximena looks like she wants to hug me, but Derek shakes his head almost imperceptibly at her, and she keeps her hands to herself.

ALL LIVES MATTER.

RIP generationkeZi.

RIP

YouTubers are always begging people to comment, like, sub-scribe, subscribe, subscribe, and when they finally get a few followers, they fall off smh.

You idiot she died a few months ago.

RIP

You did not die in vain, everyone will know your name

Love you

Over one hundred thousand followers. That's how many people clicked on that red rectangular subscribe button after coming across a video of Kezi saying something, anything, and decided, in that instant, yeah, I'll take more of this. Scrolling through the comments gives me access to another side of Kezi, something else she had to deal with. Many of the messages I'd skimmed through were neutral to positive. But not all. When you're a young, Black woman speaking up online about the prison industrial complex or voter suppression laws, a chorus of hateful, fearful, violent rhetoric rises up with you too. Frightening, yes, but also a reminder of why you're speaking up in the first place.

Genny, Ximena, and Derek emerge from the next elevator whose doors spit out the passengers of the arch. I had gone ahead of them. They look slightly unsure what to make of me standing with my phone in hand, frowning.

"People say some wild things on YouTube," I say lightly and drop the phone into my bag.

"Kezi used to keep a running list of the most insane stuff but stopped real fast once she realized they could actually be kind of creepy," Ximena says. She pauses, biting her lip as if deciding whether or not to share her next thought. Finally, she continues. "The day before Kezi was arrested, she got an email that I could tell really rattled her. She made me promise not to say anything to anyone, so I didn't, even though I really wanted to. But that account name stuck with me. *Mr.no. struggle.no.progress.*"

"What did the message say?" I ask, my skin rippling with goose bumps.

"It was so weird. The guy in the email said something about never being alone because they had each other. He went on and on about being more than a subscriber. It was strange enough, but then he attached a video to the message. It was a clip of Kezi speaking on that city hall panel a few months before. Remember that day? Kezi and I watched the video a few times but couldn't figure out if he was the one who recorded it or if he was someone in the audience. It just felt…off."

"Wow," Genny says. "I wish she would've said something."

"Me too. I tried to get her to change her mind, but she downplayed the whole thing," Ximena answers. "I didn't push anymore, because I figured it would just be another secret Kezi wanted me to keep. She always used to joke that the comments from just one of her uploads could fill an entire book."

"From what I've seen, it seems more like ten books," I say.

Genny chuckles, but there's no humor in the sound. My heart squeezes as I realize this is just another thing Kezi felt she had to go through alone.

"Where to next, y'all?" Derek asks.

Genny looks down at her notes. "The Old Courthouse."

We file out of the building and cross the well-manicured park that hovers over the highway beneath us. Clusters of lush trees flank us as the green dome of the courthouse beckons visitors to come explore. Ximena walks ahead, shielding her eyes from the yellow Missouri sun as she looks around the parkway.

I quicken my steps to reach her.

"Hey…"

"He—" She looks pained and stops herself. "Hi."

She slows down a bit, so I take it as a signal to keep talking.

"Ximena… I wish I could say I'm shocked by my parents, but I'm not. I'm really sorry about the way they acted. It's like they've forgotten that you loved her too…and maybe it's not in the way they thought but so what? Why should it matter? I—"

She squeezes my shoulder. "Dude, you don't have to apologize. *You* didn't do anything."

I shake my head. "Exactly. I didn't do anything. Doesn't

that make me just as wrong? Yeah, I believe in God, but a lot of the rest that comes with church? I can't get behind that. Telling people who they can love or that a man is supposed to run shit because of what's in his pants…it drives me insane." I didn't plan to spill my guts at Ximena's feet like this, but now that I've started, I can't stop. "Every Sunday I would file into pews just like the one at my uncle's church and tune out everything they said while I sat through service like nothing was wrong. It makes me sick to my stomach to think Kezi had to sit there too. She was right beside me sometimes and never so much as flinched."

"That's because she would hold it all inside until *we* spoke." Ximena sighs. "I tried so many times to get her to tell everyone, but she refused. She said there was no point rocking the boat at home when it wouldn't change the way your parents thought. She'd joke that coming out would be equivalent to asking them to choose between her and Jesus, and there was no way she'd win that war."

"That's terrible. But with our parents, I can't say she's wrong. You know, the most absurd thing about the Sodom and Gomorrah story is that everyone loses their minds that the men in the town demand to have sex with the two secret angels who show up out of nowhere, but everyone seems to be cool with Lot offering up his daughters to be raped instead. Like, how can we take this seriously?"

You never even learn their names. Most of the daughters in the Bible don't get a name. Except for the few, like Job's girls. Jemimah. Keziah. Keren-Happuch.

I pause and then I ask the question that's been swirling around in my head since we left Jasperilla. "Why didn't she tell me?"

Ximena doesn't say anything, the only sound being the

crunch of our steps as we continue across the pristine lawn. Finally, "She didn't know how to."

"Oh." It's all I can say. Sisters are supposed to be able to speak to one another about anything, their bond more secure than any safe under lock and key. But Kezi and I were akin to strangers.

"Don't feel bad. It was hard for me from over here too," Ximena whispers. "We were a secret from most of the people Kezi loved. Every time I saw you, I wanted to let you know, but it wasn't my place. I understood why Kezi didn't want to say anything, but it didn't make it any easier to be hidden. She deserved to share that part of herself with *both* of her siblings in her time. If I could do it all over again, I would try even harder to get her to tell you, at least."

I nod. If *I* could do it all over again, I wouldn't have been so closed off and untouchable. Though it's too late for me to make it up to Kezi in person, there's still time to get to know her, even if it is only through the eyes of other people.

"I was dumb to not realize you two were together though," I say with a smile. "Everybody else at school thinks you're fine as hell, why wouldn't Kezi?"

Ximena rolls her eyes but smirks.

I surprise us both when I link my arms through hers.

"Just go with it," I say, and she laughs. The chatter of Genny and Derek behind us pauses for one shocked moment before they clumsily stumble over their words so they don't get caught eavesdropping.

We close the short distance, and finally we're at our destination. The Old Courthouse is surrounded by modern buildings. The glittering reflections of countless windows mirror the sparkling white exterior, rounded columns, and impressive minty dome of the historical site. I stop and pull Kezi's camera out of my bag to record the next installment for her channel. I pan up and down the building, zooming in and pausing at an onyx statue of a man and a woman holding hands and staring into the distance at something only they can see.

"This area has experienced many renovations, but no veneer or new coating of paint could ever erase the horrors that occurred on these very steps," Genny reads aloud from a page of Kezi's notebook. "Human lives were sold here. Families ripped apart. Children stolen. Souls desecrated. Right here."

I steady the camera on her as she continues.

"But even in despair, there's hope. Where so many were unsuccessful in their fight, Dred and Harriet Scott were able to change the course of history. They sued for their right to liberty, and their case eventually made it to the US Supreme Court. But instead of granting them freedom, the courts ruled that African slaves could not take their grievances to court because they weren't US citizens and were of 'an inferior order' to their white counterparts. This verdict and its bigoted rationale shook the nation and became the most pivotal case in the eventual abolishment of slavery in this country."

"Wait, so they *didn't* get their freedom?" Derek asks incredulously.

"Not from the Supreme Court ruling," I reply. "It wasn't until the slave owner who they were fighting against married this guy who was anti-slavery that things changed for them. He convinced her to get rid of the Scotts, and she agreed under the condition that she receive the back pay from all the labor the Scotts had done for other people over the past decade. The Scotts were eventually sold back to their original owner, who freed their family within two months. And all of this likely only happened because they didn't want to deal with the negative press that the case had generated."

"Kezi? Is that you in there?" Derek stage-whispers in my direction.

"Ha. Ha," I reply as I pause the recording so that we can enter the courthouse.

Genny leads the way and Ximena, Derek, and I follow. Inside, the interior of the dome is more impressive than the view from outside. Beautifully drawn Italian Renaissance style images complement the elaborately decorated balconies and supporting pillars. We explore each floor of the courthouse and tour various exhibits about women's suffrage activists and restored courtrooms.

Just as we enter the gift shop, my phone rings. I assume it's Mom or Dad breaking the silence we've maintained since Sunday and checking in to see how we are. I've been doing my absolute best to avoid any interaction with them until I know what I want to say, until I have the exact words to truly tell them about themselves. But when I glance down at my phone to begrudgingly answer, it's Santiago's grinning face that looks back at me instead. I'm so stunned that I almost miss the call.

"Hello? Santiago?" I say, right before he would have been sent to voice mail.

"Hey!" he replies. "How have you been?"

There's no succinct way for me to answer truthfully, so instead I say, "Fine. You?"

"I've been great! Things are going really well on set, even though the girl who was their first choice for my love interest never showed up. They said they tried calling her over and over again and everything. She didn't have an agent though, so they couldn't figure out another way to contact her and went on to the next person. Anyway, I'm really growing more as an artist than I ever thought I could." Santiago launches into

a very one-sided conversation and shares the latest developments in his whirlwind new life of table readings, rehearsals,
and interpersonal dramas. I try my hardest to be the dutiful
girlfriend and ask the necessary follow-up questions, laugh
at his jokes. But the more he speaks, the more I remember I
am not the same girl. My earlier shock at seeing his call shifts
from autopilot to agitation to outright anger. Blood boiling.
Crimson sight. *Furious.* Not once has he paused to ask me
how this trip has been. I told him about this new way of commemorating Kezi, but he hasn't stopped for even a second to
genuinely check in on how it's going.

This is it. No more pretending our time isn't up. It's *been* up.

I make a beeline for the nearest exit, bumping into Derek as
I do. I mouth *Sorry* to him and keep moving. Finally, I'm outside and racing down the steps to put some distance between
me and the courthouse. My path leads me to where the car
is parked. I take a deep breath as I go, filling every ounce of
myself with air. Everyone knows that wind adds fuel to fire.

"Santiago." It's not a question.

"Yes, babe?"

"Do you want to ask me how I'm doing?"

"…I did," Santiago says, clearly confused. "Right when
you answered. You said—"

"I know what I said!" I snap. "But did you really care about
my answer? Because you legit just had a whole-ass, ten-minute
conversation by your damned self."

"I didn't realize—"

"Of course you didn't *realize,*" I interrupt Santiago again.
"You're always too busy thinking about yourself. Meanwhile,
I'm over here driving across the country because it was the
last thing that my dead sister wanted to do, and you haven't
so much as sent me a friggin' text message to see how I'm

doing. That's not something you forget, Santiago. The fact that your girlfriend's sister *died* isn't something that slips your mind, like a doctor's appointment."

"You're right, Happi. I haven't forgotten. But what am I supposed to say to you?" Santiago sounds upset with me, and I can't believe it.

"You've never even tried to say *anything*!" I shout.

"There isn't a handbook for this shit, Happi. I didn't sign up for this!"

"You didn't sign *up* for this?" I repeat, trying it out on my tongue.

"I didn't mean it like that, babe. I'm sorry. I really—"

"You think I did?" I ignore him. "You think I volunteered to have my sister die the way she did? To die, period? Wow, Santiago. I always knew you were self-centered, but I chalked it up to the actor in you. This is… This is disgusting. And I'm going to do you a favor and take you out of your misery. You don't get to be shitty to me and say that it's because you don't know what to do. Me and you are *done*. Now you don't have to do anything. Do you understand? It's over! Good luck on your stupid show. I hope it gets canceled after the first episode."

I rip the phone from my ear and jam the End call button. I feel a scream bubbling up in my throat, but I push it down. I've already been flipping out in these St. Louis streets, looking like a maniac yelling at this boy over the phone. I'm not going to have someone call the police on me for having a nervous breakdown as I wait by Genny's car.

But I'm trembling. I can't keep it together. It's not just the fact that Santiago and I broke up. It's the idea that I somehow knew any better than he did about how to navigate this world of grief and loss. My vision blurs, and I close my eyes for a second. I just want the earth to swallow me whole. Instead, I feel the car shift as the weight of another person rests against it. I turn to see Derek standing beside me.

"Do you wanna talk about it?" he asks.

I shake my head.

"That's okay. I'm here. And you don't have to say anything to watch my moves."

Derek jerks his shoulders up to his ears, up and down, like he's doing a weird new viral dance, and I laugh. With his mission of making me smile accomplished, he settles back beside me on the car, and I rest my head on his shoulder. Just like I used to do on long bus rides home.

"Thank you," I say.

"Any time."

He stands beside me and says nothing else. But he's there. Exactly what I need.

21

SHAQUERIA

TUESDAY, APRIL 17—
THE DAY OF THE ARREST
LOS ANGELES, CALIFORNIA

Darius's long arms wrapped around me tightly, pulling me into a big hug. A spiderweb. His embrace was meant to comfort, but I wasn't foolish enough to allow myself the false sense of security even for a second. I looked over his shoulder as I stiffly returned the unannounced display of affection, sure the busy people walking by and half paying attention thought he was my older brother or something. I tried not to flinch when he cupped my cheek and patted it. A reminder. A warning.

"I just wanted to wish you luck as you wait to hear back about that role you were trying out for. And give you a little something for you to grab a bite to eat," Darius said gently as he slipped me a crisp twenty-dollar bill. "You should try In-N-Out. It'll be the best thing your country self has ever tasted. And there's just enough time to get it before you head over to where you're supposed to be."

I nodded rigidly at his unexpected "generosity" and thanked him. Darius didn't say another word as he walked away. He stepped up to a black SUV I hadn't noticed was idling a few feet from where we stood. I watched as he swung open the door on the passenger side and hopped in. Darius rolled down the window and waved his hand at me, a terse goodbye, and drove off.

I rattled out a shudder. I knew the game he was playing then; I'd had a foster mom play it too. Mess with your prey's head by being cruel and kind. They'd never know what to expect from you and stay in check. I tried not to think about the moment when the nice act inevitably fell away and revealed the gleaming teeth of a wolf swaddled in sheep's clothing, finally unleashed and ready to rip me to shreds.

Another *Thatcher Academy* hopeful exited the building, the expression on her face clear that her audition hadn't gone well. But mine had, if the casting directors' reactions were any indication. I had turned it around. And I wouldn't let Darius take that euphoria away from me. I glanced down at the twenty in my hand, and my stomach growled as if on cue. There was a lot about LA that was blown up to unimaginable proportions, but everyone was right about In-N-Out. And it was the perfect way to celebrate this win.

The restaurant wasn't too far, so I walked, no, floated down the sidewalk to my destination. The air seemed clearer. The sky bluer. *This* was where I was meant to be. There was a freedom to success, to knowing that I was damn good. My life was going to be bigger than what any one of those people I left behind in Mississippi expected from a girl like me. They would never forget my name. And countless more would soon learn it. Shaqueria.

I just knew it.

It wasn't long before I was seated with my order, a #1 combo with a chocolate milkshake. I held the juicy burger between both of my hands and had opened my mouth to take the first bite when I noticed a brown-skinned boy about my age glancing my way. He looked at the empty seat across from me meaningfully and smiled. I didn't reciprocate. Instead, I slammed my feet down on the chair a little too forcefully and refocused on my meal. The young man frowned but didn't approach.

Perfect. It was taking me much longer than I cared to admit to get over my ex, and I wasn't about to invite any other distraction, no matter how cute. Especially now that I was one step closer to landing the role of my dreams. I had to stay committed. And maybe one day, when I'd Made It, or at the very least knew how I'd be able to consistently pay my rent, I could open up to the idea of letting someone in again. Being alone was my default and had been for years.

Although, I had to remind myself it hadn't always been that way. There was a time when I was smothered in devotion, in hugs, from people who loved me, a surplus of affection I had long since depleted in this time on my own.

I still remembered the day my parents died. Of course I did. One moment they were kissing third-grade me goodbye, off to enjoy some "couple time" while I spent the weekend with my grandma. The next, an officer my grandmother was scared to open the door for was standing at our threshold, solemnly explaining that my parents had lost control of their car. In less than an instant, *bam*. They were gone. I had an immediate vision of them turning to dust, just two piles of disintegration the wind would blow away at any second. And when that happened, how could I be sure that they were ever there in the first place?

My grandmother tried so *hard* to keep it together for me.

She went to bed with an empty tank of energy each night. But even at eight years old, I understood that she was on borrowed time. Mom and Dad were both only-children and had always spoken about having a large family so I could have lots of siblings. That had excited me, the idea of being the leader of a small pack and knowing that, no matter what, I had brothers and sisters to depend on. I really wanted sisters. But I would take anything. When they'd dropped me off that fateful day, I remembered my mom hugging my grandmother and saying they were going to work on that, and the pair of them had giggled coyly. I hadn't understood their exchange then, but when I thought of it now, I couldn't help but smile into my milkshake.

It used to make me sad, recalling the final happy moment that preceded the end of that terrible day. The beginning of my second life. I would never get a chance to see my mother as a fellow adult, chuckling over our own secret things. I would no longer be able to compare my height to my father's each birthday, wondering if I would ever catch up to him. It had been so long, I wasn't quite sure where my head would land if I had the chance to rest it beside him again.

Those are the types of thoughts you have to conceal if you don't want to be immobilized by heartbreak.

When my grandmother passed away two years after my parents, I had already decided to take my pain and hide it away at my core.

As I cycled through the foster care system in Mississippi, I created my own family, made up of the characters I performed in school plays, community theater shows, and my dreams. Maybe one day they'd be real again.

The alarm I'd set to remind me to head over to meet Tyler went off loudly in my bag. I pulled it out and silenced the phone. One day would have to wait. Today, I had a job to do.

22

EVELYN

WEDNESDAY, JANUARY 2, 1946–
72 YEARS, 3 MONTHS, 15 DAYS BEFORE THE ARREST
JOPLIN, KANSAS

Evelyn's eyes slid over Antonin's letter, pausing on the firm stroke of an *l* and the confidently rounded *o* in his favorite word: *lovve*. To someone who didn't know him well, Antonin had appeared to be composed of all mirth and swagger. His calm, measured penmanship might seem uncharacteristic of the giddy young man they had witnessed passing notes in class. Whispering through Sunday service. Strolling through St. Nicholas Park and picking flowers for his beloved. But to the select individuals Antonin let in, truly let in, well, he shared all of himself. His goals. His failures. His fears. His triumphs. No one got a bigger piece than Evelyn. His wife. She was not yet accustomed to calling herself his widow.

She had taken her time that morning to reread the letter

that changed everything, the one in which he'd announced his transfer from his miserable station in the Missouri Ozarks. Antonin had been much too overqualified for his work there but finally, *finally*, he would be moving up and becoming an illustrious member of the 761st Tank Battalion—the Black Panthers—in Fort Hood.

Some second lieutenant got fresh with a bus driver, of all people, and was pushed out! Now it's my time to get to work.

She inhaled deeply. Let the air stuff her belly round like when they'd been expecting DeeDee. The peculiar and very particular swirl of disbelief that her husband was dead a little over a year now, that she was still living in this lonely town, that she was expected to raise a child alone, that he would not be there to write them any more poems, that he would miss out on the delight of intimidating some poor boy as her father had done to him, that there were no more anniversaries to celebrate together, that his grandchildren and great-grandchildren would never have the pleasure of witnessing his joy in person, that her dear Antonin's bones might well be dust by the time Evelyn's bones just began to groan in old age… It was a taste her tongue would never be accustomed to.

Ding-dong.

She fluttered her eyes closed, then exhaled slowly as she rose from her seat. Antonin's best friend, basically his brother from the military, knew enough to call before visiting, which she appreciated. Still. The wrong man in uniform was knocking on Evelyn Cerny's door.

"Antonin was a good man," Parker Bailey said, pulling his gaze from the teacup he held and looking directly into Evelyn's eyes. She deserved that, even if it hurt him to do it. "He went out fighting."

"Thank you," she said. When she had opened the door and seen Parker, she'd let him in before he finished introducing himself. She recognized him from the letters. Remembered Antonin's description of his friend's bushy eyebrows and flat nose. His bitterness at being the only young man from his neighborhood to be drafted, and his bewilderment at learning that Antonin had attended Officer Candidate School and joined the military *on purpose*.

When Parker had asked if he could come calling that day, Evelyn had agreed. She suspected he wanted to ask her something. Something she had been pushing out of her mind for months. Evelyn hoped she was wrong and that this was a regular visit between a soldier and a widow. But when she opened the door and spied the stack of clothing still in hangers taking up a third of his back seat and the chauffeur's hat resting on his dashboard, the occasion for this visit became clear. She did not attempt to chase away the pause in their conversation.

"I... I am not good at this," Parker said finally. "My small talk is very, very small. Your husband never faulted me for that, even though he himself could talk to anyone about anything. Even the stuff he had no idea about."

Evelyn's dark brown eyes shimmered at this mention of Antonin, picturing the last argument her father and her husband had engaged in, about a sermon she knew Antonin had slept halfway through. She smiled softly. "That was Antonin."

"You might think me a coward for this admission, but I had no desire to be on any front lines," Parker began. "I was just fine in the kitchen."

Evelyn shook her head. "Believe me, I understand the hesitation. But...the idea of the double victory campaign lingered with Antonin long after he first heard about it."

Parker chuckled.

"His eyes lit up like a sack of firecrackers when I asked him why he kept adding an extra *v* to words and he explained to me that it was 'the Negro's way of acknowledging that we're fighting a war out there but right here too,'" Parker recited, pointing at the table. "It was the only way to make sense of signing up to die for a country that hates you and not too long ago saw you as three-fifths of a human."

"My husband was always good at seeing the big picture," she whispered. "There was no way he wasn't going to protect what he loved. Who he loved."

Parker rummaged through the canvas satchel he'd carried in with him.

"He left this with me."

Parker pulled out an old copy of *The Negro Motorist Green Book* and a newer pamphlet with the same title but slightly different cover. The edition: 1941. They'd paused publishing during the war. Evelyn could still feel the firmness of Antonin's chest the day she'd pressed her family's *Green Book* into it. If she closed her eyes, she could feel his lips moving against her hair as he wrapped his arms around her and promised he would keep it with him when he traveled. She stopped the memory before getting to the part where he swore to bring the book back with him. In victory.

"We had to get an updated version, just in case some of the businesses were changed. And when—when Antonin...left for Europe, he said to hold on to these for him. He wouldn't need them where he was going."

Antonin had gone all over the place, to cities and towns with names plucked from fairy tales: Normandy, Moyenvic, Vic-sur-Seille. The Forest of Ardennes was where he'd sent his last letter. It was where he fought in the Battle of the Bulge. And lost his life. Evelyn's own prince. Gone.

Parker took a breath.

So did Evelyn.

"Ma'am. He and I made plans. And I know you know about 'em, because there wasn't a kicking of dust on a field that Antonin didn't write about to you in those letters of his."

She bit her bottom lip, debating with herself. "Mr. Bailey. I appreciate you stopping by, I really do. But whatever you and Antonin had come up with…that was before…" She stopped herself. Tilted her head back slightly to temper the tears.

"It was his idea, ma'am. He was adamant about starting a new life out west, knew you liked the idea of being in California, starting fresh with Cordelia."

"Look. We moved to Kansas for Antonin's training. If anything, I would go back to Harlem."

"Mrs. Cerny—"

"Evelyn."

"Ma'am. Your husband kept your correspondence in the strictest of confidence. But he did speak proudly about your accomplishments as a nurse. Said your dreams were bigger than any of his fears. He talked about your self-assurance and how you wanted to climb mountains and visit the Hollywoodland sign up close."

"Do you understand what you're asking me to do?" Evelyn asked. "I'm already a—a widow. The short time we had as man and wife was right here. In these four walls. I don't know if I'm ready to leave those memories."

"Ev-Evelyn—"

"I can't move DeeDee to a new place all alone."

As if sensing she was the topic of conversation, Cordelia wailed from her mama's bedroom. She had her own, but Cordelia had started sleeping in bed with her mother each night since the news about Antonin had arrived. Evelyn knew she would have to encourage her to go back to her own room soon, but for now, she needed to keep her last piece of him near. Safe.

"But you wouldn't be alone! You'd have me!" Parker didn't seem to have any doubt that this fact would help his case. He plowed on. "I got a job as a chef's apprentice at Clifton's Cafeteria, a restaurant we found with the *Green Book* on one of our deliveries."

"That sounds wonderful," Evelyn said. She got up from her seat, motioning for him to stay where he was.

Instead, he followed her to the back of the house without asking if he could. Stood at the doorway and watched as Evelyn knelt beside her daughter's little desk, smoothed her wavy hair and asked, "What's all the commotion?"

"I got juice on Daddy's letter," she cried. "It was an accident!"

Evelyn reached over and examined the soggy sheet. A quick skim told her it was Antonin's missive to Cordelia where he'd made her name into an acrostic poem. He'd included a map to California with it as well. Despite being hundreds of miles away, he'd wanted to be the one to surprise her with the news.

CERNYS IN CALIFORNIA
OAKLAND
REDONDO BEACH
DIEGO, SAN
ELK GROVE
LOS ANGELES
INGLEWOOD
ANAHEIM

See you in The Golden State…!

Love,
DADDY

"This is actually wonderful," Evelyn said. "Apple was your father's favorite flavor. We'll have this hang in the kitchen, and when it's all dry, it'll smell just like your daddy when he would get caught sneaking a slice of pie before dinner."

"Promise?"

"I do, baby."

Evelyn stared at Parker from where she knelt beside her daughter for a long while before speaking.

"I'm going to need some time, some boxes—"

Parker straightened right up in the doorway.

"Got all that in the car, ma'am."

23

HAPPI

I lean forward and tap on the dashboard.

"Are we going to have enough gas to get back to the hotel?"

I've never seen an arrow so close to the *E* before. Genny wanted us to stop at the grocery store and pick up some flowers, just the two of us. No, I don't know why.

"Ooh, I guess we should stop to get some," Genny grumbles to herself. "You know what, let's just do it later."

I shrug, distracted by the missed call on my phone. "Mom called me."

"Me too," Genny says.

I give her a side-eye. "And *you* didn't answer?"

Genny looks at me defiantly. "I was trying to figure out what I was going to say."

"Well let's start with 'hello,' because she's calling again," I say, pressing answer and then the speaker icon. "Hello?"

"Hi. Your father's on the phone too," Mom says. "We just wanted to check in and see how you all were doing."

"Fine," Genny says stiffly.

"We're not going to lie. We are still doing a lot of thinking and praying," Mom continues.

I scoff but pretend to cough when Genny shoots me a threatening glare.

"Ma," I begin. "I'm not even trying to be rude, but you should get to it then. Bye."

"All right, y'all! This is it!" Genny says, smiling into Kezi's camera as I carefully hold it in my hands. I can tell she's trying her hardest to sound really excited for the sake of Kezi's YouTube followers. But there's no amount of high-pitched talking that could make this cool.

"You're kidding me, right?" I say even though the camera's rolling.

We're standing in front of the Blue Whale of Catoosa, a hat perched inexplicably atop its large head. It's an eighty-foot long, twenty-foot high Smurf-colored whale with possibly once-marshmallow-white teeth and red-lined lips stretched into a too-wide smile. Some might think it was curved into an inviting grin, a friendly way to beckon visitors to walk through and explore its hollow insides of horror.

"Man, this shit is peak white nonsense," Derek says, and I'm inclined to agree.

"I think it's kind of...sweet," Ximena says. She's looking down at one of Kezi's handwritten notes as she speaks. "It says here that it took Hugh Davis two years to build the Blue Whale of Catoosa. He worked for nearly 3000 hours using rock, concrete, and sand to construct the fixture with help from his friend Harold Thomas. In 1972, Davis finally presented the whale to his wife, Zelda, as a gift to celebrate their thirty-fourth wedding anniversary. It was originally intended to be enjoyed by just the Davis family, but soon people from all over came to see what is now one of the most recognizable roadside attractions on Route 66."

I turn the camera to face me. "You can tell Black people didn't have a say in the roadside attractions on Route 66. This is whack!"

"Come on!" Genny says, grabbing the camera from me and speaking into the lens. "Don't listen to Happi, everybody. This is Americana at its finest! Although the Blue Whale of Catoosa was created years after the last edition of the *Green Book*, Kezi included it as a reminder. A reminder of what Black people probably wouldn't be allowed to see and experience for themselves if this had been created during the Jim Crow era."

"And!" Ximena hops over to stand next to Genny. She shrugs. "It's not far from our next stop, either, which doesn't hurt. Shall we go to it?"

Genny waves at Ximena like she's swatting her words away. "Let's get a closer look." The two of them head toward the beaming mammal and leave Derek and me staring at it from afar.

"I dunno…this is still weird AF." Derek chuckles and I go on, "If my husband took two years to give me this as a gift, I have no idea how I'd react. I'm sure Zelda would've been just as happy with a nice diamond necklace."

"Maybe. But where's the romance in that?" Derek asks. "He probably got some nice brownie points for taking all that time to create something for his family to enjoy too."

I say nothing. The last time Santiago did anything romantic for me was right before the first round of auditions for our school's rendition of *A Midsummer Night's Dream*. A dozen red roses for his leading lady, he'd called it. He made a grand show of presenting the bouquet to me in front of all the other girls vying for the role of Helena. I remember squealing with glee over his thoughtfulness. Did any other actress have their boo bringing *them* a good-luck bundle of flowers? Nope. But mine had. I had gone out onstage with my gift still clutched in my hands. I remember placing the flowers on the floor next to me for luck before I began my monologue. I was right in the middle of a particularly dramatic line—*"My ear should catch your voice. My eye, your eye. My tongue should catch your tongue's sweet melody..."*—when I walked *right* into the vase. Who knew that something that was already so close to the floor could make such a loud noise as it shattered? There was no coming back from that. I promptly proceeded to bomb the rest of my monologue in front of all the people there. Including—no, especially—all those flowerless girls.

"What else is there to check out here anyway?" Derek asks me.

"Genny mentioned there's an ark or something," I say quickly. Anything to stop thinking about my terrible performance. And Santiago.

"Sheesh. First Jonah's whale and now an ark? We're definitely in the Bible Belt."

Derek and I head down the path in the opposite direction from the blue whale. There's a gift shop not too far away that looks like it hasn't been renovated since Hugh Davis made his anniversary present. There's no paint covering the narrow logs that stand vertically to create the walls of the store. The no-nonsense decor of the shop screams that it is here for function and not form. Donate to the establishment or keep it moving.

The pathway is still neatly trimmed as we move farther away from the main attraction. Even so, it gives the impression that, one bad week, and the place will be overgrown with vegetation, an invasion of untended grass and untamed weeds reverting the grounds back to their original state before there was any blue whale or mildly interested tourists.

We follow a bend in the curve, and there's no missing the massive structure that is the ark. Derek and I step closer, and the signs of rot spring into focus. I can see straight through the hundreds of small holes of decay that dot the wooden planks of the boat. It gives the impression that dozens of animals with unevenly sized eyes are staring right back at us, watching our every move. Or that someone used this place for target practice. The single string of white fairy lights draped around the ark in an attempt to make it more inviting only serves to highlight the neglect of what a sign has listed as the "Animal Reptile Kingdom."

"Oh I see what they did there," Derek says.

We peek our heads inside the now glassless windows and view signs with arrows of various sizes strewn across the floor, useless directions on how to reach the now-defunct attraction. The chunks of wood that have disintegrated look as if they've been chewed off.

"Um. Do bears eat wood?" I ask Derek.

"There are no bears here, Happi. We're too close to the highway. Besides, what we should really be concerned about are the alligators."

"Gators?!" I say and take a quick step back.

There's an overgrown tree root I don't notice until it's too late. The heel of my right shoe somehow gets wedged beneath it, and I start to go down. My arms spin like a rogue windmill but still, Derek lunges to catch me. His grip on my arms is firm and, luckily, I don't fall, but my shoe is stuck staunchly in place. I unintentionally shift all my weight on Derek for support, leaning into him. I look up to say thank you, but the words get lost on my lips. We're so close that I can see the light blue ring around his dark brown eyes. We used to stare into each other's faces as kids to try to show each other the "pretty parts" of our eyes. Before we knew better.

"You always did have gray around your irises," Derek says so softly. He must remember our childhood game too. But there's nothing childish about the look he's giving me now.

"Finally!" a familiar voice shouts. Derek and I pull away from each other like we're standing near a too-hot stove. My traitorous shoe has now sprung free.

"We've been looking everywhere for you two!" Ximena says. "We're gonna get some food from that taco truck and then get back on the road."

"Great!" I'm practically running I'm moving so fast, to put some distance between my and Derek's moment. I ignore the look of puzzlement on Genny's face as I rush past her and try my hardest not to trip over my feet again.

It isn't long before we're back on the road. I don't know *what* that was between me and Derek, and there's no way I'm going to unpack it in the back seat of a car with my oldest sister driving. I set my book bag on the seat between us for good measure. There.

When we arrive at Montgomery Baker's Filling Station and Museum, it looks like a snapshot taken in decades past. The two gas pumps are tall and rounded with a giant sticker placed on the front of each that reads *MB Gas* in large letters, with the silhouette of an old-fashioned car emblazoned in the background. The nozzle to pump the gas is placed high on a hook ready to fill the tank of any car, thankfully. I bet you could use it to travel through space and time if you lifted it at precisely the right angle.

The sound of our car dying as we putter into the station must be kismet. Genny pulls the key out of the ignition then sticks it back in and twists, but the engine doesn't start. She tries again and nothing.

Genny climbs out of the car and stands in front of one of the pumps, trying to figure out how it works. Upon closer inspection, she groans aloud and sticks her head in the Mustang through the rolled-down driver's seat window. "The pumps are just for show, y'all."

"Ugh," I moan. "That's just cruel."

Just as we get out of the car, an old man approaches us.

"I'm sorry, kids. We got rid of the actual gas part of the station about twenty years ago. It was so expensive to keep up, and it was either this or the museum. Business just isn't what it used to be."

Derek slides down in his seat in distress.

The dark brown skin of the man's scalp glistens under the late morning sun. He has a straw hat that he promptly plops onto his head, presumably to protect from the harsh light. The white tufts of hair that poke out of his ears make him look like a cartoon teapot puffing steam.

"You can try asking for a gentleman named Richard at SaloonEd a little ways away," he says apologetically. "They always have extra gas to keep their generator going. They should have more than enough to spare."

"Thank you, that's perfect," Genny says. "We actually have in our schedule to spend time at your establishment this morning. Since we're already here..."

The man straightens up and claps twice.

"Well, in that case! Welcome to Montgomery Baker's Filling Station and Museum," he says, waving his arm in a grand gesture to show off the sign above the building. "I'm Dwight Baker. Where are y'all visiting from?"

"We're from Los Angeles, but our adventure started out in Chicago," Genny says with a smile. "We're on a road trip along Route 66. Or any other road we accidentally find ourselves on, to be honest."

"Now, isn't that something!" Dwight says. "It's rare that I get people taking the entire journey on the Mother Road. Or what's left of it anyway. Come on inside and get out of this heat."

We follow Dwight into the station and see that the interior has been completely remade into a full-fledged museum. We each go our separate ways to explore. Lining the walls are pictures of Black families who stopped to refuel on their cross-country road trips. Replicas of old treats from back in the day are safely stored inside glass boxes with ten-cent labels lying next to them. As I stroll around the museum, there's no avoiding the two large signs placed high on the wall amongst pictures of grinning babies and Oklahoma landscapes. Whites Only. Colored Only.

I've made almost a full circle around the museum when I come across a photo of a grinning man wearing round glasses. His kinky hair is cut close on the sides but stretches into a rounded bouffant at the top of his head.

"That's my father, Montgomery Baker," Dwight says as he stands beside me. He's holding his straw hat in his hands as he smiles up at the picture. "He took that photo the first day he opened up this place. It was a few years before I was born, but he would talk about it all the time."

"He was a handsome man," I say.

"Oh yes." Dwight nods. "MB Gas was his pride and joy. And he had to make sure that he presented himself as respectable when he opened this gas station. There weren't too many Black business owners round these parts in Oklahoma in 1950."

Genny, Ximena, and Derek walk up to where Dwight and I stand admiring the photo of Dwight's dad.

"My father's gas station was one of the only stations available to Black people in Edmond. While white folks could travel safely throughout the state, and the entire country really, it wasn't the same for Negroes, as we were called back then. Oklahoma in particular had many sundown towns, and you're standing in one of them."

Derek looks down at Kezi's notepad. It's his turn to read her messages. "Kezi mentions sundown towns here, but she says we should ask someone at the museum to explain."

"Kezi?" Dwight says. "Who's that? The name sounds familiar..."

"A friend," Derek says with such finality that Dwight doesn't ask any follow-up questions.

There's a moment of awkward silence, then Ximena asks, "What's a sundown town?"

"Well, sundown towns were places where Black folks weren't welcome after dark. As soon as the sun went down, if a Negro was found out and about, it wouldn't end nicely for them. The person could be subjected to anything from intimidation to lynching, depending on who they were unlucky enough to come across."

"Wow," Ximena whispers.

Dwight nods. "Yup. Imagine my dad running this store and having to close up before evening came. My mother used to get worried sick waiting for him to get in. Not only would it be unsafe for *him* to be caught outside at night, but any other

Black person who might have been looking for a place to fill up would be in grave danger too, if they happened upon here after he was gone for the day."

"I can't believe things really used to be like that," I say.

"Believe it," Dwight replies. "Sometimes it feels like nothing has changed... But I guess that just means we've got to keep fighting the good fight, doesn't it?"

Genny clears her throat. Bites her lip briefly.

"Mr. Dwight... Could you please point us to the bridge? I think you know the one."

His eyes widen and he shakes his head furiously. The ripple of anxiety that radiates from the older man is as tangible as any of the artifacts he's shared with us. My chest tightens in response. There's nothing so contagious as fear.

"Oh, no, I can't—you don't need to be going there—"

"Sir. We do. It's very important we make this stop," Genny says politely but firmly. "It's for personal reasons."

Mr. Dwight's face falls. "Lord. If you're telling me your family was trying to come here back in the day... I want you to know my daddy would have stayed open later if he could've," he whispers. "He had no choice—"

"Sir, we would never blame you or your father," Genny says.

He shakes his head again. Ximena and Derek look as confused as I felt until I saw the distress on this man's face at the mention of a local bridge. My family's history collides at once as I remember that Kezi isn't the only family ghost.

I realize what it means to be where we are. Edmond. Oklahoma.

Genny waits.

"It's just a ten-minute walk from here if you head east," he says in defeat. "Right across from the restaurant I mentioned, where you can find Richard to get some gas."

We thank Dwight for being a lovely host and leave some cash in the donation jar he has at the front of the museum as we head out.

We walk in silence. Genny sighs occasionally, as if she's trying to release some of the heaviness following her conversation with Mr. Dwight. I think about whether or not things have really changed for people like us. If you had asked me a year ago, I would've replied, absolutely. But life after Kezi's death is different. I know we've made advances. Not acknowledging that would be a slap in the face to those who have worked so hard to improve our society. But we have a hell of a long way to go. It's like I'd been walking around with blurry vision, thinking that fuzzy trees were the norm. And then someone finally decided to slam a pair of glasses on my face and force me to see the world for what it was. The clarity is sickening.

The bridge is unimpressive. There are five pairs of thick towers holding up the weathered main cables on each side. The crisscrossed suspender cables lead your eyes down to the wide deck they hold up. Looks sturdy. It must be, to have carried the lifeless weight of a grown man. To carry the far-reaching calls of justice, or at the very least, revenge for the lives of all who were lost here. To hold the missing remorse of the hordes of people who witnessed these lynchings and saw them as only something to keep Negroes in line, or an entertaining spectacle.

Genny takes the now-wilted bouquet of flowers she carried in her backpack and splits it in half, then into quarters. She hands a bunch to each of us. Derek, who knows our family almost like he knows his own. Ximena, who has become family. And me, who is trying to catch up. Now it makes sense.

"Kezi wanted us to take this time to do a little introspection," she says. "Whatever you want."

We spread out instinctively, each of us clutching our roses. Genny bends her head, eyes closed. Ximena looks far into the distance, not focusing on anything in particular. Derek eyes the railing suspiciously.

I stare down into the water. Look away when the splashing of fish near the surface distracts me. Are these the descendants of fish that would crowd around a fallen body in interest? Maybe— No. Nope. I can't. My stomach can't take where my mind has found itself. I walk over to Genny, and she smiles faintly.

"How about we do this together?" I ask, letting the wind carry my voice away.

"Yeah."

"Joseph. Um. Great-Grandfather Joseph?" I pause. "We've never met, obviously, but... I know you? If I think about it, you kind of shaped our entire childhoods. The number of times I heard Mom and Grandpa Riley—oh, that's just Riley to you—talk about what a wonderful father you were. How you gave your wife red roses every week. You were just as playful as the kids you raised until you couldn't anymore... The grown folks never went into the gritty details of what happened on this bridge, but we all know, don't we? It broke Grandpa's heart. But when he finally put it back together, when Grandma helped him do that, and they moved forward with their lives together...you were always there."

I stop here, giving my sister space to speak.

"You said it all," Genny says, eyes shining.

24

Dear Ma,

When I started this assignment for my AP Human Geography class, I had no idea I would end up falling headfirst down a rabbit hole of discovery. I've learned about myself, our family, and our history. And because I didn't want to hoard all of this newfound knowledge, I've been working on a little something I'd like to share with you.

Growing up, you taught me, Happi, and Genny about what happened to Grandpa Riley's father all those years ago. And while I knew the story, it wasn't until I dug into this project that it felt like more than just a distant tale. You spared us the details as children because there's no manual for sharing such an ugly truth. But as I moved deeper into my research, there was no more hiding from what happened to Great-Grandpa Joseph. It was murder, and that no one was held accountable for it is an injustice that has no name.

I remember when Grandpa Riley died two years ago, you mentioned that he was finally at peace. And I didn't understand at the time. That was something you say when someone's suffered with an illness for a long time, and Grandpa Riley passed away suddenly from a heart attack. But now, after these weeks of learning how he was forced to grow up so quickly and forfeit the new life of opportunity that forever remained just outside of his grasp, I finally understand what you meant.

That kind of loss is one that sits with you for an eternity, a heavy blanket that constricts just as it comforts. Because you can't ever truly cast it aside. Doing so would mean that you are forgetting the person that you're mourning. Wouldn't it? Grandpa Riley carried that weight around with him from the time he was eight years old until the day he died. It informed who he was as a person. And whether he was aware of it or not, he passed a little bit of that on to you. How could he not?

You've stressed the importance of education because you learned from your father how it can open doors to spaces you could only dream about. And how when that door is slammed in your face, its impact can reverberate long after it's shut. All I want to do is make you proud. To reach the heights I know I'm capable of. To show that despite it all, we can not only survive but thrive.

I want you to know that I'm so grateful for you, Ma. You've raised your children with love and discipline. But I'm learning progressively each day that there is more to life than following rules and obeying orders. I have to go tomorrow. I can't remain seated while another family endures what ours has already endured. I want to fight for their justice, even as I know your grandfather never got his.

Love,

Kezi

25

RILEY

"Riley! Hurry up, child! We're already runnin' behind!"

Momma shouting from the front door where all the neighbors could hear meant she was serious, so he zipped through brushing his teeth and splashing water on his face in the bathroom. Last-Minute Riley, that was him. Riley ran to join his family outside, taking special care not to bump into any of the boxes marked "fragile" as he went. The house was all packed and he and Debbie had taken turns rocketing through the home moaning like ghosts, because their voices finally had enough space to bounce off the walls. Poppa even joined them in haunting last night, the gloomiest specter of them all with that white sheet over his head. Momma had made them share one among the three of them. (Riley and Debbie were pleasantly surprised she'd let them use any.)

It would've been too hard to move everything with just Ma to help and three kids. So Poppa was driving them all the way to Oklahoma to his brother, Uncle Frank. They would stay with Uncle Frank's wife, and Uncle Frank and Poppa would head back here to gather what was left behind.

When Riley got outside, his eyes zeroed in on Debbie, looking at him through the window from where she sat in the car. She pressed her face to the glass of Poppa's Oldsmobile, so much so that she resembled one of those pigs Ma would buy down at Mr. Green's butcher shop.

"Stop making faces like that, Deborah, or it'll get stuck that way," Momma said to Riley's older sister as she slid into her seat, cradling his little brother Michael while she settled in. Poppa, always the gentleman, closed the door carefully after her.

Poppa climbed into the driver's seat and looked down at the little booklet that Momma passed to him. He had been studying it for the last few days in preparation for their road trip. He'd already explained that it was going to take a long time to make their way from Virginia to Oklahoma, and the contents of that small publication would ensure that the family got to their final destination okay.

"All right, now. Does anyone *else* have something they need to do before we head out?" Riley was in the back seat with Debbie, finally ready to go. Poppa put away his book and then glanced at the both of them through the rearview mirror, waiting for a reply. Riley and Debbie shook their heads back and forth like they were on a swivel.

"Nooo!"

Poppa smiled and started the car. Riley always loved the sound it made when it roared to life, a grumpy giant stretching itself awake. He wiggled around in his seat to get one last look at the little home. It wasn't much, but it was theirs. Or had been. And he would surely miss it.

The Palmers were headed to Alpha, Oklahoma, so that Riley could attend Excelsior Academy: Educational Institution for Gifted Negroes. It had taken a little bit of acclimating, but he was now quite excited about the idea of attending a fancy school for high-achieving youngsters, as his old teacher had explained to him. This wouldn't be like those other schools where Black kids were being bussed into white neighborhoods and scared for their lives all in the name of integration. Or like the public schools the county over that were shut down because the school board preferred for their white students to attend "private academies" instead of being forced to share space with colored kids. No, this school would have new textbooks, state-of-the-art supplies, smaller class sizes, and most important of all, brown faces.

Of course, when Momma and Poppa first sat him down to discuss said school, he'd had his reservations. Would his classmates at Sabal Elementary be joining him? *No.* Would he ever see his friends again? *Perhaps.* Would he even like it at this Excelsior place? *That was up to him now, wasn't it?*

He sensed that his parents were so proud that a school all the way in Oklahoma had heard about little ol' Last-Minute Riley in Richmond, Virginia. The adults in his life were terribly pleased at this "unprecedented opportunity," and Riley didn't believe he was in the best position to share his real thoughts about all this change. (Terrible, just terrible.) So he nodded and smiled along as he packed boxes and folded comforters. His outsides were calm and serene like a duck floating lazily in a pond while his insides quaked, racing back and forth like the duck's little feet right beneath the surface of the water, splashing away.

As his last day of school loomed closer, Riley pulled more and more into himself. No one could tell, but he might have disappeared into his navel at any moment. Everyone was going to forget about him *here* and then he would go off to a new school and not have any friends *there*. Poppa picked up on his solemnness and one day sat his eight-year-old son on his knee and assured him that everything would be all right. How could it not, with him right there? And of course, Momma, Debbie, and Michael would be around for their new adventure as well. He would make friends in no time. (The Palmers were quite likeable after all.)

"Give it a few weeks, and you'll feel right at home. You'll see." Poppa was so convincing that Riley believed him. He could finally look forward to this move.

Momma was also pretty persuasive, it seemed, because it wasn't just Riley who was about to start at an all-new, first-rate school. Debbie would be too. Riley had stood a few steps before the kitchen in order to be hidden from view but still able to catch every single word his mother uttered on the phone when speaking to his future school's principal.

"It's all or nothing," she said firmly. "It's only a matter of time before they start enforcing this new law over there, and I'm not sending any of my babies to no school to be heckled and harmed by white folks. You'll take Riley *and* Deborah and even little Michael when he's old enough or we'll stay right here in Virginia." Success. And voila, they were all headed to the Sooner State.

It didn't always work out that way, but Riley tried to stay out of grown folks' business. That's what he was raised to do. But when the principal agreed, he'd cheered silently to himself, overjoyed. He'd watched white men bark at his poppa and call him boy. He'd noticed that Momma always made sure to keep her eyes down when speaking to anybody white as well. And anything (or anyone) terrible enough to spook Riley's momma and poppa scared him too. Knowing that they'd all be safe was a dream come true.

"Welcome to Edmond," he read aloud as they drove past a large brown sign along Route 66.

"We're running a little behind, but should be in Alpha soon," Poppa told them. "And, kids? I want you to hold me to this—I'm gonna get Momma *two* bouquets of roses, since I didn't have a chance to get her weekly dozen while we were prepping for the move."

Riley and Debbie nodded from their place in the back seat. Even little Michael cooed, as if he too would help in the reminding. Poppa and Momma exchanged a glance just between the two of them. They had a special way of communicating that involved nothing more than their pupils and eyebrows. More grown folks' business that Riley shouldn't be minding. He looked out the window and noticed the sun was just beginning to set. Beautiful oranges, pinks, and reds painted the sky before finally settling into darkness, the white twinkles of the stars popped into place ready to put on a show. He stared at them, mesmerized, and tried his hardest to count them all.

He must've fallen asleep, because the next thing Riley knew the car was slowing down until it rolled to a complete stop.

"What's wrong, Ma?" he asked, wiping the crusty sleep from his eyes.

"We've run out of gas is all," Momma said. She had that scared look on her face. The same one she got when they had to go to the post office and talk to those white folks.

"It's my fault for not paying closer attention to the tank," Poppa said. He rubbed his hands across his face. He was tired. Despite Momma's insistence, Poppa had decided to forgo following his list and instead kept driving so they could get to Alpha faster. They'd stopped only once the entire trip, hours ago at Mrs. E. Brown's Tourist Home in Chattanooga, Tennessee. Poppa took a quick nap, and then they were back on the road again. It was understandable that he would forget to keep an eye on the tank.

"What are we gonna do?" Debbie asked from where she sat beside Riley. She was cozy with her legs tucked under the folds of her light blue dress.

Poppa leafed through the booklet that he was looking at earlier. "It says here there's a gas station that we must've passed a few miles ago. I'm going to head back and get some fuel and then we'll be on our way."

"Joseph…do you have to go now? We could just sit here and wait until morning. We really aren't in any hurry." Momma placed a hand on Poppa's arm to stop him from leaving.

"I'll be fine, Helen," Poppa said and flashed her his winning smile. "Rather us get out of this sundown town as soon as possible. I'll be back before you know it."

Momma looked at Poppa long and hard and then finally nodded for him to go. He took her chin in his hand and gazed at her all tenderlike, as if communicating their secrets, and planted a kiss on her full lips. Riley and Debbie squealed in the back seat, and Momma hushed them to not wake up the baby. Poppa looked down at Michael, sleeping in Momma's arms, and gave him a gentle kiss on the cheek. He turned to the duo in the back seat and beckoned them forward, a kiss for Debbie and one for Riley too.

"Be on your best behavior, kids," Poppa said before stepping out of the car. He turned to his oldest son and said, "You're the man in charge while I'm away, okay, Riley? Can I trust you?"

He nodded at Poppa. His stomach was in knots at the thought. Riley could hardly sit at the kitchen table without his feet swinging. He didn't think he was old enough to be a whole man. But if Poppa said he was, then that was that.

Poppa stepped out of the car and Momma locked the door behind him. Riley watched as his father walked back down the road that they had driven on. He stared after him until his white shirt was one more twinkly star against the night.

The *tap tap tap* that woke Riley the next morning startled him so that he almost hit Debbie in the face with his elbow. It was Uncle Frank at Poppa's window. He was alone, holding his hat in his hand and twisting it like he was juicing an orange. His eyes were so bloodshot that Riley wondered if his uncle had squeezed the imaginary fruit onto his face. Momma quickly got out of the car and made her way to her brother-in-law. She bounced Michael on her hip, but she was paying him no mind. She was studying Uncle Frank. Taking in his hunched shoulders and the skinny creases that pinched his eyebrows together in a way Riley had never seen before on his usually jovial uncle's face. No, no, Riley knew he was not supposed to mind grown folks' business, but the goose bumps on his arms and the ghost in his ear were telling him that something was wrong. He rolled down the window just a crack so that he and Debbie could hear what was going on.

"Cut the small talk, Frank," Momma said. Her voice was high, wild. Like she was on the verge of shattering right before them.

"Helen." Uncle Frank's voice was deep with what could only be sorrow. "You might want to sit down."

26

HAPPI

When we step inside the bar and feel the cool draft of the air-conditioning, I could cry. But the few pairs of eyes that turn toward us as soon as we enter send a decidedly unwelcome chill down my spine.

"They don't look like they want us here," I whisper to Genny.

"Yeah, well, we don't wanna be here either," she answers quietly. "Let's just get the gas and peace the hell out."

We follow my sister to the bar, where a middle-aged white woman with dirty-blond hair and red lipstick on her teeth is working behind the counter.

"Excuse me, ma'am," Genny says sweetly. She looks down at the name tag pinned to the front of the bartender's shirt. "Is it all right if I call you Bev? Do you know if Richard is in today?"

"He's off," Bev replies curtly and starts to turn away.

"Oh!" Genny says, which stops the bartender from dismissing us. "We were just with Mr. Baker over at the Montgomery Baker Filling Station and Museum. We've run out of gas, and he said that Richard would be able to help. Since he's not in… Do you think you could assist us instead?"

"Look, if you're not gonna buy anything, then it's best you get on."

"Are you serious?" Ximena asks incredulously. "She just asked you for help and you're going to turn us away? What kind of—ow!"

Ximena stops abruptly as Genny has stepped forward and stomped down on her big toe.

"Please excuse my friend, Bev," Genny says. "We've been walking in this Oklahoma heat. Can you help us out with just a little bit of gas so that we can be on our way?"

"Fine," Bev replies in exasperation. "Let me tend to these *paying* customers first."

We wait twenty minutes before Ximena starts to complain again. Loudly. "This is ridiculous. There aren't even that many people here!"

"Ximena, cut the shit," Genny snaps. "You tryin' to get us killed out here?" As soon as the words are out of her mouth, I can tell she regrets it. "I'm s—"

"I'm going to the restroom," Ximena interrupts, and dismisses herself from where we're sitting at the bar. She doesn't turn away fast enough to hide the red spreading on her cheeks.

"Dammit," Genny sighs. "I'll be back."

Before Genny can take a step, one of the "paying customers" gets up from his end of the bar and walks over to us. The way my sister squares her shoulders lets me know that she's preparing for a fight. But the man who stands before us doesn't look that tough. He's a fairly tall white guy with sandy brown hair and a scruffy beard that looks like he forgot to shave this morning. Thin. Plain. Forgettable.

"It sounded like you all needed a little help? I'm Mark. Mark Collins." The man sticks his hand out for Genny to shake.

She takes it slowly and answers, "Yeah. Our car ran out of gas. We only need a little bit to make it to the closest station, and then we'll be all set."

"Well you're in luck. My family happens to own this restaurant, and I know for certain that we've got extra fuel to spare. I'll have Bev bring it right out. Are you all hungry? Have a seat. My treat."

We don't have the chance to reply, because Mark is already making his way back to Bev. He speaks quickly with her, and the glare she throws our way says that she's not amused to be helping the likes of us. Genny lets Mark and Bev know that we're going to freshen up, and then we head to the restroom.

The bathroom is very small with only two stalls. One of them is locked, but the sound of muffled sniffles is unmistakable. Genny knocks on the door and whispers Ximena's name. She opens it slightly.

I try my hardest not to interrupt or distract them, but it's hard in such close quarters. After a little while, Genny has squeezed in with Ximena and closes the door behind them. I think it's best to give them some privacy, so I quickly wash my hands and head outside to meet Derek, who is now seated at a table and accompanied by Mark.

Mark is chatty. He's one of those guys who tries too hard to be likeable. He laughs a little too loudly at Derek's jokes, although his smile never seems to reach his eyes, and nods eagerly at me as I speak to show that he's paying extra close attention. He rubs me the wrong way, but I can't tell if it's something he did or the regular way that white guys in general tend to make me wary at times. I slide my hands up and down my arms to chase away the ice that has settled in my bones.

Genny and Ximena join us just as the food comes out, seemingly no longer at odds with one another. Mark has taken it upon himself to order us a little bit of everything on the menu. He's in the middle of explaining why SaloonEd's barbecue pulled pork sandwich is the best thing "this side of the Mississippi" when Bev comes back to the table with two fuel containers. She places them on the floor next to Mark and turns around without saying a word. Derek and I glance at each other and smirk.

"Don't be salty, Bev," Derek leans over to me to whisper. I stuff a fry into my mouth to gulp down the laughter that is bubbling at my lips.

Finally, we finish eating, and when Genny reaches into her bag to pay, Mark stops her.

"Seriously, you don't have to worry about that. It was truly an honor to have you here," he says solemnly. "Your sister is *such* a brave young woman. Her story is going to change this country for the better."

His words are meant to comfort, but there's something about his delivery that gives me pause. And then it dawns on me. The reason that he's been so nice to us. Mark lobs a look of pity between me and Genny, and all I want is to knock that expression right off his face with one good swing. He thinks his good deed will counteract everything we've been through. Like a free lunch will make any difference in our lives, or the lives of people like us.

I look at Genny. She nods once but doesn't speak, biting

back the response I know must be trying to claw its way out of her throat.

We leave quickly after that. There's no point in tempting our resolve by staying any longer. Not when the memory of a hanging bridge erected proudly in a sundown town will remain inscribed in my mind forever. Not when every fiber of my being wants to lash out at Mark and tell him about himself.

I know white people like him. The ones who sit silently by for twenty whole minutes, watching you be belittled by their fellow white person, only to step in when it becomes impossible for them to ignore. He probably thinks that, by stepping up and saying something, he's done his ultimate good deed of the day. The whole week even. But good intentions don't mean shit when it's your very personhood that's under attack. When the simple act of asking for help is perceived as a personal affront.

I look back one last time and see Mark staring after us. He smiles strangely, clearly still feeling the afterglow of his own virtue. I turn away and follow the others out of the restaurant before I change my mind and wipe that look off his face after all.

27

SHAQUERIA

TUESDAY, APRIL 17–
THE DAY OF THE ARREST
LOS ANGELES, CALIFORNIA

It was stupid hot today, and there was no getting away from it. Not with all the people who were standing around outside, building up their collective outrage to form one cloud of heat. They had matching shirts. Megaphones. White posters with *Justice for Jamal* written in black letters. I was supposed to meet Tyler on the corner of Jefferson and Broadway, which felt like a good sign. One day I would make it to the real Broadway. But with this enormous crowd, I didn't know how I would find him. Then, there he was, wearing that ridiculous gold sweatshirt in this weather, just like Jaz told me he would be. He probably thought that having the hood up helped disguise him. Not in that bright-ass yellow. I guess he really was just a dumb kid.

"Tyler?" I asked as I walked up to him.

He looked over his shoulder like he expected to see someone standing behind him. He turned back to me and nodded.

"You got Darius's money?"

Tyler reached into his pocket and pulled out a clean white envelope. It was full to bursting. I took the brick that Darius had given me from my backpack, keeping my sweater wrapped around it, and stared at the cash that peeked through the poorly sealed flap. I'd be lying if I said that I hadn't thought about taking that money. I could hop on the next Greyhound back to Mississippi. See the country. But what would I be going back to? My ex was long gone, and we weren't together anymore. He hadn't even lasted a month in LA. Said it was nothing but fake people living above their means and broke up with me before catching a one-way flight to Jackson. It wasn't until later that I realized that he'd taken all the money we had saved. I'd called him over a hundred times, and he hadn't sent back so much as a text.

Plus, I'd dropped out, so there was no more drama class with Ms. Priscilla. I missed her, I guess, but she had a real family. A whole baby. She would forget about me soon enough.

No. I was better off staying here.

"Put your hands up!"

Shit. Of course I'd get caught on my first day working for this man. Why had I believed that hiding in plain sight would work?

Tyler didn't waste a second. One moment he was standing in front of me, and the next he'd grabbed the package and was racing down the street.

The money!

Getting robbed by Tyler was almost worse than potentially

getting caught by 5-0. How the hell was I going to explain this to Darius?

I started to run after Tyler, but I was too slow and got winded fast. He was already long gone, his stupid yellow sweater lost in the crowd of protestors. Even with him dressed in the brightest piece of clothing to have ever been worn by anyone on earth, I was the one who stood out to the cops.

The next thing I knew, I was sprawled on the concrete. I had to protect my face. I wouldn't win any roles with a busted grill. The casting directors would think I was some junkie off the street.

"Stop resisting!"

They jammed me into a van, placing me in the middle of two women. The one to my right looked to be around my age. She sat with her back ramrod-straight, like she was trying to retain all her dignity in this tiny prison. The one on my left, who seemed older, looked pissed.

There was only one guy in the truck, sitting behind a metal divider. He was thanking the younger girl for standing up for him at the rally and spitting some bullshit about heroes. If I hadn't been too busy freaking out, I would've rolled my eyes.

Bam!

The pressure weighing upon my chest got heavier and heavier as the officers sharply turned corners, carelessly slamming us against all sides of the vehicle. Over and over again. I didn't need these handcuffs or this van; I was already a prisoner of this body. My lungs constricted with each breath that I took.

The golden girl turned to me. Gasped. Released the breath that I couldn't.

My head spun relentlessly, but then I heard—

"Let's breathe together, okay? In and out, real easy."

Maybe karma was real.

Hours later, I was sitting in a cell by myself. The police had allowed me my one phone call, and the regret I felt for not having Ms. Sienna's number on me ate me up from the inside out. A social worker who worked for the county would come in really handy right now. Of course I wouldn't tell her or Ms. Priscilla what I had gotten myself into, but I would've taken her look of disappointment when she came to get me from the police station over my sole other option. I called Darius. His number was the only one saved in the phone he'd given me, and I had it memorized. He picked up after a few rings and listened as I explained what had happened. Silence. And then he was laughing into the receiver like we were old friends and I had just told him the funniest joke.

"Jaz, you fucked up with this one!"

That was the last thing I heard before he hung up on me.

This wasn't how it was supposed to be. LA was supposed to be my new beginning. I was supposed to hit it big. I knew other people came here thinking the same thing, but *I* was different. Why would I have gone through all this shit in life if I wasn't supposed to make it out on top? The underdog who rose to victory. Everyone was supposed to know my name.

My thoughts swirled into a tornado of panic and my chest clenched. Again. Breathing in was okay at first, but it was impossible to exhale. I just kept getting more and more full until I might as well have been breathing through a straw. My damn asthma was acting up, and I didn't have my inhaler. They'd taken everything in my bag when they'd processed me.

I tried my hardest to get the attention of the officer who

stood no more than five feet from my cell. Her head was turned away, shouting. Something about smoke. I smelled it too. That explained the sting in my eyes and the river of tears waiting to flood from them.

I was wheezing by then, waving my hands through the cell to get her to turn around.

"Please." My voice was a gravelly whisper, and I could barely hear myself. "Please."

Right when I was about to give up hope, the officer turned around. She walked to my cell and stared at me, now half-sitting, half-spread across the floor.

"Officer," I wheezed. "I can't breathe."

"Stop being so dramatic," she said with disapproval. "The smoke isn't that bad."

But the sudden blaring of a fire alarm told me that she was wrong. The same thought must have dawned on the police-woman, because she pulled out her walkie talkie just as a panicked voice crackled to life, every other word cutting out.

"...fire started... bathroom... spreading fast."

The officer outside of my cell cursed and sprinted away without even a last glance in my direction. Her words to me echoed in my head.

Stop being so dramatic.

Stop being so dramatic.

Stop being so dramatic.

Maybe I could act like this was one of the roles that I loved to audition for.

My grand finale.

But then—someone else was walking with purpose toward my cell. A man—the one I'd seen earlier? With the balloons and cake? I had no more air left in me to speak, my precious breath wasted on an unheeded call for help. He was bend-ing down now, reaching through the bars. Stroking my hair. Looking into my eyes like he knew me. Like he needed to be there for these final moments.

And that's how I go out. On the cold floor of a Los Angeles jail cell.

Who's going to remember me now?

PART III

"Travel is fatal to prejudice…"
—MARK TWAIN

QUOTE FEATURED IN
THE NEGRO MOTORIST GREEN BOOK
1949 EDITION

28

KEZI

I open my eyes.

At least, I think I do.

Everything is still dark and if I tilt my head just so, my eyelashes graze a blindfold. The straps around my head are not tight enough for me to bruise, but they are still decidedly knotted. The same goes with the ropes trapping my wrists and feet.

I am tied down in what I think is a back seat, and shielded from my surroundings, but the steady ride and the intermittent flashes of perhaps streetlights tell me we are on an open road. We are driving. Far. I pretend to still be knocked out to give myself time to figure out what to do.

He is speaking to me. Pauses as if listening politely to my response before continuing his monologue.

"I'm so glad that your forehead isn't ruined, Kezi," he says. "How's the pain?"

Nothing.

"Don't worry, I've got something to help you in a bit, but I can't give you too much at a time. Boy. Of course it would be a cop to hurt you like that…but you don't have to worry anymore."

I keep my breathing level, inhale, exhale, while my heart beats wildly, and sweat pools in the glands of my fingers and palms. My mouth is as dry as dust from the tight, balled-up fabric stuffed inside it.

"*We may be young but we are bold. We will inherit this earth so we must speak up and act when we see injustice.*"

My mind is a soupy mess of pain, heaviness, and confusion, but I know those words. They're my words. *Who is this man?*

"I had just rewatched that video, you know. It's one of my favorites," he says. "It was kismet. *Kismet.* I get notifications on all your social media activity and caught the tail end of your arrest."

He pauses.

"You need better friends." He laughs, bordering on a cackle. "Maybe she should've watched your video on being a good ally. But anyway. I'm freaking out, right, because you're in the lion's den. The screen went black! Who knows what they were up to? I bet their body cams were probably conveniently turned off. I was thinking of the worst possible scenarios. You okay back there?"

The car slows until it comes to a stop, and I hear a deep creak as the man leans over his seat. Tips of cold fingers graze my body and I involuntarily tense. *No.* I slow my breathing and force my shoulders to relax as I exhale slowly, to distract myself from the overwhelming desire to jerk away from his strangely light touch. Layers of what feels like thin cotton move up on my chest and I understand: he's adjusting my blankets. Thunder erupts in the sky, and then the incessant tapping of rain crashing against glass begins.

"We're in the middle of nowhere, by the way. It's just me and you, Kezi," he whispers, the little hairs in my ears surely standing on end from his warm breath. "Just in case you were...wondering."

My unknown captor pulls away from me, but I am still on edge. The redundant click of an already locked door being relocked tells me he is back at the wheel. The car rumbles to life again and the bumps on the street resume.

"So, where was I... This is where the kismet comes in. It was my last day on the job, and they were throwing me a going-away party. But let me tell you, it wasn't much of a party, just some cake from Ralphs and a pair of measly balloons. And I know the balloons were an afterthought, because the cake said 'Happy Birthday Mark.' Which I mean, I know I'm not the most social guy in the precinct but, come on, do your job right, Kathy—"

He laughs so hard he chokes.

"Anyway, I was feeling a little disappointed, surrounded by all these *strangers*, feeling so alone. I am—*was*—the best medicolegal death investigator on the team. *Every*one came to me if they needed help with a body. But the whole time, I was thinking about you, wondering if you were okay, since your livestream cut off. And then, out of nowhere, there you were, being led into the jailhouse! A gift from the heavens. I think we even made eye contact. But that's when I know. Remember. I'm not alone anymore. I have you."

The sensation of my heart sinking down, down, down as I realize who he is takes everything within me not to scream.

He's the person behind the emails. The one who was supposed to be harmless.

"I had to think fast," he continues urgently. "It was a sign. What were the odds you would be right there where I was, on the last day we would share Los Angeles as a city? I was moving back home to take care of my sick dad and run the family business. And the idea comes to me as soon as I see her walking in right after you. I take those stupid birthday candles and then I go to the bathroom to escape any cameras and well, let's just say toilet paper rolls are very flammable."

I have to get out of here. I have to get out of here.

"Things heat up fast... It's a mess. You can't see much through the smoke, but I am on a mission. There are prisoners being escorted from the holding cells, some run but don't get far. I'm trying to listen for your screams in the midst of all the ruckus, but you're mysteriously silent. And anyway, I have to make sure that our girl is going to die in this fire— sorry to be so callous, you just get so desensitized in my field of work—and bam, there's another moment of kismet, because when I get to her cell, it is very clear that our girl is going, going, *gone*."

His pace quickens with each progressive sentence; he's almost tripping over his words in his desperation to get them out. To me, a person he thinks is asleep or unconscious.

"I will preface what I'm about to say with this: I'm not like those cartoons that make the Black characters the same color. Or those white people who think all Black people look the same. But she really was the same complexion as you—it was uncanny. She had the same short, thin build. By the time I got close enough, she was almost dead, so I couldn't tell if she had the same brightness in her eyes. I supposed that was a small mercy, because it meant she didn't feel any pain once the flames reached the cell."

The strangled gasp of horror that pushes its way out through my cloth muzzle reveals me. Even as my mind races to understand what's happened, information shifts into place. He watched someone die instead of trying to help because it was…convenient for him. Because he knew he could get away with using this person's body as if it was nothing. Because that someone looked liked me.

"Don't be scared, Kezi. There's nothing to worry about," he says. "I'm Mark, by the way."

This time I feel the car ease to the right, my bent legs pressing into the door as my trapped body slides slightly down the wide back seat. Memories of being in the police van overtake my mind. I am yet again in a vehicle, being shuffled this way and that against my will. A gentle rough ride. He pulls over to the side of the road.

"It's surprisingly easy to fake someone's death when you've got a body to switch it out with," he chuckles. "Especially when everything's on fire and one of the people involved is, hate to say, a bit disposable. There was a quick moment when I thought I had missed my window of opportunity. There was a policewoman standing by her cell. But she didn't stick around long since things were really starting to heat up. And when she passed by me, I knew that everything might go my way for once. Even pushed the limits a bit when I asked the officer what our girl was in for. Distribution of narcotics. Let me tell you, she was *not* one of the good ones, like you. Once I knew she was gone, I scooped her up and took her right over to where they were holding you and made the swap. Everything was pure pandemonium then, so I didn't even have to hide you until it came time to walk out of the precinct. And I let the fire do the rest. Knowing my old bosses, the last thing they'd admit to is losing some girl that no one is even missing."

I hear him shift and then his fingers are on my face, lifting my blindfold. He pulls the gag from my mouth. I spit, but nothing comes out. The pain from my sore throat is overtaken by the sharp stabs of streetlights assailing my hazy vision. As my eyes slowly adjust to this new reality, darkness slowly engulfs me from every angle. It is night. Who knows how long we've been driving.

"It's funny. In another life, I thought I'd be an anesthesiologist—in that line of work, you want your patients *nearly* dead but not completely. Even though life took me somewhere else, I've kept an avid interest in atropine, ketamine, and all the other chemical-ines that make you fall asleep, stay still, and eventually wake up again. I expected you to come to about fifteen minutes ago, so we're right on schedule."

I whimper.

He smiles. "Hi, Kezi. Isn't it great to be alive? Don't feel bad about what happened—"

"Why would you do this?" My words are barely audible over the pounding of rain on the windshield.

"Hmm. The lidocaine is wearing off," he says to himself. He rummages in a large black bag that I can just see in the passenger seat and pulls out a plastic mask. "Please don't move. It'll be much easier if you stay still."

I squirm as much as I can, but it's no use as he gets closer and places the mask over my face. My eyelids droop and my breathing slows. I am surrounded by darkness once again.

29

HAPPI

"Uh, hello, Happi. This is your father. Malcolm. Please return this call when you get a chance."

Beep.

Genny and I are sitting on her bed staring at my cell phone in awe. This is perhaps the fourth time in my entire life that I can remember my father calling me. Definitely the first voice mail.

"What do you think he's going to say?" Genny breathes.

"I...have no idea."

We are certain that this involves the revelations from church on Sunday. But the fact that it was our dad who called, and at eleven thirty at night to boot is...mystifying. Since our last phone call, the check-in-every-day, twice-a-day rule had been modified on our end to become a quick once-a-day text message. The parents hadn't tried to reach out any more than that either. Did this message mean they had done enough "thinking and praying" to finally speak with us? We weren't exactly eager to find out. And after our bad experience at the saloon in a former sundown town and the major moment of vulnerability we had commemorating Great-Grandpa Joseph on the bridge, we had been more than ready to get to bed as quickly as possible and start over fresh in the morning.

But it's been months and months since I've slept soundly through the night. I'm grateful when I get any rest at all. And I was unsurprised when I found myself awake at 3:00 a.m. but flabbergasted, no, gobsmacked, at the voice mail notification from *Dad (Malcolm Smith) Obvi.*

So much so that I'd picked up my phone and called Genny.

"Hey are you awake?"

"Wow did my own baby sister just 'u up' me?"

"Ew. I'm coming over."

Her voice had been clear despite the late hour, like she had also been spending quality time with insomniac monsters in her closet.

After replaying the voice mail again, I turn to her where we sit on the bed. "What are you doing up anyway?"

Her room looks like it's still waiting for a guest to check in, minus the suitcase on the floor. But her desk is littered with lab notebooks and pens and highlighters. She has a half-full jar of trail mix open, and it's clear she's already eaten all the chocolate pieces and is now left with the boring raisins and peanuts. Her laptop is on top of it all, in an attempt to hide the mess.

"Couldn't sleep so I figured I'd get some writing done."

Genny is always on her grind. She's smart but makes it clear that she puts in effort. A lot of it. She graduated high school early and eventually became the youngest Black woman to earn her PhD in integrative biology at Caltech. Kezi was going to be valedictorian. And I...begged my elementary school principal to let me skip a grade too when Derek was promoted, and she laughed in my face. I never told anyone. Too embarrassed.

I don't even want to think about the work Genny's going to get back to after our trip. She's had the responsibilities of research, teaching, grading, office hours, and writing up grants for her lab added to her load.

"You're much more productive with your nights than I am," I say. "I personally split my time between staring at the wall and the ceiling."

"Girl, bye," she retorts. "Does that pile of junk over there look like I'm doing anything worthwhile?"

"Oh, uh, I thought it was your process."

My sister grins. "Thanks. That's just me being over-whelmed...it still feels like she was alive a few days ago," she whispers. "I keep waiting for her to text me."

I tuck my feet under my legs as I nod. "I know what you mean. Time keeps passing, but I'm not ready to be six months, then one year without Kezi, and two years, and then another and another. I need the world to slow down."

Genny takes a breath. Gazes at me uncertainly.

"My therapist is helping me work through the circum-stances of her death. Sometimes exploring those emotions makes me feel a bit better, but other times I get so defeated. There's so much systemic injustice that I feel so tiny. What happened to Kezi could've happened to anyone else—and it does. It seems like it'll never stop."

I didn't know Genny was in therapy, but it makes sense. The principal reached out to my parents and strongly encouraged them to take me to "talk to someone" after everything happened. I attended a couple of sessions. Even though I saw a private therapist, I knew the school psychologist was busy with students wanting to come in and speak to her as well. In my own sessions away from Thomas Edison Senior High, I wondered what my peers could say about my sister that I could not. The intruding thoughts became too much, and I stopped showing up. But I know I need to go back. I don't want to spend the rest of my life running. Avoiding.

"Even dealing with this bullshit from Ma and Dad," Genny says. "You would think they'd show some growth."

I sigh. "Should we call him back? Maybe he won't answer."

The phone hardly rings, and then Dad is on the line, insomnia linking us all even with miles between us. We greet each other but say nothing else for a while. Finally he speaks.

"I've been thinking about your question, Happi."

Genny and I wait for him to continue.

"And my answer is no," he says quietly. "I don't believe she's in hell."

Genny and Ximena's truce still stands. Derek and I are Switzerland, neutral bystanders who happen to love chocolate. Genny keeps us on a strict schedule, and we are packed and ready to go to our next destination by eleven in the morning.

"Would you like me to drive, Genny?" Ximena asks politely as she watches my sister balance a bowl of instant oatmeal from the hotel's continental breakfast on her lap when she gets in the car.

"That would be great, thanks," Genny says.

They switch places as Derek and I raise our eyebrows at each other.

Ximena unhooks her Supreme bag from her chest and throws it in the back seat.

"Dude, did you just unclasp your fanny pack seat belt just so you can put on another seat belt?" Derek asks.

"Like I've told you fourteen times, it's a waist bag, not a fanny pack," Ximena says.

"Keep your bag in front," Genny says sharply. "Please."

Ximena appears stricken.

"You want it nearby, in case an officer stops you," I explain. "Don't be caught with your back turned, so they don't have a reason to think you're up to something sketch."

"Oh," she says softly. "I never thought of that."

"It's not your fault you don't have to," I say.

"Sorry. I'm still a little on edge from yesterday," Genny mumbles. "I felt way more standing on that bridge where my ancestor was murdered than I expected to. Like, you hear stories growing up, but the characters seem so far away. Knowing his feet had once been where my feet stood rattled me... And plus hearing what Dwight from the gas station museum said, and running into that rude waitress who didn't want to help us until the owner made her...it's exhausting. I'm just trying to go on a road trip to commemorate my sister, dammit."

We drive the two hours to Elk City in pensive silence, everyone exploring their own thoughts. When we get to the National Route 66 Museum, we drag ourselves out of the car, but our enthusiasm for the 1981 Miss America displays, the pioneer chapel, and the windmill collection is very limited.

"Just four or five more states to go," I say, consulting my itinerary packet.

It takes us a little over two and a half more hours to get to Amarillo, Texas.

I won't even front. The sound of a guitar from Jason Aldean's song "Amarillo Sky" has been strumming in my head nonstop since we drove past the Welcome to Amarillo sign fifteen minutes ago. It's not something I talk about a lot, but I love country music. All the crooning about tilling a small patch of land, riding a tractor, driving a truck, dancing in cutoff shorts, kicking your feet up on the dashboard. Doing your best to stretch a dollar so ends can almost meet. So much of it is about falling in love with the girl next door, living an entire life in that same twenty-mile radius of a small town. That's what high school feels like. It's the same people coming in and out of each other's lives, building things up and burning things down. Sometimes it feels like we're all going through life in a country song—different lyrics, maybe, but humming the same melody, and nobody's listening closely enough to notice.

The next stop on our list is not far from the new hotel we check into. The *Green Book*'s Amarillo lodging options, Watley's Hotel and the Tennessee Hotel, were demolished years back.

It should take five minutes to get there (three since Ximena's driving).

But even she slows when she sees the sign for a park we pass on the way, standing right beside an elementary school with a different name: Robert E. Lee School Park.

"Daaaaaannng."

Genny flips to her Amarillo notes page and reads.

"Named tributes and monuments to Robert E. Lee are being taken down (or conversations have begun for their removal) across the country, stretching from California to Florida. We've finally reached a point where enough people in power agree that naming public areas after a Confederate Army general is in, to put it lightly, poor taste."

I suck my teeth impatiently.

"That's what pisses me off," I say. "Have as much Southern pride as you want, 'cause I'm gonna rep West Coast, Best Coast all day. But don't pretend like the Civil War wasn't about keeping Black people enslaved."

Yes, girl! I can practically hear Kezi crisp and clear in my brain.

Genny folds up her notebook and smiles. I know her thoughts are in the same place.

I don't know what time we expected the Wonderland Amusement Park to close on a Wednesday night, but when the ticket seller wished us a "wonderland wonderful" hour, we decide to split up. Genny and Ximena laser in on the funnel cakes and Derek and I are relegated to the Ferris wheel, where we can record aerial shots of the entire park for Kezi's channel.

It's Derek's turn to hold up the camera to capture the roller coasters, water slides, and people eating candied apples and popcorn down below. As we lift higher into the air, I take out my phone and go to Instagram's Discover page. He peeks at the screen.

"Yo, you watch those too?"

"I love a good ASMR video."

"I watch like five before I go to bed," he confesses. "Is that weird?"

"You have so many other characteristics that make you weird, Derek." I smile. "What's your favorite kind of video?"

"Hmm. I'm a classic kind of guy. Slime. But I'm not afraid

to shake things up so I amend my answer to slime with shaving cream. You?"

I think.

"Honey being scraped from the comb for sure…and soap being scored into different shapes and shaved off or crunched up by hand."

"They're so calming. I mute the squishy noises though."

"Oh my gosh, I know right? The creepy sounds take it too far!"

We watch the clip in amiable silence for a few seconds.

"You know what's even weirder? The random text that goes with the posts," I say. "Comment with the name of the second pet you truly ever loved."

"Comment with which finger you'd cut off if you had to lose one," Derek replies without missing a beat.

"What is the maximum number of fire ants you'd be willing to eat for $100,000? Share below!"

I scroll down to see what strangeness awaits us and am not disappointed, albeit a tad spooked.

Where do we go when we die? Comment below!

My phone beeps and jolts us apart. The three short buzzes send messages in quick succession.

Hey.

How are u?

I miss u.

The message is unexpected. And unwanted. Santiago.

"You're still entertaining that dummy? After all that?"

I blink. Mask on.

"That is so far from your business I'm not sure they even make maps from where you are to over here."

"Well, I'm just surprised you're still in touch with him. You should think more highly of yourself. You're really—"

"We've been having some fun on this road trip but don't get it twisted," I say. "We aren't cool enough for you to be sharing unsolicited commentary on my life."

"I'm not trying to make you angry, Happi. It's just an observation. Wait—"

Without another glance in his direction I pull the Ferris wheel's handlebar over my head. The park attendant comes over to help us exit the ride that has returned to the ground not a moment too soon, but I'm already gone. Derek's mouth is still hanging open as I leave him swinging in the chair.

30

KEZI

It has been three months and fifteen days since I died. The giant calendars of April, May, June, July, and August taped to the walls of my prison tell me so. Surely, I am no longer the lead story on the evening news. I imagine I don't show up at all. But still, I am the only thing the devil thinks about. Jotted on the last square of July and the early days of August are words like *Chicago, St. Louis, Amarillo, Edmond, Taxa, the Grand Canyon…* I am an idiot for sharing my entire road trip schedule online, to have given him one more thing to know about me and obsess over. I teased meet-and-greets in various cities with my fans and revealed so many stops, down to the general vicinity of the campground I would stay at in the Grand Canyon. Made a video about it being the best spot for catching the sunset. I wasn't foolish enough to post the exact places I would be sleeping each night, but now I regretted even revealing the days I would visit particular *Green Book* locations and public Route 66 attractions.

"*O, Edmond Bridge.*
the heart of town.
Hear it callin'.

O watch it all.
come tumbling down.
Hear it caaallin'."

The old man pauses to catch his breath. He is ancient. His blue eyes are glazed over by a white film, cataracts dulling the icy orbs. His jowls sway with each word he sings. We are alone, but I am unafraid. He usually keeps to himself, although we spend hours and hours in this now nonfunctional freezer-turned-fortress. He mutters constantly, humming warbled nonsense under his breath. We may both be prisoners, but we are not the same. I am trapped with rope and tape, and he is trapped by his own mind.

He laughs until he gasps when he gets to that line about tumbling down. Every. Single. Time. I glare at him—Ellis—and he continues to howl himself into a stupor. He thinks my anger is about the song, but it's much more than that. Over time, Mark has shared nuggets of information with me, perhaps hoping I will trust him if he shows that he trusts me. So I know the reason I am in Edmond, Oklahoma.

As we drove for hours, Mark shared his family story with me. Ellis had thrown himself into the upkeep of the restaurant after the passing of his wife, possessed with the idea of preserving it in her memory. But that all changed when a waitress came down to the then-working freezer in search of more ice cream, only to find Ellis shivering in a corner. He'd forgotten why he'd gone there in the first place and had been unable to find his way out. She'd called Mark up right then and demanded he "do something" about his father, because she "didn't get paid enough to deal with this crap," which he admitted was true.

In his brief moments of lucidity, Ellis screams and screams for someone to rescue him. Until he realizes he is not alone. My unfamiliar young Black face sends him into a frenzy every time, and he shouts even louder. Cursing. Calling me dirty names that chip away at my resolve, each word latching itself on to me like a raised palmprint following a slap.

"You're behind this! You...you...you filthy piece of shit. Let me go!"

Somehow, in his warped mind, he believes I am the one holding him against his will. Although I am tied up and useless on the floor. The first time this happened, I prayed someone would discover us. Certainly there'd be a person curious enough to find the source of this commotion? But, like Mark promised, no one can hear us down here. Not with five inches of urethane insulation and steel standing in between my voice and the outside world. And no one ever comes.

"You see those holes? That's so you don't suffocate. And of course I turned up the temperature so you won't die of hypothermia like Dad almost did," he'd said, smiling.

If it weren't for the calendars, I would have no sense of time. There are no windows to show me when the sun shows its face, or when the moon takes over. I know that I am underground only from the shuffling of feet and laughter and occasional fighting that go on upstairs. After all this time, I haven't decided if they would even care if they knew I was right below their reveling. This is hell.

My fingernails dig deep into my palms as I ball my hands into fists at the sound of clicks and slides of bolts and latches unlocking. I've broken skin so many times, the scars make it harder to bleed now.

"Kezi."

Just the breath from his whisper electrifies the hairs on my neck and jolts my senses. The scream that is trapped in my throat blocks my inhale and exhale.

"Hi, Kezi."

Every utterance of my name fills me with revulsion. I want to snatch away his tongue, to eliminate the pleasure he gets from using it.

"Kezi." There is the hint of annoyance this time, even as he strolls leisurely to reach me.

In his twisted perception of the world, Mark thinks he is a nice guy. A good guy. An ally. He hands me my lunch, a soggy burger and fries, and water. Once a week he does exercises with me while I am still weak. His hands slide over my legs and bend them at the knee to keep them "nimble." He rotates my arms so that my muscles don't atrophy in their bindings. When I take the food, he wags a packet of multivitamins in my face and tears it open to give those to me too. ("There's no reason why you should be Vitamin D deficient just because you don't see the sun!")

The pot he left me to relieve myself in is still empty, so he relaxes. I know there is a bathroom mere feet from this door. When Mark decided to move back, he said he had hired a contractor to make the basement area more livable for him. He does not seem to have visitors or friends or family besides Ellis. Each night I hear the same creak of a bed and the flow of water from a sink. The dings of the game shows he has saved on his DVR. I wonder if anyone thought twice about his request to keep the freezer.

"You won't believe who I just saw."

My shoulders leap up as his clammy fingers caress my chin. I yank my head away, but he steadies it firmly. This freezer, the only world I've seen in three months and fifteen days, shrinks even smaller when he gets this close. I can count every line on his thin face and each strand of gray peppering his sandy brown hair.

"You've been crying, Kezi." He tuts in disapproval. He pulls a handkerchief from his pocket, probably stored there from some distorted idea of chivalry, and dabs at the trail of tears on my cheeks. "Well, here's some good news. I was just talking to your family upstairs! They look good."

What? No. He's lying— My eyes must betray my shock, because he grins.

"Yes, I met Genny," he says. "And Derek...and Ximena... and Happi too."

I freeze.

"Oh, I know them all, Kezi."

I don't think about the straps and the ropes tying me down. I lunge.

31

KEZI

I am all rage as I pull against my restraints, fury guiding me forward. The binding around my right wrist rips from where it's secured to the floor, and I use the momentum to slam a fist into Mark's face. He screams and grabs hold of where his skin has already begun to redden, taking an involuntary step back from the force of my hand. I recoil clenched fingers to strike again, but he's quick and slides out of my reach.

Ellis stands by, watching in stunned silence, until I curl the restraint that is trailing from my wrist around my hand like a lasso, a whip. In two strides he is in front of me and smacks me across the cheek. My eyes water and I yelp from the pain, shocked that he can still deliver such a blow in his condition.

"I've been dealin' with your kind since I was a little boy,"

Ellis shouts at me, spittle flying from his lips. "My daddy taught me just what to do with you n—"

"Dad! No!" Mark interrupts as Ellis raises a hand to hit me again.

I bring my arm in front of my face to block the incoming blow, but it never lands. Mark is standing in between me and his father. Ellis attempts to step around his son, pouncing on me with hate etched in every fold of his wrinkled paper skin. He doesn't have time to pivot when Mark maneuvers himself between us again and shoves his father back. Ellis's arms circle as he tries to find his balance, his right foot a few inches off the floor while his left leg teeters back and forth like a tree that's been hacked away at the base. He topples and lands on his side with a sickening crack, and howls from what is surely a broken hip.

"Look what you made me do," Mark says, turning to me. His expression is one I haven't seen yet. Wild. If I was scared before, I am in pure terror now.

Mark walks to his father and kneels beside him. "I'm going to call an ambulance, Dad. Don't worry. You're okay."

A sole whimper escapes Ellis's lips.

I try to crawl away, but the restraints keep me locked in place. Mark is done consoling his father and turns his focus in my direction again. He steps toward me and pulls a key out of his pocket to release me only to grab my arm roughly to keep me still.

"Why would you behave this way, Kezi? I thought we had an understanding," he snarls in disgust.

I say nothing as he drags me through the doorway that I've stared at for months in the hopes that someone, anyone, besides Mark would come through. My eyes are wide as I take in my surroundings. Mark's quarters are so…normal that it

almost makes me want to burst out in hysterical laughter. A
guest would never know that just on the other side of this
rustic living room, filled with beautifully polished chest-
nut pieces and expensive-looking tapestry, lies a prison more
locked down than any high-security cell.

Mark opens another door, and I am in his bedroom. An
elaborate wooden bedframe is the focal point. The other fur-
niture, a bedside table, dresser, an ottoman bench, are all se-
lected to perfectly complement it. There are no pictures on
any of the walls, nothing to suggest that he has ties to other
human beings. Mark flings me onto the bed and I freeze,
paralyzed with fear at what he might do, wanting desperately
to follow the advice of my brain screaming *run* on repeat. He
looks at me with disgust again, clearly repulsed that I would
think he was capable of violating me. He races to open up
his closet as I unsuccessfully attempt to move myself on the
mattress. Rows of immaculately kept clothing dangle from
matching wooden hangers. There's a large box on the floor
next to his shoes, and he riffles through in search of something. He stands when he finds it, cords and a large roll of
duct tape in hand.

Mark makes quick work of tightly wrapping the bindings
around me again, even as I attempt to break free. My legs
are tied together from my ankles to above the knees, arms
bound from wrists to over my elbows. He secures my hands
and feet together for good measure, making me a sitting duck,
trussed and ready to await what comes next. Mark opens up
a drawer and doesn't say a word as he takes a balled-up sock
and shoves it into my mouth.

"I didn't want to do this, but you've given me no choice,"
he says as he unfurls the adhesive and places it over my lips.
"I need to get my father some help and can't risk you slip-

ping away. I'll be back okay?" He's speaking in that pleasant tone of his again, like we're good friends catching up over a nice cup of tea.

He leaves me alone in the room, locking the door behind him. I fight the urge to break down right there on the bed. Tears flow from my eyes uncontrollably. I have to think. I have to get out of here. I breathe deeply through my nose, hoping to calm myself. I need to use my head and not pass out from fear. It's time to act. I'm wracking my brain to come up with a plan when I hear the sounds of people walking down the stairs and into Mark's living room.

The paramedics! I attempt to sit up on the bed.

Maybe I can make a noise to let them know I'm here. I scream against the sock in my mouth until I'm hoarse but can barely hear a sound through the gag. The living room grows silent again as the paramedics disappear through another door that's slammed loudly behind them. They must be in the freezer area now. I'm running out of time to get their attention.

I try to straighten myself again but fail.

I'm so close, I think frantically. *What can I do? What can I do?* And then it comes to me. I shift my body on the bed until I am lying horizontally, the sheets bunching beneath me as I do so. After I stop a moment to catch my breath… I rock. It's ever so slight at first, and then, as I push my whole weight harder, I gain enough momentum to roll over. And over. I roll and roll until I advance across the bed, until I'm on the edge, where I fall onto the ottoman and then the floor.

The wind is knocked out of me from the impact, but I don't stop. I can't afford to miss my chance. I continue rolling, traveling across the floor of Mark's bedroom until I'm lying right in front of the door. I have just enough space to pull my feet back as far as I can and kick toward the wall.

Thump.

There. That should be loud enough. I bring my feet back again and ram the wall. I'm not able to pull my legs back as far as I'd like, since my hands are tied to my feet, but it will have to do. I hear the paramedics open the door to the freezer room. Yes.

Thump. Thump. Thump.

"What's that noise?" an unfamiliar voice says.

I try not to sob into the sock in my mouth and keep banging against the wall.

"What noise?" Mark asks. He sounds jittery. The paramedics will think it's because he's worried about his father.

"*That* noise," the same paramedic says, and they all quiet as if they're listening.

Thump.

Thump.

Thump.

"Oh, that? We're below the bar. Someone's probably had too much to drink."

Thump.

"No, it sounds like it's coming from that room over there." The unfamiliar voice moves closer to Mark's bedroom. My heart pounds in my ears. I bring my feet back and echo the noise against the wall faster.

Thump. Thump. Thump. Thump.

"It's my dog. I put him in there so he wouldn't get in the way." Mark's impatient voice draws closer as he walks with the paramedic.

I'm sweating against the restraints and trying my hardest to not let my legs tire from the strain. I'd fling my entire body against the wall if I could. I bring my feet back again, ready to slam it and—

"Mark? Mark? Where are you?" Ellis's voice rings out, thick with pain and confusion. "Everything hurts."

"Please," Mark says to the paramedic. They're right outside the door now. "My father needs to see a doctor. He has dementia and is easily startled. We need to get him help and calm him down."

A pause.

"Okay, fellas. Let's go."

I scream against the sock until the sounds grate weakly against my throat's raw flesh. Fling myself against the wall until I ache. Cry for help.

But they're already gone.

32

HAPPI

THURSDAY, AUGUST 2—
3 MONTHS, 16 DAYS SINCE THE ARREST
AMARILLO, TEXAS

I don't just hold grudges. I nurse them. Swaddle them lovingly in cloth. Whisper nursery rhymes to them as I rock my resentment gently back and forth against my chest. I could be crumbling on the inside, but you would never know it. When we get in the car and head to the famous Chevy Ranch, it is very clear who I have beef with.

"Good morning, ladies!"

Genny looks over her tumbler of coffee in surprise from her shotgun seat.

"You're in a good mood."

"Well, life is beautiful, so why shouldn't I be?" I say, batting my eyelashes.

Ximena grunts and leans her head back with her headphones on.

In the driver's seat, Derek is silent, but I'm not done.

"You don't mind if I—"

He leans all the way over away from me and toward the door when I reach forward to connect my phone's Bluetooth to the car. The ethereal chanting of Beyoncé's "★★★Flawless" floats in, and I sing until it switches to "Dirt Off Your Shoulder" by Mr. Knowles-Carter. It takes me shouting the words of "My Prerogative" loud enough that Bobby Brown could probably hear them from all the way in California for Genny to look at me sideways. But I explain nothing and rap along innocently as I pretend to like my enemies in Drake's "Energy." Ximena finally pulls her headphones out when "Shake It Off" comes on and Derek doesn't sing along.

"Isn't Taylor your girl?" she asks.

"Her early discography, yes," he hisses.

I cackle internally as Ximena glances between the two of us and smirks.

Derek exits I-40 and drives down Frontage Road for about a mile before stopping in front of an open gate. Despite the name, the Chevy Ranch has no horses. It is just a deep field of browned grass until we spy the rows of classic automobiles arranged in a wide circle with four lines of cars inscribed within it like a chicken's foot; the peace sign. The heady chemical scent of paint reaches our nostrils before our eyes can take in the colors.

"This is giving me serious Cuba vibes," Ximena says. We get out of the car and walk up to the enormous art piece, clouds of dust exploding into the air with every step we take. Half of each car's body is burrowed into the desiccated ground, as though this caravan's journey to the center of the earth was stopped midway. Frozen. Must've ran out of gas. But the spirit of antiquity is still clear through the long, rounded

trucks and thick exhaust pipes. There is a majority of epony-
mous Chevys, but Chryslers, Dodges, Mustangs, Cadillacs,
and Buicks also make a strong showing. Not a bit of the cars
are the original hues. They are coated in layers and layers of
spray paint.

"Which isn't a coincidence," Genny says, reading from her
notes. "The art collective that created this installation wanted
to bring attention to the need for peace during the Cuban
Missile Crisis in 1962."

"My grandparents arrived in the United States as exiles just
a few years before, but I remember growing up and hearing
them talk about how scared they were when that was going
on," Ximena says.

A group of people who appear to be in their early twenties
and visiting from Europe based on their British accents and
loud conversation about Americans "driving on the wrong
side of the road" several cars down rummage through a wagon
of cans and begin tagging a few feet from the *ATTN: Do Not
Paint the Cars* sign.

"Why do the cars make you think of Cuba?" I ask.

"These classic types are still all over the place there," she
says. "The country's been frozen in time ever since the em-
bargo started. My cousins WhatsApp me videos flexing on
the Malecon, and I see these old cars rumbling by in the background. They make for a cute picture on Insta when you're
on vacation, but they're also a huge reminder of how locked
away everyone is." She looks down. "Kez and I started talking
about us visiting my relatives over there. If we would still be
allowed into the country, that is. The rules keep changing."

Derek pulls her into a hug, and I look away. Ignoring my
sister's best friend seems stupid now.

"Oi!"

We look to where the tourists are waving us over. Genny shakes her head and screams, "What do you want?"

The guy (bloke?) who shouted first says, "Want to paint some cars? We brought way too much."

My sister opens her mouth to presumably turn down his offer when I hear myself say, "Yes!"

"What are you doing?" she says. "The signs say not to paint the cars!"

"What signs? Come on, check Kezi's almighty packet. Did she tell us if it's all right?"

Genny flips to the page on Chevy Ranch and skims. She's quiet as she walks toward the Brits. I grin.

"What colors you got in there?" she yells over to them.

Minutes later, we have the help of Harry, Liana, Oliver, and Thomas with painting massive letters on four cars at the bottom of the peace sign where the three prongs meet. It takes us over two hours to outline a *K* on one car, then *E, Z,* and *I* on the others. Ximena runs to our Mustang and grabs her portable speakers, and we blast Celia Cruz, who sings that the carnival of life isn't as cruel as you think, and about Black girls who have *tumbao* (*Azúcar!*). As we wait for our streams of red, orange, yellow, green, blue, and purple within the letters to dry a bit, Ximena gives the group a quick salsa lesson and then throws us at each other.

"May I have this *bailar*? I'm sorry if I said that wrong, I took GCSE German back home," the one named Harry says to Genny, who is beside me on the ground. We've been sitting in silence, knees to chin, shoulders touching, staring at our sister's name inscribed on the metal trunks. Soaking it in for her. She looks at me uncertainly, and I smile.

"God, yes, please take her," I joke.

Derek hops down to where Genny was and waves the camera in explanation of his presence. He pans up and down the cars and then leaps back up to walk through the sculpture to get more angles. Nods at me. I nod back.

I go back to wishing Kezi could see this herself.

HAPPI

At first, the news stories would remind me in weeks: *a Black teen activist—valedictorian and student body president—died one week ago on her birthday…two weeks ago…three weeks ago.* When they moved on, and all that was left was the ghost of our final conversation and the spirit of heartbreak throughout the Smith household, I would count the time that fluttered by myself. Today Kezi would have been a day closer to nineteen years old, that funny age that is technically teenage but still adult, like eighteen, except without the pomp. She will never get to celebrate those uneventful birthdays, the twenty-threes or forty-fours. Instead she is three months and seventeen days dead, with an eternity to go.

Getting out of bed, pulling the curtains back to expose the

sun, showering, and making myself presentable to a world I do not want to interact with today feels impossible. I have—we all have—been moving nonstop for almost a week. I have embraced Kezi more these past six days than I have in years. I have kept her words close, meditated on them night and day like a psalm. I have attempted to get into her head to better understand my sister. But I have kept the why of it all, the *why* she is not with us, at an arm's distance. Guilt seeps into my skin when I ask myself, *Why her?* When I know that perhaps that would mean someone else would lose a sister, a daughter, a girlfriend, a best friend. And I know that Kezi would give her life up to prevent anyone from undergoing what she went through, what her loved ones went through in losing her. The why of *why did this happen* is a sticky web with many threads. Do I mean:

Why did she go to the rally?

Why did they arrest her?

Why did she get sent to that jail?

Why did she die?

Why do Black people get disproportionately killed by law enforcement?

Why did this fact weigh heavy enough on Kezi's heart to speak up about it?

Why didn't I pay attention until it happened to me?

Why did it feel like the world only cared about her death because of "everything" she had "going" for her?

Why did that matter?

Why does it feel like she's not really gone?

I can barely lift my head from my pillow this morning, let alone pick up my phone when I hear a buzz beside me on the nightstand.

Hey, hey. Are you almost done? We're waiting downstairs and checkout is in a few.

I didn't bother to change into sleeping clothes when I got to my room yesterday. The drive to New Mexico was smooth, but I am starting to miss home, the couch I sleep on down-stairs… I am considering moving back into my room, even with the memories of Kezi steps away from my door. I no longer believe they will suffocate me.

Not gonna lie. Haven't started packing. Feeling…introspective.

It is still uncomfortable to be open with Genny, but I force myself to do it. We are the two remaining of Job's three daughters. So many of the women in the Bible are faceless. Even some of the genealogies list just the men and boys, like they populated the earth alone. But Jemima, Keziah, and Keren-Happuch are noted as descendants of a man who ex-perienced the worst events of his life as a bet between God and the devil, and was then gifted with three daughters as consolation for all his suffering.

Genny and I survive Kezi. Who she was will live on with us and Derek and Ximena. Even when I wake up with a mind full of *whys*, I have to remember that.

The knock on my door brings me back, and I creak it open slightly to see Genny, her black suitcase in tow. I open the door fully to greet her, but before I can she starts talking.

"So," Genny says nervously. "Kezi had an idea that she hoped you would like. She wanted to have you play the part of Great-Grandma Evelyn from that project she was work-ing on. She even reached out to a *Shakespeare and the POC* troupe to record them for her YouTube channel and everything. They perform Shakespeare but add their own twist to it. And they also incorporate the works of authors of color whose pieces should be considered classics too. But then when she…when she…when all of this happened, they never got to finalize anything. It was a long shot, but a few weeks ago I reached out to them myself. To see if they'd be open to doing something in her memory."

"What did they say?" I ask tentatively.

Genny smiles. "They said yes. And they agreed to have you play Evelyn."

"What? Why would they do that?"

"Well, Kezi recorded you practicing at home for the audition you had around the time of her birthday, without you knowing, and sent it to me. I remember her saying that you were driving her crazy reciting Helena's lines for days on end, but you were pretty good. When I reached out to the troupe, I sent them the clip. They were eager to commemorate her, and after they saw you practicing, they were even more excited."

Whoa.

"It's for a podcast recording, so you'll have the script the whole time," Genny continues. "We wanted it to be a surprise that we could share with you together. But…"

My sister's ghost squeezes at my heart. "Genny, this is… this is amazing."

"When Kezi first mentioned she wanted to go on this road trip, we both knew you wouldn't really be down for it. So we thought of something you might like, something just for you. And I know I don't say it enough, but you are so talented, Happi. Kezi thought so too. This was going to be our way of showing that we support your dreams. And if there's anything I've learned from all of this, it's that we need to share how we're feeling with each other while we have the chance."

I knew my sisters *loved* me, but in recent years it had felt like it was in that mandatory, familial way. As we grew further and further apart over time, I became uncertain about whether they were proud of me or even *liked* me. But as I watch Genny hold out a script to me and bite the side of her lip, I realize that my fears were unfounded.

I throw my arms around Genny and hold her tight. We stand together, silent, as we find strength in each other's embrace, the weight of Kezi's presence hanging over us even in her absence.

"Welcome, Happi! Or should I say, 'fair Helena'?"

The theater director, Lionel Khan, shakes my hand firmly as Genny, Derek, and Ximena sit in the stands watching eagerly, as though this interaction were the show itself.

"I'm so happy we were able to make this happen," he says. "It's truly our honor to commemorate Kezi and to have you with us. The clip that Genny sent of you was spectacular."

"Thank you so much for this opportunity," I say bashfully.

There is a sizeable crowd of diverse young families and couples here for the performance. A few people are just arriving, while others have settled in, baskets of picnic foods spread out to be eaten. There is even a camera crew from a local news station.

The other actors are already seated in a semicircle, microphones poised in front of them like miniature disco balls. I walk to the empty seat located in the center of the performers and shuffle into place. I'm nervous, the pages of the script trembling in my hands as I adjust and readjust them. I look out at the audience and make eye contact with Genny. I can tell she is so proud, but there's an undercurrent of sadness sitting right below the surface of her pleased expression. I know she is thinking the same refrain that has been echoing through my mind for this entire trip: *Kezi should be here.*

Lionel stands before the audience, and the conversations slow until it is completely silent.

"Greetings, everyone. Thank you so much for joining us for this recording of the *Shakespeare and the POC* podcast episode of *A Midsummer Night's Dream.*"

Everyone claps in response. A few guests cheer.

"Before we begin, we wanted to share a last-minute addition to the program that we think everyone will enjoy. A few months ago, we received an email from a young lady named Keziah Smith. She had a project she was working on that she wanted our help with. We were so excited for the chance to collaborate, but soon after, Kezi's life was cut short."

I stare ahead, above everyone sitting on the ground in front of me as Lionel tells the crowd how saddened the troupe was to learn of what happened to Kezi, and how honored they are to have the chance to commemorate her today. He continues, sharing his thoughts on the importance of uplifting the voices of people of color, but I'm no longer listening. If I'm going to play my part, then I need to remember why I'm here. Because Kezi and Genny care about me. Because they want me to be happy. I take in a deep breath and release it, the tension sliding from my shoulders, down my arms, through my fingertips, until it floats far and away from me. I'm going to do this. And I'm going to do it well.

"Happi? Would you like to say any words?"

Lionel is looking at me expectantly and I smile, lean forward into my mic.

"Hi, everyone. Thank you for being here today." I clear my throat. "So, I learned about this project just a few hours ago when my sister Genny came to my hotel room and shared what she and Kezi had planned months before. I'm not exactly a…road trip kind of girl." Members of the audience chuckle. "But my sisters figured out a way to make me feel like this adventure was something I could enjoy too. And for that I am grateful. I've learned so much about my family, my friends, and myself throughout this trip. I never would've imagined that I'd be in New Mexico performing a piece my sister Kezi wrote to honor our own ancestors as a way to honor her. But here we are. And I'm going to do my best to help bring her words to life and make her proud."

I look over at Genny, Derek, and Ximena. They are firecrackers on a hot summer night, shimmering bright with joy. Crackling with anticipation.

"Thank you, Happi. We know you will do just that," Lionel says kindly. He waves his hand with a flourish to begin. "Without further ado, we bring you the story of Evelyn Hayes."

I begin. "Oh, how I miss my hair."

34

HAPPI

One way in and one way out. That's all we've seen for the last few hours as we drive down the two-lane road that's taken us from New Mexico to Arizona. The windows are down, and fresh air fills the car, Ximena's playlist crooning softly in the background. I look to my right and see wide open fields of brown. Bunches of fluffy white clouds flirt with the rocky sienna mountaintops while others kiss them outright. Even in this sparse land there are signs of life. If I look closely, tufts of green grass fight valiantly through choked earth as if to say *I'm still here*.

I'm in the back seat with Derek again, and I glance at him. He's humming along to the song that's playing, his fingers *tap tap tap*ping against his leg in time to the music. I smile, and he turns to me at that exact moment. I don't like that

I'm caught staring, but he gives me a quick wink and turns to look out his window, still jamming.

Derek was all smiles after my *Shakespeare and the POC* performance. He pulled me into a tight embrace and said, "I'm sorry for what I said. Of course you can hold your own. That was stupid to get jealous." I nodded, and he grinned at me so wide that I could feel my face warm to 100 degrees from all the brightness. Any trace of our argument is long gone now.

"We're almost there, everyone," Genny says from the passenger seat.

I look straight ahead through the windshield and see a short line of cars waiting to enter the Four Corners Monument. We pay our fee and park our car in a row next to the other people who've come to be in four places at once. The ground crunches beneath our feet as we walk past stands of food, jewelry, and other crafts. A sign lets us know that the monument is administered by the Navajo Parks and Recreation Department. Derek holds the camera and captures our every step.

"This is only a quick pit stop," Ximena says into the lens when Derek pans to her. "But we couldn't pass up the opportunity to be here. The Four Corners Monument is where Arizona, Utah, Colorado, and New Mexico all meet. It's the only place in the US where four states intersect."

There aren't too many people left to take photos, so the four of us stand together and wait. I glance around at the wide expanse and think how strange it is that the point of overlap for multiple territories is so…unassuming. I could easily imagine it being overrun by skateboarders, each daredevil using the ramps, benches, and guardrails as catapults for their outrageous tricks. A young couple walks up to take their picture and they stand across from each other, each of their feet planted on a state's name, and kiss over the brass circle on the ground that marks the intersection point. A family of six is next, a harried-looking mother and father quickly corral their four small children together for their photo and they're done in a matter of seconds, surprisingly efficient. Then, it's our turn.

The four of us position ourselves so that we are each on our own section. We look up and grin at the camera Derek hovers above us. We start to step away but stop when someone behind us offers to take a group photo. We turn to see an elderly couple wearing coordinated outfits smiling at us. The husband's shirt reads I'm Looking for Trouble while the wife's has Hi, I'm Trouble. Derek starts to give the camera to them, but Genny puts a hand on his shoulder and pulls out her phone instead.

"This'll be easier," she explains.

Derek walks over and shows "Trouble" how to take the picture, and we pause for a second time and smile.

"Perfect!" Mr. Trouble says as he surveys his wife's photo-taking skills.

"Thank you very much," Ximena says.

"You're wel—Oh, you have an incoming call."

"I'll take it." Genny steps up to retrieve her phone. "It's my mom."

Genny greets Ma on the phone and pauses for a moment. "*Seriously?* Mom. That's amazing! Kezi would—" She steps away from us to get a bit of privacy from Double Trouble, whose ears seem to have perked up at her excitement.

Derek, Ximena, and I stay to chat a bit with the couple after moving out of the way of the other visitors eager to take pictures. Everything is fine until the woman pulls Ximena to the side and asks in a whisper if Genny and I are the sisters of "that girl who passed away out in California—the name sounds familiar, you know the one."

I can't fight the feeling that I'm about to become another thing to ogle at this roadside attraction, so I excuse myself and walk around the stands. I stop at one of the jewelry tables to look at handcrafted bracelets, necklaces, and other pieces. A row of delicate silver cuffs with an embedded turquoise teardrop gem in the center of each band catches my eye.

"So beautiful," I say to myself as I touch it gently.

"It is," Ximena says as she walks up beside me, Derek in tow.

"Y'all finally got rid of that couple?" I ask, masking my disturbance with a smirk.

"Finally," Derek says with an exaggerated sigh. "Man, those people could talk!"

"Genny wants to get some footage of the landscape with us in it, so she sent us to look for you. You ready?"

"Yeah." I follow Ximena as Derek trails behind us.

We find Genny standing alone, waiting for us where we entered the monument. She's admiring the Arizona scenery, southwest plains rolling out to meet craggy mountains in the distance.

"Who knew dirt could look so amazing, right?" I say to get her attention.

"It's beautiful in a desolate kind of way," she answers.

Genny adjusts the camera in her hands and takes a few moments to film the four of us hanging out and admiring the world around us. Derek and Ximena are chatting quietly, so I pull out my phone to check Kezi's YouTube page. I make my way through the latest comments, answering each one as I scroll along. I stop when I come across a post from a *prissyhoward*.

Have you seen this girl?

Name: Shaqueria Jenkins

Age: 18

Race: Black

My sister works for the district and learned that Shaqueria was arrested the same day as Kezi. They were taken to the same jail, but no one has heard from her. We've tried reaching out to the police department, but they say she was released. However, we recently learned that her personal belongings are still at the jail. No one has had any contact with Shaqueria, and we have reason to believe that she is missing or worse.

There is a link included at the end of the comment, and I click through. The window opens...and my heart seems to freeze midpump as I am greeted by the smiling face of someone I recognize. It's the girl from the *Thatcher Academy* audition. I was so wrapped up in my own drama that day, I hadn't taken a close look at her. But now that I'm able to see her clearly, I notice she looks startlingly like Kezi—full lips, high cheekbones, warm, bright brown eyes.

Something twists in my chest as I remember my last phone call with Santiago. "*...the girl who was their first choice for my love interest never showed up. They said they tried calling her over and over again and everything.*" My stomach churns, becoming a tangled mess of knots as my mind works to make sense of it all.

I'm still looking at my phone when Genny walks up beside me. She gingerly places the cover over the camera's lens, apparently satisfied with the footage she's recorded. Derek and

Ximena join us, and I can tell they're all restless and ready to wrap up our time at the Four Corners.

Just as I open my mouth to share the comment on Kezi's page, Ximena speaks. "How'd your call with your mom go?"

"It was good. *Really* good," Genny answers. "There are some members of Congress rallying to introduce legislation that will be named in Kezi's honor."

"That's amazing!" Ximena exclaims.

"So dope," Derek agrees.

My instinct to speak up about the post on the page disappears, replaced by a large lump in my throat as I try to respond to this latest news. The feeling of loss that is usually so close to the surface whenever I think about Kezi is still there. Just as wide, just as deep. But now I have a bit of hope budding right alongside it.

"She would've liked that," I finally choke out.

Genny pulls me into a hug, and I hold on tight. "Yeah she would," she whispers into my hair.

35

KEZI

The chicken is unseasoned and dry, but I take a teeny bite anyway. My head weighs about as much as ten bags of sand, and I'm not sure my neck can support it much longer. My right ankle is rubbed raw from a rope that Mark keeps knotted around it. The other end of the rope is securely tied to the foot of the bed. It's just long enough for me to walk throughout the cabin we're in but short enough to keep me from walking out the door.

The days since Ellis's accident have been cloaked in mist. I try and I try to sieve through my memories for a full picture. But all I come up with is losing the fight against my closing eyes and waking up here. *Welcome to Arizona*, Mark had whispered this morning. I was just one state away from home. An image of the maps papering the walls of my freezer prison flashes in my mind, and I think I know where we're going. I made a separate video months ago about my excitement over visiting the Grand Canyon and founding a new tradition for me and my loved ones. If I am learning the machinations this man is capable of, then I think a crooked, rotted extended olive branch by way of a visit to a national park is in my immediate future.

We are face-to-face, seated at a small wooden table in the cabin. There's not much else here: a drab gray bathroom, a queen bed probably festering with bedbugs, and a clunky old television that needs an antenna to work. For the past three hours, I have been clutching my midsection and moaning quietly to myself. I know he's heard me. I can see the *tick, tick, tick*ing of his brain as he debates whether to acknowledge it. A thick forest surrounds us on every side and largely blocks our one window, but we can't be that far from civilization, because Mark looks more agitated than usual. He's trying to appear calm, but I have followed the shifting of his eyes from left to right throughout our lunch and since we arrived in Arizona early this morning. Maybe somewhere in the pit that is his mind he's realizing the irrationality of his actions. *I've abandoned my hospitalized, injured, elderly father to run off with my captured victim who is believed to be dead. Help, I've run out of ideas. Think, think, think, think, think.*

"I'm sorry about this," he says, motioning to the feast of soggy rotisserie chicken, boxed golden raisins, and sour-cream-and-onion potato chips. His cell phone hangs precariously off the edge of the table, and I try not to think about how help is lying on the other side of a phone call. "Even the saloon's food is better than this slop."

I breathe deeply and shut my eyes. "Is that really what you're sorry for?"

I am so tired. So, so tired. But as I have drifted to and from this world over the past few days and months, I have held on to a lifeline. And I need answers.

"Mark." I place down my fork. Since waking up from the last time he put me under, I have tried to smile often. Not make any movements that would make him nervous. Or angry. I can't take any more of whatever he's been using to knock me out. My eyelids are still only half-open, and I need, need, need to get back to myself if I want any chance of escaping this monster.

"Yes, Kezi?"

I contain the shudder at the sound of my name from his chapped lips and look down at the table, hoping I look ashamed. "I have my period."

Mark blinks and stares at the ceiling. Groans at the disruption my biology causes him. He has asked about my menstruation from the beginning of this nightmare, but it's been missing since my birthday.

"Can you use toilet paper?"

No, you cruel, stupid, idiot, I cannot. Do I look like a confused middle schooler to you?

I hang my head low to give my neck some respite and to wipe my eyes. My shoulders heave up and down silently.

"Hey, hey, don't cry! I will be right back," he says. "And I hate to be that guy…but there really isn't any point in running, okay? The convenience store is right across the street."

I nod. Sniffle.

He walks toward the door and my spirit soars. But it comes crashing back down to earth when he returns to the table to grab his cell phone. And then he's at the door again, locking it behind him as he leaves.

I exhale, trying to center my raging emotions. My legs are lead and jelly at the same time. They wouldn't be able to carry me two yards past the doorway, especially since I'm tied to the cabin's bed like a ship moored to a dock. I'm scared to think of what Mark would do if he found me outside, frozen in my mission to escape. I'm not going anywhere.

Mark's laptop is open on the bed. When we entered the cabin, he made a big show of promising to be "respectful" and offering me whichever side of the mattress I wanted. My face remained neutral as I shrieked inwardly and pointed stiffly to the side farthest from the door when I realized he was waiting for an actual answer. He'd nodded, pleased.

I hobble over to the computer, careful not to trip on the rope at my feet, and tap the keys desperately to wake it up. My stomach drops. Of course there is a password. I pause and think. And type. The box of concealed letters shakes to tell me I'm wrong. I try again. Same thing. I pause to collect my thoughts. I can't have the computer lock me out and keep me from what may be my one shot out of here. Maybe…

generationkeZi!

My hands start to tremble when the computer twinkles to life, pulling up the last thing Mark must have been watching while I was knocked out. I see my once-hopeful face staring back at me. For a flicker of a second, I wonder if the unsettling messages to my account have stopped, since he has the real thing right here. But I'm not using the priceless few minutes I have to figure it out. YouTube is up, and the boxes of images on the *Recommended* section are all from my channel. I click one to get to my page and choose the most recent video. I gasp.

"Hey, y'all, we're at the Chevy Ranch!"

Derek's voice flows from the speaker as the camera points at a row of painted cars. He zooms in on the letters that spell out my name while Genny, Happi, and Ximena, who stand before them, present their handiwork with arms open wide. The screen cuts to them dancing salsa at various levels of skill along with four white people I don't recognize. This time, I tear up for real. They haven't forgotten about me. Happi is even there, looking, well, happy. When Mark said he saw them, I knew it had to be because they were going on the road trip I planned. But he didn't mention anything about them filming it for my channel.

The slam of a car door jolts me. Mark is going to be here any second and I've wasted precious time watching YouTube videos. I consider sending an email. How simple would it be to send a mass message screaming *I'M ALIVE*? But who would believe that it was me and not some cruel monster who's hacked my account? Keys jingle at the front door. Mark curses as the doorknob jams. I scroll down to the comments and type the first thing I think of.

I press Send.

The spinning wheel of death pops up, and I choke back a scream.

My message doesn't go through.

36

HAPPI

"Who's ready for an amazing show?!"

Genny, Derek, Ximena, and I sit side by side in the third row of the annual Black Rodeo Extravaganza put on by the National Association of Black Cowboys. The MC is doing a great job hyping up the crowd. The audience, full of people of all ages, cheers for the nine individuals who stand in the center of the rodeo ring.

"I'm Cowboy Rick, and these are your performers for today!" Rick goes down the row and has each person introduce themselves. Eight men, and a woman named Cheryl. Each of them waves a temporary goodbye to the audience and heads to the sidelines to wait their turn to show off their skills.

"Now a true rodeo show is risky business." Cowboy Rick

speaks clearly into his mic. "Each of the cowboys and cow-girl are trained professionals. We ask that everyone remain in their seats and out of the ring for their own safety and for the safety of our performers and livestock."

With that final warning out of the way, the show begins.

The performance is mesmerizing. One after another the entertainers try their hand at bareback horse-riding, barrel racing, calf roping, and more. Each time they succeed with their tricks, the crowd explodes with applause.

Our attention has been glued to the ring for over an hour when Cowboy Rick's voice booms through the speakers, "All right now, everyone. It's time for the grand finale and what you're all here for—bull riding!"

The audience members jump to their feet as soon as the first cowboy bounces into the center of the ring hanging on for dear life on the back of a bucking bull. His right arm whips back and forth with every jerk of the animal, but he holds on tight. For a brief moment, I wonder if the bull is okay with all of this, just as it stretches its hind legs and kicks them both back in the air with all of its might. The cowboy flies off and lands flat on his back. The wind must be knocked out of him, because he lies there, stunned.

"Get up! Get up!" the members of the audience chant.

The bull seems disoriented from the weight of the rider now being off its back, and it faces in the opposite direction. But then it gives its head one good shake and turns toward the cowboy, who is still lying on the ground. The bull lowers its large head and charges straight for the fallen man. The audience's screams are deafening as the cowboy lifts himself off the ground just in time to avoid being impaled by the bull's horns. He races to the sidelines and jumps over the fence in one leap, safely putting a barrier between himself and the provoked animal.

The crowd erupts with cheers at the narrow escape.

"That was a close one!" Cowboy Rick exclaims. "Our cowboy was on Black Lightning for a total of four seconds. That's the time to beat. Let's see how our other competitors fare."

"Only four seconds?!" Derek blurts out from where he sits at the end of the row. "That felt like an eternity!" He's enjoying himself and hasn't taken his eyes off the ring once.

The show ends with only two minor injuries and as the audience trickles out, I see little Black and Brown kids mimicking the moves they just witnessed. We follow everyone out of the rodeo ring and watch as people make their way to different stations. There are guests swinging lassos in the air in one corner, and others being helped onto the backs of horses in a small ring.

We stand close to the horseback riders and wait for the host to meet us. Genny, who's been recording since we arrived at the rodeo, has the camera fixed on Ximena.

"Wasn't that amazing?" Ximena says excitedly. "The National Association of Black Cowboys puts on a traveling show every summer. Kezi kept everything about this trip a surprise but she was so happy to learn that their Arizona stop would happen while we were in town that she couldn't help but share her excitement with me. Witnessing this myself, I can see why!"

"Hey, y'all!" Cowboy Rick walks over. He is, of course, using his very large ten-, twenty-, fifty-gallon cowboy hat to wave at us. "Thank you so much for coming to our Black Rodeo Extravaganza. We're beyond pleased and honored you're here." He sticks out his hand to greet us, and we each introduce ourselves.

"Thank you for having us," Ximena says. "That was a fantastic show."

Cowboy Rick takes us around the ranch that the National Association of Black Cowboys has rented for the day. He's a country man through and through, from his slow drawl when he speaks down to the sharp spurs on the back of his boots.

"How did you get into the rodeo business?" Genny asks from behind the camera.

"Well, we've had cowboys in my family for generations. My father is a cowboy and his father before him was one too. It's in my blood."

"I had no idea there were Black cowboys," I say, impressed.

Cowboy Rick nods. "I'm not surprised. But that's what the NABC is here to help change. Black cowboys are as American as apple pie, but we haven't seen that reflected in the mainstream. At the height of cowboy culture, one in every four cowboys was Black."

"Are you serious?" Derek asks. "I wish I had known that! I used to watch Westerns with my brother and my little cousins all the time. A Black cowboy would've changed the game."

"Absolutely. The crazy thing about it is that during the Civil War, African Americans were the ones tending to the ranches while Southern and Western whites went to fight for the Confederacy. After they lost the war, you had white folks coming back to their farms in need of help taking care of the land and minding the animals, and that's where Black cowboys came in. There was no barbed wire or mass transport at the time, so Black cowboys worked alongside white ones to herd animals, manage stampedes, and even fight Native Americans as they crossed through their lands."

"Wow. Nothing like fighting folks in their own homes to rally people together," I say sarcastically.

"It was a different time," Cowboy Rick says simply. I try not to roll my eyes.

"What were Black women doing during this time?" Genny asks for the sake of the rolling camera.

"Black women were there, holding down the home and doing other activities they traditionally did back then," Cowboy Rick answers. "But there were a few women who were pretty notorious in their own right. One woman in particular, Mary Fields, or better known as Stagecoach Mary, was the first African American woman mail carrier for the United States Post Office. Before that, she worked at a convent but was asked to leave."

"Why's that?" Derek asks.

"Well…she was a two-gun-wielding, hard-liquor-drinking, shit-talking badass who wore men's clothing. Not exactly convent material. According to legend, the offense that got her kicked out was when she and a janitor got into an argument and they pulled their guns on each other."

Ximena clasps her hands above her heart and laughs. "Oh my goodness, I think I'm in love."

After the tour with Cowboy Rick, we sit down to eat. It's one of the best meals we've had since embarking on our road trip. Fried catfish, collard greens, and a side of mac and cheese that has Genny running around asking anyone she can find about the recipe. It's a heavy lunch, but we worked up an appetite spending a whole day trying to be rodeo people.

As I finish my second plate of food, I scroll through the comments on our most recently posted video and think back to the last time I was on Kezi's page. Have there been any developments in the two days since I learned of Shaqueria's disappearance? Once we got to our hotel that night, I'd done an internet search and found that *prissyhoward* was Priscilla Howard, a high school drama teacher in Jackson, Mississippi. But as for Shaqueria, it was almost like she didn't exist—the one social media account I found of hers was devoid of pictures and there was a single video of her uploaded on YouTube by the county's public school drama program over a year ago. The caption explained that the clip was of *District Independent Events Winner Shaqueria Jenkins* performing a monologue as Beneatha Younger, the ambitious daughter in *A Raisin in the Sun.* Her performance was…breathtaking. Still, I had clicked out of the window quickly; seeing an echo of my sister's face on another body was too much.

I keep an eye out for anything else now as I continue reading the comments and leaving short messages for the subscribers who have shared their love for our road trip. Others ask questions that I do my best to answer:

Q: Where do you all sleep?
A: Hotels and motels but we'd love to stay at a "tourist home" that was once listed in the Green Book. They were like Airbnbs for Black people and are incredibly rare these days

Q: Who picked that car y'all are getting around in?
A: That was allllll Kezi! Very lowkey and modest decorating I know

Q: Who does the most driving?
A: Definitely Genny but mainly because she's such a back seat driver otherwise

And then…my eyes fall on a comment that has my entire body breaking out in goose bumps.

You don't get tired of always being so woke? Go take a nap sometime, damn!

There's no way I could ever forget the last words I said to Kezi. I've been playing them on repeat since the moment they rolled off of my tongue.

The account name shouldn't mean anything to me—*mr.no. struggle.no.progress.*—but I pause on it as something tickles at the back of my mind. Would one of the students who was around when I said the most regrettable words of my life leave this comment as a prank? Why would someone be so cruel? But the more I think about it, the more I wonder if that's not it at all. I open up a separate tab, my pulse pounding as I type the username to see what I can find. The blood that was so swiftly running through my veins freezes as I see pages and pages of comments on Kezi's YouTube channel. Some seem normal but others are decidedly off. I realize then that I've come across a few of them myself in the time since we began the trip. Not too long ago, Genny, Ximena, Derek, and I were talking about the strange posts that Kezi would receive. But to see a complete record of this one user's interactions is chilling.

I know I'll sound ridiculous, but I type up a response and barely want to think as my heart pummels my chest. Could Kezi be—

"You ready?" Genny claps a hand on my shoulder, and I stifle the scream that bubbles up to my throat.

"Whoa," Genny says looking at me, her eyebrows furrowed. "Are you all right?"

"Y-yea-yeah. I'm good. Let's go get Ximena and D."

★ ★ ★

We say our goodbyes to Cowboy Rick and the other performers and pack ourselves into the car. It's my turn to drive. I settle behind the wheel and take a deep breath to calm my nerves. I don't want to worry the others and tell them about the bizarre comment that I came across, but it's taking all of my strength to stay focused. I adjust myself in the seat again and check my mirrors twice before heading to the hotel where we'll be spending the night.

I don't argue with Genny when she asks to choose the playlist. As I drive, my thoughts hone in on the likelihood that one of my classmates hates me enough to cause me emotional distress. While I haven't always been the friendliest, I don't think there's anyone who would try to hurt me in such a way as to relive one of my least-proud moments. But if this isn't the work of some unidentified enemy, then who could it be? Because the alternative is impossible. Isn't it? To think that Kezi could be...alive? I can't even *begin* to let myself imagine something as wild as that. One mention of this to Genny would definitely have her cutting our trip short and marching me straight into a doctor's office.

I'm still trying to contain these absurd thoughts when the red-and-blue lights of a cop car reflect off the windshield and snap my attention back to the road.

"Aw shit," Derek whispers from the back seat.

I was distracted, that was certain, what with thoughts of Kezi swirling like a cyclone in my head. But I know I wasn't speeding. My nails are digging crescents into my palms as I pull over. I turn down the volume of the radio. Genny switches the music from Cardi B to Carole King. She must see how tightly I'm gripping the wheel, because she peels the fingers of my right hand off, one by one. She holds my hand in her lap and tells me to look at her.

"We're okay," she says. I nod and wait for the officer to get to my side of the car. He taps on the glass, and I move slowly to press the button to lower the window.

"Hello, Officer," I say as politely as my nerves allow me.

"Hello, young lady," the officer says. "Do you know why I'm pulling you over?"

I can feel the tears welling in my eyes at the simple question. I need to calm myself down. Some officers don't take kindly to emotional Black girls blubbering behind the wheel of a car.

"N–n–no," I stammer.

"You just switched lanes back there and didn't use a signal." The policeman bends down to get a closer look at my face and I suck in a breath. I think back to seconds earlier, see myself maneuver the car to the right lane without warning, submerged in my thoughts. He stares at me a little longer, and then glances at Ximena in the back, his gaze lingering on Derek beside her before moving to Genny beside me. "Wait. I know you guys."

Genny tightens her grip on my hand.

"You're sisters of that girl who…who died recently. You're on a road trip in her honor."

"Yes, Officer," Genny answers, stepping in because I am trembling like a leaf beside her. "But…um. How do you know that? Sir," she adds.

"Paul, call me Paul," the officer says. "But yes, I saw it on the morning news. They had a really touching segment about it. Where did y'all stop today?" If Officer Paul notices me trying my hardest to keep it together in the front seat, he doesn't acknowledge it.

Genny tells the officer about our time with Cowboy Rick, but I can tell she's on edge too. She and the others' laughs sound hollow as they politely listen to the policeman joke about his first time attending a rodeo.

He's talking about his favorite Western films when he cuts himself off. "Where are my manners? You all must be exhausted! Let me escort you to your hotel. Where are you guys headed?"

Officer Paul walks back to his car and soon drives ahead of us so that he can guide us to our destination. I'm on autopilot as I follow him. All I have to do is make it to the hotel, and we'll be all right. In a few minutes, we're in front of the building. Officer Paul drives up beside us and rolls his window down.

"All right, y'all. Have a good night. And have a safe rest of your trip, you hear?"

He waves at us one last time, and Genny, Derek, and Ximena mirror the motion. As soon as he drives off, I crumple in my seat. The anxiety that I've kept from spilling out from my insides is now rushing off my body in waves. Tears are dripping down my face, and I hiccup from how hard I cry. My shoulders shake with sobs that have been buried deep inside me from the moment I learned Kezi was gone.

Is this how my sister felt in her final moments? Pure terror had coursed through my body from only being pulled over. What must it have been like for Kezi to have an officer restrain her? To put her in the back of a police car? There was no denying that the officer's gaze had stayed a bit longer on Derek in the back seat as he inspected us. I don't even want to consider how differently things could've turned out if the policeman hadn't recognized us, if he wasn't a nice man, if he perhaps didn't think we were some of the "good ones."

I'm wailing now. What do people who don't have a You-Tube page with a formidable fan base rely on when they're pulled over? I know I should keep quiet, since we're parked in front of the hotel, but I can't plug the avalanche of grief that has been weighing me down from dislodging itself from where it's hidden for the last few months. These demons are being purged right now.

"I was so scared," I say through my sobs.

Genny pulls me into an embrace and lets me cry until every tear is shed.

37

KEZI

Go, go, go, go, go. I press on the comment button one last time to see if the message will post and sigh in heavy relief when it ultimately goes through after I refresh the page. I turn to stagger back to the table but realize I haven't closed the window. I click to the home page and put the computer to sleep.

The knob finally turns.

"Oh, you're up," Mark says, carrying a plastic bag full of snacks. His gaze darts to his computer, which appears untouched.

"I was trying to open the door for you," I say quickly, my hand on my stomach. "You were struggling."

He smiles and walks toward me. I force myself to stand in place.

"I told them these were for my wife," he says, holding up

another bag full of pads and tampons. He laughs to himself. "So it wouldn't be weird."

Holy shit.

I take them and nod. "Thank you."

"You can say my name, you know." The monster stands before me, with his mouth turned up at the corner. Waiting.

"Thank you... Mark."

"You're very welcome, Kezi. I'll see you in, oh, let's say three minutes?"

He motions to the bathroom. Shows his teeth in what I'm sure he thinks is a smile. It's more than the two minutes he usually gives me, but apparently menstruation makes him generous. I still haven't actually gotten my period. I suspect that's due to a mix of the stress of this entire experience, my weight loss, and the drug cocktail he uses to keep me down. But I need some more time alone. Even if it's sixty seconds.

The only window in the bathroom is a small rectangle way up on the wall near the showerhead. It's so high that I'm too short to even attempt to crack it open, even when standing on the edge of the tub. I can't waste any more time on escape plans that won't work.

I unwrap a tampon.

"Feeling any better?" Mark shouts through the door. I swing it open before he does it himself.

"I get terrible cramps, but I should be okay," I say, arranging my lips into what I hope looks like a grateful smile pushing through pain. "Thank you again."

I move to the bed, pull back the stiff, dingy comforter and sit down gingerly. All I want is for my body to get back to normal. To know that, when I try to run, I won't pass out, and he won't catch me.

"Mark?"

He looks up from his computer, surprised. I usually refuse to speak to him. But I need him on my side. And that means making him believe I've accepted my fate as his hostage.

"Could you please tell me more about the girl who…you found in the jail?"

He gets a look on his face as if he's debating in his mind, and then he relents. "It's not a very interesting story, Kezi. I've told you that already."

I hear the exasperation and push a little further. Clutch my middle and bend over, in pain. "Please, Mark? Just to distract me?"

"Okay, okay. When you two walked into the jail, I saw the resemblance immediately. She looked, you know, rougher, but so similar in face and body type. After the fire," he continues as though he was not the person behind the conflagration that destroyed a police precinct, "I had to act fast. So after she died, I pulled her out of her cell and into yours. I compared bodies—don't worry, even though I had to do it quickly, I was incredibly respectful," he says earnestly. "Being a medicolegal death investigator was very, very useful. I'm the guy who calls up families and confirms identities and assembles histories…and explores bodies to get more information for cases."

I tug the comforter up to my chest, to block this invasion of privacy. But it is too late.

"I rummaged through my investigation kit, found a permanent marker to dot a smattering of moles exactly like the patch on your right shoulder blade. Parted her hair to the left to match your hairstyle that day. And switched her into your clothes," he explains.

I breathe out, hopefully pushing my revulsion away with the air.

"Didn't anyone notice she was gone? Or that she was… *dead* and I was passed out?"

"I'm no Usain Bolt but I'm speedier than I look." He barks out a laugh. "Trust me. Common sense flies out of people's heads when they're running for their lives. And who was going to believe anything some thuggish prisoner said if they happened to see anything on their way out? It was a hectic day. I know those guys. The police had no desire to point out that they had a missing body, in the middle of what was already a public relations disaster. That building was overdue for an upgrade, and everyone knew it. Anyway, a kid that age getting busted for dealing drugs? You're not doing that stuff if you come from a good place. Kismet. Nobody missed her."

He looked up to the ceiling, as if checking to see if he remembered everything.

"As for your parents...when they came to claim you, her body was burned so badly that what they saw of her looked like your identifiers, so..."

Oh God.

The thought of my parents, filled with grief, trying to pull themselves together to inspect the body of someone who they believed to be their daughter is too much to bear.

"What was her name?" I whisper.

"Boy, I don't know. It's not important," Mark says, sliding his thin hands through his hair, looking awestruck that I am still speaking. "*You're* important. She—she's Claudette Colvin. You're Rosa Parks."

I can't stop the tears flowing down my face. I am disgusted and angry, but first, I am sad. For this girl whose name I don't know, who no one knows. Mark might not have killed her, but he desecrated her body and killed her memory. I understand *exactly* what he means by comparing this young woman from the jail to the teen girl who refused to give up her seat to a white woman on a bus in Alabama nine months before the more socially palatable Rosa Parks did the same thing. Colvin was darker skinned. Became an unwed mother a little after the incident. The protestors fighting for change who prayed at the altar of respectability politics, along with the rest of the world would have said her "baggage" was a distraction.

"She got booked for drug dealing," he spits out. "Not exactly helping the cause or fighting the prevailing stereotype about Black people. You, now—*you* mattered. Straight-A student. Class president. Internet following. Gorgeous face. Beautiful, beautiful future. You were one of the good ones!"

Mark says this all with a wide grin. It's clear he believes I should be flattered at the idea that my loss would be felt, but not that of another human being. How could someone who's watched and rewatched all of my YouTube videos as much as he's proclaimed to these last few months not see how *wrong* this is? *One of the good ones.* How does he not realize that, in order for him to see a young Black girl's humanity, she must have a list of accomplishments to justify her existence? It's not right.

"I also want to apologize," Mark says, tears pooling suddenly in his wild eyes. The temperature of the room has become intolerable, and beads of sweat are forming on his greasy forehead. He continues, revealing his warped thoughts to me in full. "Not just to you. But to all African Americans who have passed through Edmond. I've known about my family's participation in the mistreatment of your community my entire life. I know it was wrong. I do not condone their actions."

I stare at Mark in confusion. But then, I recall his father and his ceaseless verbal abuse. That racist litany rained down on me like clockwork as the days melted into months in the freezer. And yet, it sounds like Mark is talking about something more.

He pats his pockets and pulls out his cell phone. The screen flashes white as he looks for something on it.

"But I've... I've wanted to make up for their wickedness ever since I learned about them. And today... Well, today, I did that."

"...What do you mean?" I ask slowly, keeping my voice level and the venom contained.

"Congresswoman Anushka Patel of California introduced the Kezi Smith Bill in the House of Representatives on Monday, to address the national issue of police brutality, in honor of the slain teenager," he reads. "That's you."

But I'm alive. I want to scream.

"You're young, Kezi, so you may not understand how much of an impact your death has made on the world. How many times has a Black person been killed unjustly by police? Tell me."

Mark hops out of his chair and paces back and forth, mumbling more to himself than speaking to me.

"But I mean, really, what do you expect to change? When you're dealing with thieves and drug dealers and suspicious-looking people? We're supposed to have sympathy for *them*?"

He stops.

"Everything you've gone through is for the greater good— you know that, right? This is what your community needs! 'If there is no struggle, there is no progress', exactly like Frederick Douglass said. You're so brave, to be this sacrifice, just as I told your sisters."

The phone he has been waving in his hand vibrates.

My heart sinks when he looks down to read the alert, his face contorting into a disbelieving frown. When he speaks, I know my time is up.

"*generationkeZi* has replied to your comment?"

38

HAPPI

The Grand Canyon, in all its majestic, exhausting, imposing glory, is technically not a part of Route 66. But when one of the seven natural wonders of the world is only a short drive away, Kezi will make you stop. And yet, I know it's more than that—I know she thought about how homogenous our national parks' visitors are, how many Black people in particular don't feel welcome in them, and she wanted to be an example to the country that nature is for everyone to appreciate. That doesn't mean I won't do a little complaining anyway.

"So. You're kidding, right?" I ask the three pairs of eyes that are locked on my face. Genny, Ximena, and Derek stare at me expectantly in hopes that I will change my mind and agree to their absurd idea. "You want us to *pay* to sleep on the ground?"

"It's a campsite!" Genny says. "I said at the very beginning of this trip that there would be some camping. It's not my fault if you weren't paying attention."

"I didn't think you were *serious*!" I reply.

I can't believe how eager my road trip companions are to sleep outside.

"We'll be under the stars. It'll be beautiful." Ximena tries her hand at convincing me.

"It's what Kezi wanted," Derek adds matter-of-factly.

I sigh, relenting like everyone knew I would. "Fine, fine. Y'all win. But I get dibs on the best of everything. The comfiest piece of ground, first drink of water, biggest piece of chicken, all of it!"

The three of them cheer in unison, and I roll my eyes to the late-afternoon sky. Lord help us.

We make for the campsite that Kezi reserved months earlier. It's situated at the south rim of Grand Canyon National Park and, according to the person at the visitors' center, it's the most frequented part of the park. He points out the lavatories on our maps and gives a quick rundown of the rules of the canyon.

Once we're at our campground, Genny unlocks her Mary Poppins bag of a trunk and pulls out some of the supplies we'll need: two tents, and sleeping bags for each of us. I'm surprised to see there's running water not too far from our site, and a bit farther out, there's even a shower. We have to pay to use it, but a shower's a shower.

Getting a campsite ready is a lot more work than I imagined, because we spend a good deal of time putting together our sleeping arrangements and finding the public bathrooms (which I'm hoping I can hold off using until we're back in civilization). Finally, we have to set up the campfire.

"Can you all go grab the wood from the car?" Genny asks us just as I sit down.

I groan. "You couldn't say that before I got comfortable?"

"Come on. This fire isn't going to start itself," Genny says, pulling me up.

"I'll go with you," Derek volunteers.

We head to the car and grab the different sizes of tinder and kindling that are stowed in the trunk. Before arriving at the Grand Canyon, we made a stop to pick up some firewood. Just as I started to comment on the strangeness of paying for wood when it would be in high supply at the campground, Genny had explained that picking up the wood around the campsite was prohibited, because it messed with the ecosystem of the park.

Derek stands close to me as we gather the supplies, but I don't move away. I get the feeling there's something he wants to say, but he doesn't. I figure he'll share whatever it is when he's ready, so I don't ask.

We return to the camp, hands laden with our wooden gold, and it takes Ximena and Genny an hour to get the fire started in the allotted fire ring. But it's there, a small spark coaxed and prodded into a full flame. We sit around the heat and light, each of us lost in our own private thoughts as we eat the chunky vegan chili Genny made. The mood is comfortable and reminds me of home.

"The sun is going to start going down soon," Genny says. "You all should go catch the sunset."

"Come with us!" I say as I stand up. It must be the natural beauty of this place, of being surrounded by the rocky gradients of brown, rusty red, and amber, but suddenly I am breathless. Exhilarated.

"It's okay. Go on without me. I'll keep an eye on the fire,"

Genny replies. I can feel her sadness, and I know she is thinking about Kezi. About how much she would've enjoyed the whole trip. And now her on-the-road love letter is nearing its final sentence.

Derek and Ximena start walking to the path that will lead us to the canyon, with their flashlights in tow just in case we stay at the cliff longer than we anticipate. But I linger. I don't say anything as I sit down beside Genny and pull her into an embrace. She's been with me every step of the way, a welcome support this entire trip. And I have something I need to tell her.

"Thank you," I say to my sister as we separate from our hug.

"For what?" she asks.

"For getting me to come on this adventure. If it wasn't for you, I wouldn't be here."

"You're welcome," Genny says with a small smile.

We sit like this for a moment, the crackling of the fire ringing out as the wood snaps from the heat. Finally, Genny speaks again. "You know, it *still* doesn't feel like she's gone to me. Even after we've been on this entire trip in her honor. I don't know when it's supposed to get easier."

I don't answer as I debate whether or not I should finally give voice to the thought that has remained unformed because I refused to let myself go down that path. To hope. But then I give in and speak it aloud. "Would it be crazy to think that she's not really gone?"

"Well, none of us are ever really gone," Genny starts. "She'll always live on—"

"No, I mean, what if Kezi is actually alive?"

My question floats on the air.

"Happi… I don't know how you could think that. We were all there at her funeral."

"Yes, but she was cremated. Mom and Dad didn't even let us see her one last time. And I didn't get a chance to mention it yet, but we've gotten some *really* weird comments on the YouTube page."

"Yes," Genny says gently. "But we talked about that. Remember? Kezi would get all kinds of strange people on her channel."

"No, these feel personal."

I pull out my cell phone and show Genny the comments on Kezi's page from *mr.no.struggle.no.progress* and my reply to him asking who he was. And I tell her about *prissyhoward* asking about the girl I met the day of my audition. The day of the protest. Kezi's birthday. When we click the link, and the image of Shaqueria pops up, Genny gasps.

"She really looks like Kezi, right?" I ask Genny, trying to keep the hope that is threatening to overwhelm me from escaping.

"Let's call Mom and Dad," she says in reply. I try not to think about the last time we were all on the phone, but I nod.

Our mom answers on the first ring, and we can hear our dad speaking in the background. "Is that the girls?"

"Yes," Mom says. "You're on speaker, ladies. How have you been?"

We give our parents a quick update, and then Genny suggests I recount what I just told her. I do as I'm asked and then wait for them to answer. They must've had us on mute, because we don't hear anything for a long time and then—

"Happi…" It's Dad's deep baritone speaking through the phone.

He speaks carefully, the dissent in his tone cushioned by his need to let me down gently. He's stumbling over his words, searching for the right things to say, but the gears are shifting in my mind. There's something I need to remember… and then it clicks.

"But what about the user *mr.no.struggle.no.progress*? That was the name of an account that Ximena mentioned to me and Genni not too long ago." I explain the cryptic message Kezi received, the one we only learned about because Ximena went against Kezi's wishes. The line is silent.

"We know how hard Kezi's death has been on you," Dad says softly. "We can understand why you would want her to still be here with us, and even why you would think she might be, after everything you shared. But we have to accept that Kezi is gone."

"And I acknowledge that we haven't always approached this situation with grace," Mom says. I can imagine her sitting beside Dad on the couch, her hands safely enveloped in his. "But I promise that we—*I* will do better, be better for you all… Your father and I have been going to therapy. We started shortly after our last phone call."

Genny and I glance at each other. This revelation is a shock, but we don't interrupt.

"It was hard for me at first, because I didn't think I needed it. If it wasn't for your father, I might have never realized how terribly I was handling everything. I had been going nonstop since we learned of Kezi's death, and whenever I slowed down, I… I started to drink to numb the pain. I'm so sorry for not being there for you the way you needed."

I look up at the sky and let the tears run freely down my face. Maybe this was part of the reason I had so desperately latched on to the idea that Kezi might be alive. If she was alive, then things would go back to normal. I could get another chance to be the type of sister she deserved. I could be better toward my whole family.

"And while I don't understand everything about Kezi, our therapist is helping me to accept and love her for who she really was and not who I made her out to be. I have a lot of learning to do."

The flicker of hope that Kezi is alive goes out gently, like the extinguishing of a candle's flame. I wanted so badly to have my sister back that I was willing to let the impossible take root in my mind to combat the unimaginable grief my family has gone through.

I have to accept that Kezi isn't coming back.

At last our parents say their goodbyes, and it's just me and Genny again. We agree that I should restart my therapy sessions to help me cope. If our parents can do it, I can too.

"I love you, little sis." Genny hugs me one more time.

"I love you too, old lady."

She swats me on the shoulder, and I get up to join Derek and Ximena. It doesn't take me long to find them, settled side by side on a large log overlooking the Canyon's southern rim. I take a seat beside Derek. When the sun continues its descent, the sky bleeds into a rainbow of yellows, oranges, pinks, and reds. The rock is awash with light and mirrors the kaleidoscope of colors in its peaks and valleys. I have never felt so minuscule. I don't mean this in a bad way either. A sense of peace falls over me as I look around and just take in how big the world is. We are so small, not even a dot to be seen from an airplane, but the lives we lead are big and real and powerful. Everything is silent, as if the world itself has held its breath to behold this moment with us.

"Wow," I whisper. I look at Derek, and he is staring intently at the undulating display of nature. Ximena pulls out her phone as if to record but stops. That can wait.

We sit like this for a long while, as the sun descends and

the shadows lengthen, until Ximena gets up and excuses herself. "I'm going to check on Genny."

She glances at Derek before walking away, using her flashlight to illuminate the path. Derek and I are alone, and I'm suddenly aware of how close we're sitting on this old, fallen piece of wood.

"I'm really glad you came on this trip," Derek says quietly.

"Me too," I reply. "It would've been a shame if I missed out on all of this because I was being a little hardheaded."

"A little? Nah, you were being a lotta hardheaded," Derek chuckles.

I smack his knee, and he grabs my hand playfully in his. His laughter stops as our eyes meet. "At least you came around... It really wouldn't have been the same without you, Happi. I've missed you."

I don't know what to say to this, so I sit, quiet as the earth around us.

"Don't freak out, but I got this for you," he says nervously. I stare at him quizzically, but then he pulls out a silver cuff with a single turquoise teardrop gem in the center of the band. I gasp.

"Hey, I saw this when we were at the Four Corners! It's beautiful," I breathe.

"Yeah, I noticed how much you liked it, so I decided to get it for you. I hoped it would make you smile," he says.

My heart feels...full. "Thank you so much, Derek."

"Can I tell you something?" he asks me. He looks down at my hand, still held gently in his own. He laces his fingers through mine, and tingles shoot down my spine.

"Yes?" I whisper. My heart is beating fast in my chest. Because all I want him to say is—

"I've wanted to kiss you for the longest. But now that I've

given you this bracelet, I don't want you to think this is some weird transactional—"

I laugh in bewilderment as I shake my head. "Jesus, Derek, just do it."

He sighs in relief and pulls me closer, his free hand cupping my face lightly as he looks down at me. We close our eyes together, and the space between us disappears. Derek's lips are butterflies fluttering so gently against my own. I smile and wrap my arms around him. We breathe each other in, and my heart pounds until I'm lightheaded with intoxication. Slowly we pull away. Rest our foreheads against each other and grin.

"Where'd you learn that, Mr. Williams?"

"A gentleman never kisses and tells."

We stay a little longer and stare out at the Grand Canyon before us. I could fill it with my joy.

"We should probably get back before Genny comes looking for us," Derek says. I can tell that he's not looking forward to leaving our little spot, but his sense of responsibility kicks in even when he doesn't want it to.

"You're right," I agree.

Derek helps me up from the log, and as I step away to head back, he pulls me against him. He kisses me again until I'm breathless.

"Okay. *Now*, we can go," he says looking down at me goofily.

We walk hand in hand as we make our way back to the camp, a little different than how we started out on this journey.

"Can I tell you something else?" Derek asks.

"Anything," I say.

"I asked Ximena to leave us alone when you stayed behind with Genny so that I could do that."

My laughter rings out just as we reach our campsite.

"Oh, so that's what was taking y'all so long?" Genny says as Derek and I walk to our campsite, which is bathed evenly in a wash of orange, yellow, purple, and blue as day twilights to night. The Blue Hour. Ximena turns to look at what my sister is talking about and gasps exaggeratedly when she sees me and Derek approaching. We're holding hands, fingers laced.

"What's all this?" Ximena asks casually.

"Mmm hmm," I say with a grin. As if she doesn't know. "Mind your business."

39

KEZI

"Dammit, Kezi."

It has been one day since Mark received that message on his phone, and these are the first words he has spoken to me. Before that, the last thing I remember him saying was, "You keep giving me no choice," as he pushed those chemicals into my system and I fell into a pool of black. My world has slowly stopped spinning at its highest velocity.

Mark runs his fingers through his hair. The oily strands stick up at odd angles, as though he's been electrocuted. He looks up into the sky. Even wrapped in the deep indigo embrace of night, the Grand Canyon is stunning. The rust-colored cliffs that I remember from pictures and videos are now cloaked in darkness. And although I cannot see them, I know they stretch on for hundreds of miles. But the main attraction right now is not the surrounding peaks and valleys. It's the stars, their tiny pins of light shining brightly, breaking through the darkest hour of my life.

"In the beginning, I really thought that the world *believing* you were dead was going to be enough to effect some change," he says. "Maybe after a year or so we would be able to reveal ourselves. But that seems so ridiculous now."

Mark carries a small lantern with him, its manufactured gleam no match against the pitch black of night. I suspect he was careful to awaken me from my unconscious stupor only after he was sure any nearby campers had crawled blissfully unaware into their tents for the evening. Mark looks at me, and I let my head hang loosely. The noxious cocktail that he pumped me with hours earlier has long since left my body. But he doesn't need to know that. Even as I try to focus on the hideousness of who he is, my eyes can't help but take in the more subtle beauty of the canyon around us. The purple petals of lupine wildflowers, the silk strands of spiderwebs stretched between two rocks glistening in the moonlight. And for a place that is famously popular to visitors, it is surprisingly quiet. We might as well be the last people on earth. But I know we're not. I know Happi, Genny, Ximena, and Derek are here too, following the plan that I left behind. And I'll do anything to see them and my parents again. Hold on to my sisters and never, ever let go. I want the chance to kiss Ximena, hold her hand, and not look around to see if anyone's watching. I want to tell her I love her and pray she says it back. I want to live my life as fully as I deserve to.

"I just wanted to do something nice for you, you know?" Mark says, lifting my chin roughly so that I must look at him. I keep my lids heavy, like I'm fighting to pry them open. "You made all these videos online, teasing, saying how you wanted Black people to be treated with respect, threw out those buzz words. Justice. Freedom. Equality. *Equity*. But what have you done since then?"

I say nothing, my breathing even and deep.

"Complain!" He continues. "I was hoping to keep you alive. Maybe my dad was right about you people all along."

"What are you...what are you talking about?" My voice sounds thick even to my ears. I can feel my terror starting to build but I push it down, refusing to let my facade of fogginess fracture in this moment.

He scoffs. "You must have figured it out after all the time you spent with him."

He hums softly, that damn "O, Edmond Bridge" melody.

"Did he ever get to the next verse of that song?" Mark asks himself thoughtfully.

"Lynching bridge,
weighed to the ground.
Hear them callin'.

Spirits ring.
the reckoning sound.
Hear them caaallin'."

His voice is surprisingly sweet, souring an already dreadful song. A shower of icy-hot realization shatters inside me as I realize what he's talking about. It was more than a morbid song that Ellis sang to me. It was an oral history. Could it be?

Mark nods as he sees the tension creep into my limbs, the dread invading my body, the din seizing my mind with ques-

tions and shouts and overwhelming panic at what I've figured out.

The pieces are still fractured but clear. Mark Collins is a
descendent—*the* descendent—of the monsters that murdered
Grandpa Riley's father. His blood ripped my family apart.
When the sun rose again that next morning in 1955 and they
had retreated to their respectable places in society, a wife was
without her husband, a brother without his brother, and three
young children were left fatherless and forced to see the world
for what it was. Those realities reverberated for generations,
fragments of trauma echoing against each other for an eternity. The truth seems impossibly cruel, but I know it is fact
by the sensation deep in every cell of bone marrow in my
body. Our ancestors are tied.

Here we are today. Still linked.

It must end.

I force myself to calm down, to remember that I am supposed to be in a stupor. Even though I finally understand
what I must have known all along but was too trapped and
distracted and dazed to realize.

"What exactly...what was your father saying about what
his dad taught him? Did he...?" I ask. A man who knows the
truth of my great-grandfather's demise, a man who descended
from the monsters responsible for Joseph's destruction stands
before me now.

"Did he lynch anybody? No," Mark says. Laughs bitterly.
"But my grandpa...well, that hanging bridge by the saloon
was my grandpa's favorite spot. You don't know how many
times my own dad described the gore he witnessed as a little boy. Those poor people. One time there was a pregnant
mother and her son...another was a man all alone on his way

to the gas station that had closed hours ago…ah, yes, you get it now, don't you?"

My stomach clenches in terror. Disgust. I have to keep him talking. But he cuts me off before I can say a word, lost in his hand-me-down memories—

"They took pictures, Kezi," Mark whispers. "They put all these destroyed bodies, torn-up faces, on postcards and—and passed them around like trading cards. But my dad said the horror of those pictures was nothing compared to the real thing. They weren't scratch and sniff—you couldn't smell the copper from all the blood, or hear the crunching of bones breaking."

I inch away from him reflexively. I can't take this much longer. He grabs my wrist. Does not let go.

"The first lynching he went to stayed with him the longest. He was just eight years old. So young," Mark says. He bows his head before catching my eye. "He was obsessed with it, really. Made my grandfather tell him the guy's name over and over, because he was still wiping the sleep from his eyes and hadn't caught it when my grandpa and his friends started questioning the man about being in town after the sun went down."

Grandpa Riley was around that age, too, when his father was murdered.

Mark lets go of my wrist, and I am still. The eye of a hurricane.

I've been dealin' with your kind since I was a little boy.

"You know how these things just poison our bloodlines, like we haven't learned after all this time. That experience wrecked my father. He pretended to be okay, and everyone believed him, because no one but me was around to hear him scream 'Joseph Palmer' every night in his sleep after my mother died. They didn't see his folder of clippings—anything he could find about Joseph Palmer and his family. An obituary. A short mention in an African American newspaper about a revival in a congregation led by a Riley Palmer. A new church breaking ground out in Los Angeles by Naomi Smith née Palmer. I took my dad's work a bit further, if you will, moved to LA for nursing school and stayed in town to work. I felt…restless. I needed to be near your family. The Palmers. Our ties are unbreakable."

He pauses.

"And then I found a YouTube page by a *generationkeZi*."

My daddy taught me just what to do with you—

"Maybe we could have built a family one day," he says. He is far away. I need him even farther. "That would've been the ultimate reconciliation of our pasts… If we changed your face a little, so you weren't recognizable."

He turns to touch my cheek lightly. His thumb slides down to my jaw. I grind my teeth to prevent myself from biting off his finger. "But now you've made my choice for me."

There's no mistaking what he means. He finally got to where he was going, to the end of me. He shakes his head slowly, his gaze already far away from the destruction he is waging right here.

"I can't trust you. You're always going to try to escape," he says. Disappointed. Heartbroken. "That'll get me in trouble, and the world won't understand what I did for you people. I can't let that happen… And I also hate that it's come to this. So, I thought I'd do this last thing for you and bring you here. To take in the splendor of the stars right above the Grand Canyon. I remember when you announced your road trip stops…you were so excited to visit, even though it was a detour from Route 66. It must be a comfort to know that your family is nearby in these last moments, right?"

Mark turns to me. I can see him taking in my features. "You won't look the same at the end of this," Mark says sadly. "But I promise it won't hurt at all. It'll be just like taking a nap."

My palms are sweating, clumps of dirt adhering to my hands as I dig my fingers into the earth to ground me. I thought I had more time. But I see now that the perfect moment will never come.

I must live.

So I act. It takes seconds for me to pull the shank from my bra. I created it from the plastic applicators of the tampons Mark purchased for me. The pointed, contoured tips of the long barrels that I had smashed to reveal ragged edges are bundled together by the string of the cotton cylinders. I dragged them along the grout of the tiles in the shower that morning to make them razor-sharp. Deadly. In this moment, Mark sees his life bared before him, realizing too late that I'm more alert than I've been letting on. But he recovers quickly, hisses as the back of his right hand strikes me so hard across the face that I fall. He meets me on the ground, landing roughly on his knees beside where I am crouched on all fours. He uses his shoulder to knock me onto my back, leans in to close his hands around my neck.

"I'm going to miss you, Kezi," Mark breathes. "I wish you were more grateful. But know that you've done more in death than you ever could in life. That's noble. You're already a martyr. Maybe they'll make you a saint."

My mind floats to so many others who have died, the ones who have been attacked and forgotten, the ones whose time on earth was noted by just their families, and to the monsters who ripped their souls away. I pause at the ones who have made their marks in our society through the grave, through their ashes drifting in the wind, through their bodies in the rivers, necks on the line. Something was taken from them. *Life* was stolen from them. I want to learn the name of the girl whose life mattered just as much as mine. She wanted to live.

I want to live.

No.

This is *not* the end.

Even as my throat burns in its collapse, I trust the surge of adrenaline devouring my exhaustion and urging me forward. I refuse to die like this, or any way. I shouldn't have to sacrifice my existence so that my—no—*any* people are treated with respect. I can't have gotten this far to die alone in the Grand Canyon. Mark is still on top of me, squeezing harder on my neck. I use my right hand to hold him off, pushing against him as my other hand fumbles frantically in the dark. A sharp prick reaches the tip of my index finger. *Yes.*

I scream, finding strength that I didn't know still lay within me. Mark's eyes are saucers, bulging when he realizes the ball of makeshift knives is now lodged deep into the side of his neck. He opens his mouth to speak, but a wheeze escapes instead. He battles against my hand, but I do not relent, twisting my weapon farther, deeper, so that death will not come for me instead. A fountain of blood erupts from his skin and showers me in sticky red until I'm blind, but I've already seen my target. His body collapses on top of me, and I shout, relief, anguish, and grief rolled into one.

It is not my time to go.

40

HAPPI

It's just after midnight when we gather around the camp-fire again. We'd taken showers earlier and set up our sleeping bags only to find that none of us were ready to call it a night. The campground is silent and Ximena's chuckle at me and Derek sitting closer to each other than we need to rings out just a little too loudly. We settle down and listen as the flames crackle and spit, the smell of burnt wood wafting over us. We don't say it, but I can tell we are savoring these final hours together.

Genny heads to the car for a moment and returns with a few mugs and passes them around. We sit silently, introspective. Genny gets up and stokes the flames, placing a kettle of oat milk over the heat long enough to boil. She fills each of our cups with the warmed drink and carefully hands them back with a packet of cocoa mix. We sip slowly, the moon watching over us like a guardian. Leaves rustle from a breeze as crickets play their songs. I finally feel like I have my own song to sing, with Genny, Derek, and Ximena there to join the chorus.

"We should do HLLs for our trip," I say, breaking the peaceful silence.

"You've both been to dinner at our place enough times," Genny declares to our companions. "Highs, Lows, and Lessons. Let's hear them."

Ximena is contemplative and then, "Okay. I'll go first." We all nod for her to continue.

"My high has been feeling Kezi's presence throughout this entire trip. She took such care putting this together and it was so *her*. The low has definitely been going through this without her. I miss Kezi every day. Sometimes it feels like I've come to terms with her being gone and then—wham—I'm punched right in the gut with so much sadness. But I guess that leads me to my lesson. I've learned that I don't have to feel so alone with my grief. We have each other."

"That was beautiful, Ximena." I say. "I'll go—"

The words are snatched from my lips, because beyond Ximena I see a figure in the forest, walking toward us. But it can't be. I stand up, and the others turn to see what it is that has captured my attention.

I step forward and a wail erupts from deep within my spirit. That bit of hope that I had suppressed even just today races through every fiber of me, manifesting before my eyes.

It's Kezi. Coming toward us.

Each step makes her more real.

She glistens in the moonlight. And then she's close enough for me to see why.

Kezi is covered in blood.
Filthy.
Shaken.
Alive.

EPILOGUE

Dear Self,

Therapy is rough.

Like, you better rub some extra strength lotion and avocado oil on your elbows rough.

Like, kissing Ximena one last time in the airport security line before she starts her new collegiate life and then I walk back to my parents' waiting arms rough.

Like, the noise my brand-new emotional support dog Jubilee makes ruff (ruff!).

Dr. Opal calls what I just did "deflecting," which is "totally understandable" and something we'll keep "working on." Because we have much to sift through as we unpack the months that felt like years, where the histories of two families intertwined, stretching across generations, culminating in a final reckoning brought down by my own hand. Dr. Opal told me to write a letter to myself for my birthday. To examine how I'm feeling one year since my arrest. My death. My resurrection.

I know in an objective, cerebral way that I have a lot of work ahead of me in order to get to a place where I don't wake up in the dead of night screaming. Or feel the nauseating urge to vomit whenever I look at rotisserie chicken and golden raisins. Or want to fight, take flight, or freeze at just the sight of a white guy with sandy brown hair.

I haven't sought pain since being discharged from the hospital, but I appreciate its sharpness nonetheless. A wisdom tooth growing in. A menstrual cramp from the period that has finally come back. I relish these aches because it means that I am here. Alive. Aware. I never want the dullness of being drugged, trapped in my own body, to return. But I've relented some in recent weeks. We aren't built for eternal suffering after all. So I take over-the-counter pain relievers for the migraines that I get from time to time. It's progress.

I've found that it takes constant work to make peace. Especially since the monsters will still show up, unaware or indifferent that they've long overstayed their welcome. Sharp fangs in pointy heads hiding just around the corners of my soul. If there is a way to release the guilt of surviving when others have died, I have not found it yet. But I try. And feel ashamed for doing so. The cycle repeats.

Some days I want to hide away in my bed, surrounded

by all the posters and trophies my parents hadn't had the strength to throw away. There's comfort in knowing they weren't ready to let me go just yet. When I arrived home, my room looked the same as the day I was arrested. Untouched. But I am not the same girl who stacked up those piles of notes, curated that collection of books, set up a DIY YouTube studio.

I haven't turned those bright lights on since I've been back. I haven't looked into the little red dot to share my thoughts on where the world is going. Where it should be going. I'm not over the sensation of being stared at and discussed and debated to the point of no longer being a real person. Sometimes by the media I avoid. Sometimes by my sisters at our weekly lunch when they think I'm not paying attention. Sometimes by Derek, who just wants to talk and make sure I'm okay. I don't know that I'm ready to look into a camera just yet. But I'm working on it. I'm almost there.

Because I do still have thoughts, even though I don't broadcast them. I am so close to regaining my voice. And when I do, I will speak up. For Shaqueria Jenkins, who died senselessly. Who was commemorated at a funeral of her own. Who is missed. Who is loved. Who is remembered. Whose life mattered. Whose name I will make sure everyone knows. I will stand for her, and all the others like her, and unlike her, when I testify on Capitol Hill in a few weeks' time. I'll be ready when I stand before our country's elected officials, discussing the treatment of Black women by the police. I'll make them listen at this congressional hearing.

I know that existing as a human being on this earth should be enough to deserve respect and justice. But it isn't. Instead, we focus on those we deem worthy, for whom we allow ourselves to feel the weight of their loss. We mention potential not reached or promise of greatness gone unfulfilled, while others are erased from existence all together.

But we are more than the good ones.

We are the bad ones.

We are the okay ones.

We are the amazing ones.

We are the nothing-to-write-home-about ones.

We are the beautiful ones.

We are just…ones.

Love,

Me

★ ★ ★ ★ ★

AUTHORS' NOTE

In 2013, our family laid to rest our great-aunt Tant Moul. She was our grandmother's best friend and older sister. Grieving was as hard and painful as expected. But, because she was an older woman with chronic illnesses, we knew what to expect. After her casket was pushed into the crypt, we paid our final respects and said goodbye. As we walked away, our eyes swept over the countless other plaques and names of the departed on that mausoleum wall and one name stopped us where we were.

Trayvon Martin.

We had never known him, but we grew up with boys just like him. He was only four months older than our youngest sister, and at different points in their journeys, they had even attended the same middle school. Miami is a big place, full of everything from glamorous beaches and nightclubs to ignored and under-resourced neighborhoods. But his Miami was our Miami. He had gone to the schools that were our "home" institutions, the ones we would've attended if we hadn't been bussed away to magnet programs. His high school was less than two miles from our house in an ethnically diverse community not unlike The Retreat at Twin Lakes in Sanford, Florida. The place where he died.

There on that wall was another reminder of a stolen young Black life, a life not in our orbit but a part of it all the same. We have shed countless, heavy tears for the verdict of that case and for the other Black boys and men who shared his fate in some form or another: Ahmaud Arbery, George Floyd, Tamir Rice, Michael Brown, Eric Garner, Philando Castile, Tony McDade, and Freddie Gray. We saw irrelevant details about their lives brought up and dissected as if in explanation for what happened to them.

And we were scared. For ourselves as Black women, and even more so as older siblings of two younger sisters. We wrote this book because enmeshed in our shared memories are Sandra Bland, Breonna Taylor, Atatiana Jefferson, Charleena Lyles, Rekia Boyd, Layleen Cubilette-Polanco, and Aiyana Stanley-Jones. There are countless individuals we haven't listed but we lift them up too. They aren't as well-known as others perhaps, but they were here just the same.

A report by the Georgetown Law Center on Poverty and Inequality found that "adults view Black girls as less innocent and more adultlike than their white peers" and these Black girls are more likely to be disciplined and suspended. Let's not forget the young people who *do* end up growing up too fast when they are left behind. The teens who lose weight and miss one hundred days' worth of school after their twelve-year-old brothers are killed. The toddlers who comfort their mothers as they mourn the death of their loved ones in real time.

We chose the title *One of the Good Ones* because it's something that "well-intentioned" people say all the time without realizing how harmful it is. "One of the good ones" is usually code for a person our country deems worthy. That importance is usually tied to level of education, income, class, zip code, gender identity, sexual orientation. If most or all of those acceptable boxes are checked, *then* we care. Mark was an aggrandizement of those people who believe they are doing good when they elevate a Black person with Kezi's background, in lieu of Shaqueria's. But there is no competition. There is no allotment for who deserves justice and who does not.

All this really serves to do is divide and dehumanize us. Too often, when police brutality is discussed, the world asks the wrong questions. Did the victim smoke weed? Had they ever been arrested? Did they get into trouble while they were in school? If the answer to any of these questions is yes, then they were not one of the good ones. There is the implied justification for the brutalizing of their bodies.

We also use "one of the good ones" a few times throughout the story to depict how it all depends on who is looking through the lens. Kezi and Happi each internalized what it means to be "good" in different ways. Kezi was working on casting aside the bigoted teachings of her parents and church while learning to fully embrace herself, sexuality included. Happi was consumed by the brightness of her sister's future and the strong relationships Kezi had with their family—two things she believed she lacked. We hope that by the end of our book, readers leave reminded that being human is more than enough to deserve life and love.

Kezi was just about perfect by our society's eyes, and her Black skin still made her a threat, dangerous. If we're honest, a tiny worm of a thought has stayed with us (and, before that, our immigrant parents), our whole lives: if we were respectful—respectable—and soft-spoken and polite and good-natured and *yes, ma'am* and *no, sir* and smiling, perhaps we would be safe. But the truth is, that can't save us. It takes a systematic disruption of how the world views us. Unfortunately, it takes books like this to humanize Black people and show that, like everyone else, we deserve to have peace. And because this was our story, we decided to let someone our society expects to die, live. To breathe. To thrive. And to have the chance to help her sisters do the same.

FAMILY TREES

EVELYN HAYES CERNY + MALCOM WALKER SMITH

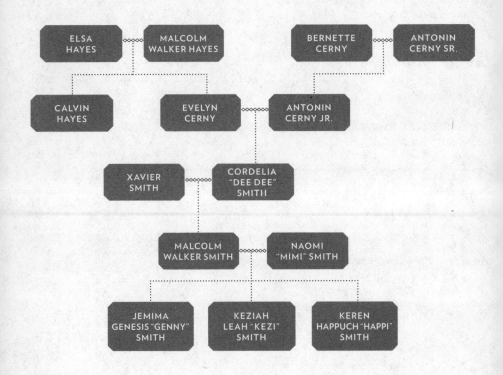

NAOMI SMITH + RILEY PALMER

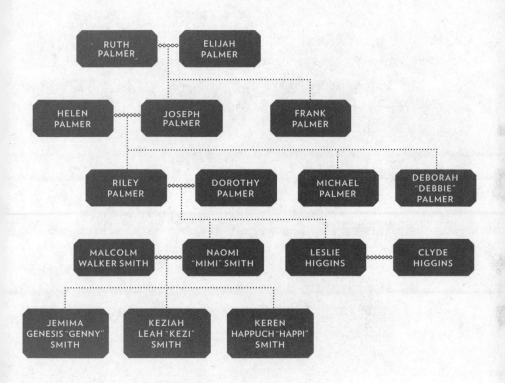

MARK COLLINS

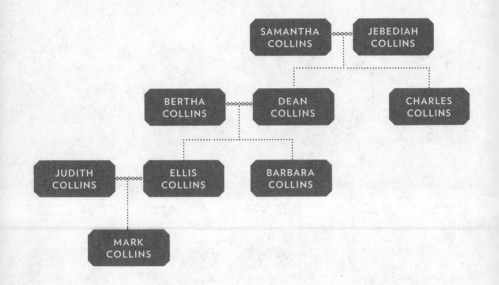

MAP

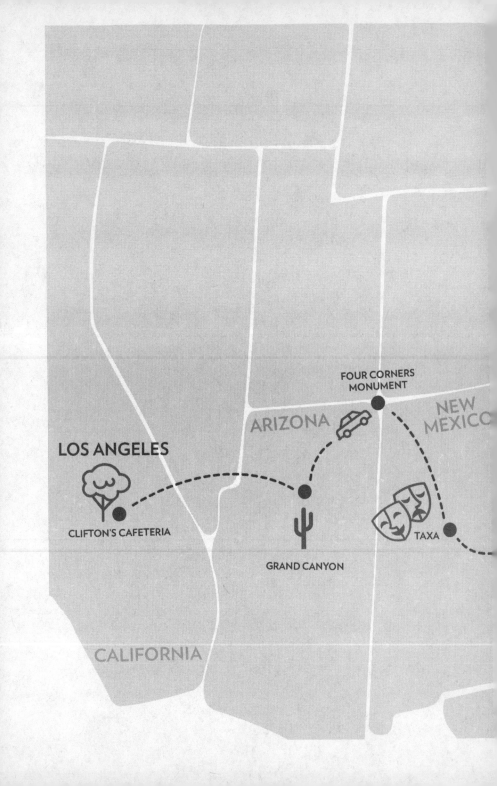

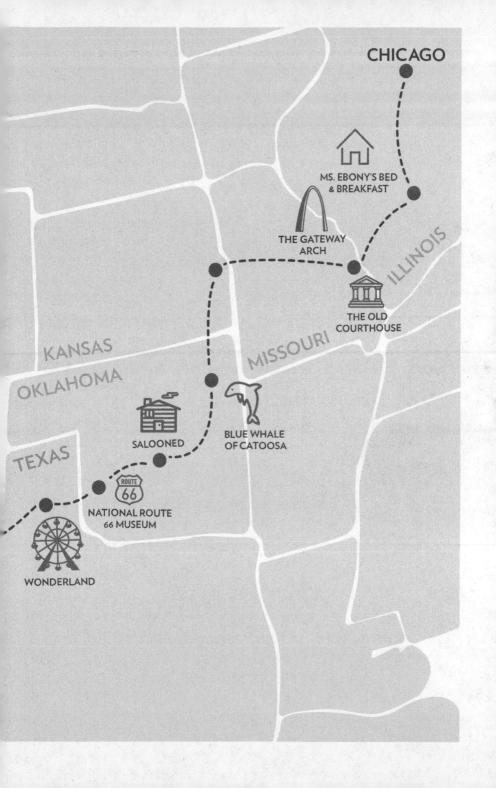

CHICAGO

MS. EBONY'S BED
& BREAKFAST

THE GATEWAY
ARCH

ILLINOIS

THE OLD
COURTHOUSE

KANSAS

OKLAHOMA

MISSOURI

SALOONED

BLUE WHALE
OF CATOOSA

TEXAS

ROUTE
66

NATIONAL ROUTE
66 MUSEUM

WONDERLAND

ACKNOWLEDGMENTS

Getting a book published is an amazing dream that feels nearly impossible to accomplish. So many things have to go right and so many people have to say yes. To have the opportunity to do it twice is absolutely mind-blowing and we wouldn't have gotten here without a few remarkable people.

First, we'd like to thank our fabulous agent, JL Stermer, for navigating us through the twisty-turny road that is the publishing journey. We are two of the luckiest girls in the world to have you on our team and to call you a friend. You are so much cooler than us. You are also da MVP! JL, you get us in such a perfect way and we are forever grateful to you!!! #SmartyPantsLadies. And of course a very special shout-out to Veronica Grijalva, Victoria Hendersen, and the entire New Leaf Literary team for their support. We love being Leaves.

We'd also like to thank our thoughtful editor, Natashya Wilson, for being a champion of *One of the Good Ones*. Thank you for asking questions. Thank you for listening to us. Thank you for helping us make this novel everything we wanted it to be. You push us to keep growing.

Thank you to publishing director extraordinaire Bess Braswell, hardest-working publicists in the game Laura Gianino and Justine Sha, unparalleled library marketer Linette Kim, and ultimate marketing maven Brittany Mitchell. Thank you for your passion and kindness and our meetings and for listening to us gush about whatever our latest obsessions are (cosmetic refrigerators, procrastibaking, the 2005 version of *Pride & Prejudice*, etc.).

We'd also like to thank Gigi Lau and Rachelle Baker for the beautiful cover of our dreams, and the wonderful team at Inkyard Press/Harlequin/HarperCollins. We literally couldn't have done it without you, and we are eternally grateful.

We are especially appreciative of Laura Ruby. First, for being hilarious and sincere. Listening to you speak at Children's Institute was a major highlight for us because we are such huge admirers of your work. So your beautiful words about *OOTGO* mean the universe to us.

Damon Young, you've already perfectly described the process of soliciting blurbs: *"It feels like asking the finest girl in school to your prom, except if A) you go to different schools and B) she's never met you before and C) your ask has to be a haiku and D) if she says 'no' you're not going to college."*

So thank you! Thank you for taking the time to read our story and write nice things about it and helping us get to college.

And Brad Meltzer. BRAD. BRAAADDD. When we reached out to you to tell you about *Dear Haiti, Love Alaine* (can you believe we have two books?!?!) we could have never in an infinite number of years known how much of a mentor you would grow to be. Thank you for letting us bounce ideas off you, squeal about your fancy accolades, and pick your brain about this world of publishing. (And obviously, Go Chargers.)

Cristina Russell, thank you for all of your support and for being your amazing self, in person and online.

To our Las Musas hermanxs, thank you for always making us feel welcomed and supported in this big ol' publishing world. ¡Abrazos!

We are library girls at heart and are eternally grateful to the New York Public Library/Schomburg Center for digitizing more than twenty editions of the *Green Book*. Thank you to Brian Foo for creating a visualization of the *Green Book* journey across the country. (It is very cool—you should check it out.)

A special thank-you to Candacy A. Taylor, author of *Overground Railroad: The Green Book and the Roots of Black Travel in America*, for creating a thoroughly researched book about the implications the *Green Book* had for Black travelers in the past and today.

Thank you to Yamiche Alcindor for reporting on the struggles that the children, siblings, and younger relatives of those killed by law enforcement experience during and after these moments of tragedy. Thank you to the protestors calling for better, and to all the other journalists who are elevating their voices and stories.

We'd never forget our amazing family for standing with us at every step of this adventure—Mommy, Daddy, Gramma, Jessica, Lydi'Ann, Ginger, and Lily. Sabiné Oh! We are so happy to have you in our lives, Bini (and hi-hi, Cinnamon and Frank!). We put the finishing touches on this book as we sheltered in place together during a time of extraordinary uncertainty. And while we didn't know how everything would turn out, there's one thing that always held true. Our love for one another. Nou renmen nou tout. Yè, jodi a, e pou tout tan.

Thank you to all of our friends, extended family, coworkers, students at Gulfstream Early Learning Center (who probably won't be reading this for another, oh, ten years), Ms. Stacy Burroughs for screaming "My Yeezy's!" and making everyone laugh whenever someone's tiny feet got too close, Steve Aubourg, Kristi Patterson, and Becca Hildner for your love, amazing text messages, and even better phone calls, and for being the greatest sounding board/ride or die, and everyone in between who has listened to us squeal with excitement over our sophomore novel. Thank you to our classmates and professors at Howard University and the University of Pennsylvania. We're so happy that you haven't gotten tired of partaking in our joy.

And thank you to you, dear reader. Yes, you. Sharing this story has been our greatest honor. And we hope to share many more for years to come.